SIR
THURSDAY

Arthur snapped his head forward, got his fingers in his mouth and pushed the ring under his tongue, cutting his lip in the process.

Blood trickled down his chin as he was hauled up on to his knees, the golden rope securing his arms behind him and his ankles together.

Arthur looked up and saw the fizzing, sparkling crown coming down.

I'm Arthur Penhaligon, he thought desperately. *Arthur Penhaligon, my parents are Bob and Emily. I'm the Master of the Lower House, the Far Reaches, the Border Sea –*

The crown was wedged tight upon his head – and Arthur fell silently screaming into darkness.

THE KEYS TO THE KINGDOM

SIR THURSDAY

GARTH NIX

HOT
KEY
BOOKS

First published in the USA by Scholastic Inc 2006
First published in Great Britain by Collins 2006

This edition published in Great Britain in 2021 by
HOT KEY BOOKS
80–81 Wimpole Street, London W1G 9RE
Owned by Bonnier Books
Sveavägen 56, Stockholm, Sweden
www.hotkeybooks.com

A CIP catalogue record for this book is available from the British Library.

ISBN: 978-1-4714-1021-5
Also available as an ebook

1

MIX
Paper from
responsible sources
FSC® C018072

Typeset by DataConnection Ltd
Printed and bound by Clays Ltd, Elcograf S.p.A.

Hot Key Books is an imprint of Bonnier Books UK
www.bonnierbooks.co.uk

To Anna, Thomas, Edward and all my family and friends. With special thanks to David Levithan, most patient editor.

PROLOGUE

The westernmost extent of the Great Maze ended in a line of mountains. Sixteen thousand feet high, the mountain range merged into the ceiling of the House, and there was no valley or gap or crevasse that might lead through to the other side. For what lay beyond the great barrier of stone and ice was Nothing. The mountains were a wall of the House, a bulwark and buttress against both the corrosive effects of the Void and attacks by Nithlings, creatures that emerged from Nothing.

There was only one place where Nithlings could enter the House. Long ago, when the mountains had been shaped, a tunnel had also been made. An arched tunnel, seven miles long, two miles wide and half a mile high, blocked by four enormous gates. The outermost gate, on the House side, was gilded in inch-thick gold, sealing in the metal by Immaterial forces that could not be breached easily by raw Nothing or sorcery. The next gate, half a mile further down the tunnel, was of silver gilt. The third, another half mile in, was of bronze. The fourth and final gate, the one that led out into Nothing, was called the Cleargate. It was purely Immaterial and entirely translucent, except for a shimmering that was painful even to immortal eyes.

Despite this pain, the Denizens who guarded the Cleargate looked out through it at the strange, constantly changing region that lay beyond, the transient lands where some of the House's virtue still shaped the Nothing into some semblance of solidity. It was the periphery of Nothing, but the Void itself was never far away. Sometimes Nothing almost touched the Cleargate, and sometimes it lay far distant, out of sight.

The purpose of the tunnel was to admit a controlled number of Nithlings into the Great Maze at particular times. These Nithlings would provide training and sport for the Glorious Army of the Architect, which was based in the Great Maze.

The routine for such admissions never varied. If a small number of Nithlings – only a thousand or two – was required then the Cleargate was opened just long enough to let that number in. Then it was closed and the Nithlings were admitted through the Bronzegate, which was closed behind them. The process was repeated for the Silvergate and the Goldgate, through which the Nithlings emerged into the House proper. It was a rule that all four gates must never be open at the same time, and only twice in the entire history of the House had three gates been opened simultaneously, to admit more than one hundred thousand Nithlings.

The gates were opened and shut by means of giant clockwork gears that were wound by subterranean rivers that coursed within the mountain walls. Each gate was operated by a single lever, and all four levers were contained within the switch room of the Boundary Fort, a complex of rooms and chambers built into the mountain above the tunnel. The fort was entered via a series of ramps that switchbacked up the mountainside, all heavily fortified with bastions and ravelins.

The Boundary Fort was defended by a detachment from either the Legion, the Horde, the Regiment or the Moderately Honourable Artillery Company. The guard changed every century of House Time.

Currently, a little more than ten thousand years after the disappearance of the Architect, the Boundary Fort was garrisoned by a cohort of the Legion, under the command of Colonel Trabizond Nage, 13,338th in precedence within the House.

Colonel Nage was in his office, donning the ceremonial silvered cuirass and plumed helmet of his rank, when an orderly knocked on the door.

'What is it?' asked Nage. He was a little distracted, since within the hour he would be commanding the Cleargate to open and admit up to ten thousand Nithlings, the chosen amount of enemy for the Army's 108,217th campaign.

'Visitor from GHQ, sir,' called out the orderly. 'And Lieutenant Corbie wants to make an urgent report.'

Nage frowned. Like all superior Denizens, he was very handsome and very tall, and his frown hardly altered his features. He frowned because he hadn't received any message about a visitor from the Army's General Headquarters, and he had received no warning from any of his friends and old comrades there.

The colonel fastened his chin strap and picked up his copy of the 108,217th Campaign Ephemeris. It was magically tuned to his hands and would explode if anyone else so much as touched it, which was why its red leather cover was stamped with his name in three-inch high capitals. The Ephemeris not only listed when the gates were to be opened and in what sequence, it was also a guide to the movement of the individual tiles of the Great Maze.

Apart from a few fixed locations, the Great Maze was divided into one million mile-square tiles, on a grid one thousand miles a side. Each tile moved at sunset to a new location according to a plan laid down by Sir Thursday a year or more in advance. To get anywhere in the Great Maze you had to know where the mile-wide tile you were on was going to go – or not go. The Ephemeris would also tell you the terrain and other features of each tile, and where to find water and stockpiled food, ammunition or any other special information.

After tucking his Ephemeris into a pouchlike pocket at the front of his long leather tunic, Colonel Nage picked up his savage-sword and slid it into the bronzed scabbard at his side. It was a service-issue blade, one of the standard weapons of the Legion. It looked just like a gladius, copied from the Roman legions of the world Earth in the Secondary Realms, but it had been made in the workshops of Grim Tuesday. Its blade was curdled starshine, the hilt gravity-hardened amber. A grain of ensorcelled Nothing encased in the pommel provided the sword with several useful powers, including its rotating blade.

Nage opened the door and called out to the orderly.

'Send the visitor in. I'll see Corbie in a minute or two.'

The visitor was a staff major, wearing the dress uniform of the Citadel, which housed Sir Thursday's

General Headquarters (or GHQ) and was one of the regions of the Great Maze that didn't move. His red tunic with its gilt buttons and the black varnished hat on his head were copied from the nineteenth century era of Earth, that favourite place which provided so many ideas and things for the Denizens of the House to imitate. He carried a short, whippy swagger-stick under his left armpit, which was probably an ensorcelled weapon of some kind.

'Hello, Colonel,' the Denizen said. He stood at attention and gave a very smart salute, which Nage returned with a clash of his right wrist bracer on his cuirass, the armour plate that protected his chest. 'I'm Major Pravuil. Carrying dispatches from GHQ. Modification to your Ephemeris.'

'Modification? That's never happened before!'

'Change of plan for the campaign,' said Pravuil smoothly. 'Sir Thursday wants to really test the lads this time. Here we are. Just sign on the bottom right please, sir, and then lay the page on your Ephemeris.'

Nage quickly signed the paper then took out his Ephemeris and put the sheet on top of the book. It lay there for a second then shivered as if a breeze had swept through the room. As the two Denizens watched, the page sank into the book, disappearing through the binding like water into a sponge.

Nage waited a few seconds then picked up the Ephemeris and opened it to the current day. He read what was there twice, his frown returning.

'But what's this? All four gates open? That's against standing orders!'

'Which are overridden by direct instruction from Sir Thursday.'

'I don't have a full garrison here, you know,' said Nage. 'We're under-strength. I have only one cohort of the Legion and a troop of Borderers. What if the fort comes under attack while the gates are still open?'

'You will defend it,' said Pravuil. 'It'll just be the usual Nithling rabble. Only more of them than usual.'

'That's just it,' Nage argued. 'The Borderers have been reporting that something peculiar is going on in the transient region. There has been a solid landscape there for the last few months, and you can't even see the Void from the Cleargate. The last report said there are columns of Nithlings marching into that region from somewhere. Organised Nithlings.'

'Organised Nithlings?' scoffed Pravuil. 'The Nithlings are incapable of organisation. They appear from Nothing, they fight stupidly – with one another if they can't get into the House proper – and they go back to Nothing when we slay them. That is how it has always been and always will be.'

'Begging your pardon, Major, that's not how it is right now,' said a new voice from the door. A Denizen in the sand-coloured tunic of a Borderer, his longbow slung across his back, stood at attention there. He bore the scars of several old Nothing-inflicted wounds on his face and hands, typical of the Denizens who patrolled the regions where the House bordered Nothing, not just in the Great Maze but also in other demesnes. 'May I make my report, Colonel?'

'Yes, do, Corbie,' said Nage. He reached under his cuirass and pulled out a pocket watch, flipping open the case one-handed. 'We still have forty minutes.'

Corbie stood at attention and spoke to a point somewhere slightly above Nage's head, as if there was an audience there.

'On the seventeenth instant, I left the sally port of the Cleargate with four sergeants and six ordinary Borderers. The sifters indicated a very low level of free Nothing in the region and the Void itself lay at least fourteen miles distant, as measured by Noneset. We could not see it, nor much else, for everything immediately in front of the Cleargate was obscured by a highly unusual haze.

'We marched straight into this haze and discovered that not only was it twenty or thirty yards wide, but it was generated by means unknown, presumed to be sorcerous. It was emanating from bronze chimney-like columns that were set at intervals in a line a mile long, opposite the Cleargate.

'Moving through the haze we discovered that an enormous grassy plain had formed from Nothing, with a broad river close to us. On the far side of the river were thousands of tents, all of a uniform colour, arranged in rows of a hundred, with a banner at the head of each row. It was completely different from the usual rough Nithling camp and we immediately noted that there was a very large parade ground of beaten earth beyond the tents, where a force I estimated at between two hundred thousand and three hundred thousand Nithlings was parading in battle formations.

'Parading, sir! We moved closer and through my perspective glass I was able to make out that the Nithlings were not only wearing uniforms, but had remarkably regular physical attributes, with only minor variations of shape, such as a tentacle here or there, or more elongated jaws.

'At that point, a Nithling sentry hidden in the grass sounded an alarm. I must confess we were surprised by the presence of a sentry and by the swift response, as a hidden force immediately emerged from the banks of the river. We were pursued back to the Cleargate and only just managed to get back in through the sally port without suffering casualties.

'End of report, sir!'

Nage stared at him for a moment as if he couldn't believe what he was hearing. Finally, he blinked several times and spoke.

'This is very disturbing! And it obviously changes things. We cannot open all four gates with such a host of Nithlings waiting to attack!'

'Are you intending to disobey direct orders from Sir Thursday?' asked Pravuil lazily. He tapped the palm of his left hand with his swagger stick, small purple sparks crawling out of the stick and spilling over his fingers. 'You should know that I will have to relieve you of your command if that is the case.'

'No . . . no,' said Nage. He looked at his watch. 'We still have time. I will call General Lepter.'

The colonel retreated to his desk and opened a drawer. There were half a dozen small lead figures inside, model soldiers, each painted in different uniforms of the Army of the Architect. Nage selected a figure wearing the long-plumed helmet and gilded cuirass of a legate of the Legion, a rank equal to general in the other commands of the Glorious Army of the Architect.

Nage put this model soldier into a small ivory stand that looked like a dry inkwell. As the figure connected with the stand, its edges blurred for a second before it became a tiny duplicate of the real, living, breathing legate. This little soldier looked up at Nage and spoke, her voice sharp and penetrating, as if she were in the room and life-sized, not four inches tall.

'What is it, Nage?'

Nage clashed his cuirass with his bracer before speaking.

'I have received a change to my Ephemeris from GHQ, delivered by a Major Pravuil. It calls for all four gates to be opened for twelve hours. But we have sighted an organised force of disciplined Nithlings waiting in the transient region, numbering at least two hundred thousand.'

'And your question is?'

'I wish to be entirely sure that the change to my Ephemeris is authentic and not some exceptional Nithling trick.'

'Major Pravuil is known to me,' said Lepter. 'He is one of a number of couriers delivering changes to all officer Ephemerides. Sir Thursday wishes to test the Army as it has not been tested for millennia.'

'In that case, I request urgent reinforcements,' said Nage. 'I am not confident I can hold the fort with the current understrength garrison if the Nithling force attempts an assault.'

'Don't be ridiculous, Nage,' said Lepter. 'Those Nithlings might look organised, but as soon as they're through the tunnel they'll go wild. A dozen tiles with

11

abundant wildlife were moved last night opposite the Goldgate. The Nithlings will go hunting as they always do, and the tiles will move them away at nightfall and separate their forces. Tectonic strategy, Nage! I'll talk to you later.'

The little legate froze and was a lead figure again. Nage plucked it out of the stand and threw it back in the drawer.

'The matter seems straightforward, Colonel,' said Pravuil. 'Hadn't you best issue your orders for all four gates to open?'

Nage ignored him. Going to a slender walnut-veneer cabinet that stood against the wall, he opened its glass door and slid out a shelf that had a telephone perched on it. Picking up the earpiece, he spoke into the receiver.

'Get me Thursday's Noon. Urgent military business.'

There was a crackling whisper from the phone.

'Colonel Nage at the Boundary Fort.'

There were more crackling whispers then a booming voice filled the whole room.

'Marshal Noon here! Nage, is it? What do you want?'

Nage quickly repeated what he'd said to General Lepter. Before he could finish, Noon's strident voice cut him off.

'You have your orders, Nage! Follow them and don't go outside your chain of command again! Put Pravuil on the line.'

Nage stepped back, letting the earpiece of the phone hang down. Pravuil slid past him and picked it up. This time, Noon's voice did not fill the room. He spoke quietly to Pravuil for a minute. Pravuil whispered back, then there was a very loud click as the major hung up the phone.

'I am to return to the Citadel at once,' said Pravuil. 'You are ready to fulfil your orders, Colonel?'

'I am,' confirmed Nage. He took out his watch and looked at it again. 'The Nithlings will not take long to get through the tunnel, Major. You may not get clear.'

'I have two mounts waiting,' said Pravuil. He tapped the Ephemeris in its canvas pouch at his side. 'And there is a tile six miles away that will take me halfway to the Citadel at dusk.'

'Go then,' said Nage, not attempting to hide his disdain for an officer leaving imminent battle. He waited until Pravuil had left his office then snapped a series of commands at Lieutenant Corbie and the orderly who stepped in from outside.

'Corbie! Assemble your men and leave the fort immediately. You are to harass and skirmish with the enemy as they leave the Goldgate and attempt to lure them out on to those wildlife-heavy tiles, away from the fort. Do you have communication figures for anyone outside the fort?'

'I only have my immediate superior, Captain Ferouk. He's at the White Keep, not GHQ.'

Nage rummaged in the drawer of his desk and handed him two lead soldiers, one in a bright scarlet uniform, the other in a subdued blue. The scarlet-clad figure had a tall hat adorned with feathers; the blue-uniformed one wore a flat leather cap.

'Friends of mine. Colonel Repton of the Regiment and Major Scaratt of the Artillery. Both are at GHQ and may be able to help you if everything goes as badly as I suspect it may. Now get going!'

Corbie saluted, spun on his heel and marched away. The orderly stepped forward as the Borderer left. He had a long trumpet by his side, a bronze instrument at least four feet long.

'Sound the general alert,' said Nage. 'And officer assembly.'

The orderly raised the trumpet to his lips, pointing it at the wall. His cheeks puffed up and he blew, but no sound came from the trumpet's bell. It wasn't until a second later that its peal reached in from outside, echoing here as it echoed in all parts of the fort, no matter how distant.

The trumpeter blew two different calls twice. When the last peals faded, he lowered his instrument and stood at attention.

'How long have we served together, Hopell?' asked Nage.

'Eight thousand four hundred and twenty-six years, sir,' said Hopell. 'That's time in the Legion. Not counting recruit school.'

'How many of our recruit class still live?'

'All but six, I think. Ropresh came good from that Nothing wound in the end, so he doesn't count. Light duties only of course, with his leg melted off –'

'Do you think we will fight as well knowing that there is a much greater chance than usual that we will get killed?'

'What do you mean, sir?' asked Hopell. 'We are legionaries of the Glorious Army of the House. We are prepared to die if we must.'

'Are we?' Nage didn't sound so sure. 'We're prepared to get hurt certainly, but not many of us get killed – and we always win. I fear that is soon to change. When the four gates open, there will be a battle for the fort, and we will be fighting organised, disciplined Nithlings for the first time. Nithlings who must be led by someone . . . or something . . . intelligent.'

'We are Legionaries,' said Hopell stolidly. 'We will fight to the end.'

'Yes,' said Nage, 'we will. But it may not be an end we like.'

Heavy footsteps sounded outside the door, the beat of a dozen or more officers marching down the corridor, called to the colonel by the trumpet signal.

'Do not speak of my doubts,' said Nage quickly. 'It was a moment of uncertainty, no more. We will fight and we will win. The Nithlings will fail before the fort, as they will be defeated elsewhere in the Great Maze by our Glorious Army.'

'Yes, sir!' shouted Hopell. He saluted as the first of the officers marched in, several others hard at their heels.

'Gather round,' said Nage quickly. 'We don't have much time and we must organise a defence. I have received and confirmed an order to open all four Gates – yes, all four gates. Shortly after that happens, I expect the fort to be attacked by several hundred thousand organised Nithlings. We must hold out for twelve hours, when we are ordered to shut the gates again. Whatever else happens – no matter what casualties we suffer – the switch room must be held and the gates must be closed on time.'

'Surely it's not that bad, sir,' suggested one of the centurions with a little giggle. He was a recent replacement, who had spent the last thousand years at GHQ. His cuirass was bare of gallantry medals, but had several stars awarded for efficiency in managing House paperwork. 'Once they come out of the Goldgate, they will have to climb up the ramps under a rain of power-spears and firewash from the engines on the bastions, get through the fort's own gates . . . We'll easily hold them. They will not stay organised, anyway. Nithlings always run wild –'

'I am glad of your confidence, centurion,' interrupted Nage. 'You may have the honour of commanding the Forlorn Hope I am placing at the base of the ramp.'

The centurion's bracer clash acknowledging this order was less strident than it should have been, quiet enough that the chime of the Colonel's watch was louder.

'Twenty minutes. I shall take five to outline my plans and then you will return to your units. I will command from the switch room myself. Our battlecry will be –' The colonel hesitated for a moment then said, 'Death and the Legion!'

His words were echoed immediately by the gathered officers, their shouts making the teacups on the colonel's sideboard rattle.

'Death and the Legion!'

CHAPTER ONE

'Hurry up!' Arthur Penhaligon called out. 'We have to get to the Front Door before Dame Primus shows up and tries to talk me out of going home.'

'OK, OK,' grumbled Leaf. 'I just stopped to look at the view.'

'No time,' said Arthur. He continued to lead the way up Doorstop Hill, moving as quickly as his crab-armoured leg would allow. His broken bone was still not fully healed.

Leaf started after him, with a glance over her shoulder. They'd run straight out of the elevator that had taken them down . . . or across . . . or sideways . . . from Port Wednesday on the flooded shores of the

Border Sea. She hadn't had any time to look at anything in the Lower House.

'There's the Front Door!' Arthur pointed up ahead to the huge, free-standing door that stood on the crest of the hill, supported by two white stone gateposts that were about thirty feet apart and forty feet high.

'That's a door?' asked Leaf. 'Must be tough to push it open.'

'It doesn't exactly open,' said Arthur. 'You just walk in. Don't look at the patterns on it for too long though.'

'Why not?'

'You'll go crazy,' said Arthur. 'Or get stuck looking.'

'You know I'm going to have to look now,' said Leaf. 'If you hadn't said anything I probably wouldn't have bothered.'

Arthur shook his head. 'You can't help it. Just don't look too long.'

'Which side do we go to?' Leaf asked when they were only a few yards away. 'And do we knock?'

'It doesn't matter which side,' said Arthur. He tried to look away from the wrought iron curlicues and patterns on the door but couldn't quite manage it. After a second, the shapes shivered and began to change, each image fixing itself in his head before it morphed into something else.

Arthur shut his eyes and reached out blindly towards Leaf, planning to tug her elbow or the back of her shirt. But she was much closer than he had thought and his questing fingers poked her in the face.

'Ow! Uh . . . thanks.'

Arthur turned his head away from the door and opened his eyes.

'I guess I was getting hooked,' Leaf said as she rubbed her nose. She kept her eyes averted from the door, instead looking up at the high domed ceiling of silvery metal that reached its apex several hundred feet directly above them. It was night in the Lower House, the only light provided by the strange clouds of glowing purple or orange that drifted across the silver surface.

As Leaf looked up, a beam of light shot down, marking the path of an elevator from another part of the House. It was quickly followed by another two beams striking down from above.

'So do we knock?' Leaf asked again.

'Not yet,' Arthur replied. He looked across at the fading trail of the elevator beams as he spoke, acutely aware that they had probably delivered Dame Primus and her entourage, come to give him a hard time – though he had half expected she would already be ahead of him, having used a Transfer Plate. 'We wait for the Lieutenant Keeper of the Front Door first.'

Dame Primus would want him to stay or at least hand over the Third Key, which was supposedly needed to keep the Border Sea in check. But Arthur didn't want to part with the only weapon he had. He had finally accepted that he must go up against the Morrow Days, that avoidance was not an option. The whole gang of Sir Thursday, Lady Friday, Superior Saturday and Lord Sunday would not leave him alone. They would interfere with destructive results in his world or any other world; they would hurt and kill whoever they wanted; they would do whatever they thought would help them retain their Keys and their authority over the House. The only way to stop the Morrow Days was to defeat them.

Arthur knew he had to fight, but he wanted to do it on his own terms. Right now, he wanted to check up on his family and make sure everything was all right back on his own world. Then he'd return to the House and do whatever had to be done to release the Fourth Part of the Will from Sir Thursday and claim the Fourth Key.

They waited in front of the Door for a few minutes, looking at the spires, towers and roofs of the city below. When Arthur had first seen it, the city had been cloaked in fog, but there was no fog now and he could dimly make out a few Denizens wandering about the streets.

As he watched, a large group came out of one of the closer buildings, milled around for a few seconds then headed towards the new-mown slopes of Doorstop Hill.

'Maybe we should knock,' he said. 'Here comes Dame Primus and the whole crew.'

He took a step towards the Door and, still averting his eyes, rapped smartly on the strange surface. It didn't feel like wood or iron, or in fact like anything solid at all. His fist sank into it as if he'd knocked on something with the consistency of jelly, and at the same time he felt a tingling through his knuckles that travelled up into his wrist and elbow.

But it did make a knocking sound – a hollow, sustained noise that Arthur could hear echoing inside the door with several seconds' delay, as if the sound had travelled a long way before coming back.

The knock was followed a moment later by a voice Arthur now knew quite well. The Lieutenant Keeper's speech was deep and slow and solid, but this time strangely distant.

'One moment, one moment. There is trouble at the crossroads.'

Arthur could see Dame Primus leading a pack of Denizens, already at the foot of the hill. She was hard to miss, being seven and a half feet tall and wearing a long-trained dress of pale green that fluoresced with shimmers of blue. With her were Monday's Noon (who used to be Dusk) and a black-clad Denizen he didn't recognise at first until he realised it was the new Monday's Dusk (who used to be Noon). Following them was a whole host of clerks, Commissionaire Sergeants, Midnight Visitors and other Denizens.

'Arthur!' shouted Dame Primus as she lifted her skirts and began to climb the hill. 'Wait! There is something you must know!'

'Hurry up, hurry up!' muttered Arthur to the Door. He really didn't feel like arguing with Dame Primus.

'I thought you said they were on your side,' said Leaf. 'Who's the tall woman in the cool clothes?'

'They are on my side,' said Arthur. 'That's Dame Primus. She's the Will. The first two parts anyway. Probably three parts by now, since the Carp has probably just caught up with her. I guess that would explain the green dress. And she is taller, and her eyes have got kind of bulbous –'

'Arthur! You should not be here!'

Arthur spun around. The Lieutenant Keeper had emerged from the Front Door. He didn't look as calm and collected as he usually did. His long white hair was a mess; his blue coat was splashed with mud and a darker blue that might be Denizen blood. Instead of his usual shiny kneeboots he was wearing sodden, thigh-high waders. His sword was naked in his hand, the blade shimmering with an icy, pale blue light that hurt Arthur's eyes and made Leaf look away and shield her face.

'I shouldn't be here?' protested Arthur. 'I don't want to be here! Leaf and I need to get home right away.'

The Lieutenant Keeper shook his head and at the same time, sheathed his sword in a scabbard that appeared out of the air.

'You cannot return to your world, Arthur.'

'What?!'

'You are already there. Or rather, a copy of you is. A Spirit-eater. I wondered when I felt you pass through the Door so swiftly, without a greeting. But whoever sent the Cocigrue had planned its crossing carefully, for I was distracted, both by a sudden influx from the Border Sea and by several unlawful openings.'

'I don't understand,' said Arthur. 'A copy of me is back in my world? What did you call it?'

'A Cocigrue or Spirit-eater.'

'That doesn't sound good,' said Leaf. 'What does one of those things do?'

'I cannot stay to talk,' said the Lieutenant Keeper. 'There are still unlawful travellers within the Door. Good luck, Arthur!'

Before Arthur could protest, the Denizen had spun back into and through the door, drawing his sword again. The outline of the sword was shaped by the ironwork decorations before it dissolved into a complex tracery of climbing roses.

Arthur pulled Leaf's arm as she was once again entranced by the patterns on the door.

'Oops! Sorry, Arthur. Guess you'll have to talk to the big tall green woman now.'

'I guess I will,' said Arthur grimly. 'This had better not be a trick she's set up to keep me here.'

He turned to look back down at Dame Primus and collided with someone who materialised just in front of him, stepping off a fine yellow and white patterned china plate. Both of them fell over and Arthur instinctively hit out before he realised that the person who'd appeared was his friend Suzy.

'Ow! Watch it!'

'Sorry,' said Arthur.

'Got here as quick as I could.' Suzy stood up with a clatter, revealing that the pockets of her long and grimy coat were stuffed with yellow and white Transfer Plates. 'I nicked all the Transfer Plates for Doorstop Hill, but Old Primey's on her way, so you'd best get through quick –'

Arthur pointed silently down the hill. Suzy stopped talking and looked over her shoulder. Dame Primus and her entourage were only a dozen yards away, the personification of the Will scowling at Suzy.

'Dame Primus,' called out Arthur, before the Will could start scolding Suzy or deliver a lecture. 'I just want to go home for a quick visit and then I'll come straight back. But there seems to be a problem.'

Dame Primus stopped before Arthur and curtsied. When she spoke, she first sounded like a normal woman. Then her voice became low and gravelly, with something of the Carp's self-satisfied booming tone in there as well.

'There is indeed a problem. There are many problems. I must ask you, Lord Arthur, to come back to Monday's Dayroom. We need to hold a council of war.'

'This isn't some sort of trick, is it?' asked Arthur suspiciously. 'You haven't put a copy of me back home yourself, have you?'

Dame Primus took in a shocked breath.

'Never! To create such a Spirit-eater is utterly forbidden. And in any case, I have neither the knowledge nor the craft to create such a thing. It is clearly the latest move of the Morrow Days against you, Arthur, and against us. One of a number of actions that we really must discuss.'

Arthur clenched and unclenched his fists.

'Can I go back through Seven Dials?'

Arthur had returned to his world once before using the sorcery contained in the strange room of grandfather clocks known as Seven Dials. He knew it was the other main portal for Denizens to leave the Lower House and enter the Secondary Realms.

'No,' said Dame Primus. 'As I understand it, the Spirit-eater has sorcerously occupied the place you should have in your Secondary World. Should you also return, the interaction of yourself with the Nithling would cause an eruption of Nothing that would likely destroy you and, come to think of it, your world.'

'So this Spirit-eater is kind of like an antimatter Arthur?' asked Leaf.

Dame Primus bent her head and looked at Leaf, sniffing in disdain.

'I don't believe we've been introduced, young lady.'

'This is my friend Leaf,' said Arthur. 'Leaf, meet Dame Primus.'

Leaf nodded reluctantly. Dame Primus lowered her chin a quarter of an inch.

'What's this Spirit-eater going to do?' asked Arthur. 'Besides preventing me from going back?'

'This is not a good place to discuss such things,' said Dame Primus. 'We should return to Monday's Dayroom.'

'OK,' said Arthur. He looked back at the Front Door for a moment, then away again. 'Let's go then.'

'Hang on!' Leaf interrupted. 'What about me? I want to go back. No offence, Arthur, but I need some time at home to . . . I don't know . . . just be normal.'

'Leaf can go back, can't she?' asked Arthur wearily.

'She can and should return,' Dame Primus replied. 'But it had best be through Seven Dials. The Lieutenant Keeper has closed the Door until he deals with the intruders. Come, let us all return to Monday's Dayroom. That includes you, Suzanna. I trust you have not broken any of those plates.'

Suzy muttered something about a few chips and cracks never doing any harm, but not loud enough for Dame Primus to acknowledge her.

As they descended Doorstop Hill, Arthur noticed that there was an outer cordon of Metal Commissionaires and Commissionaire Sergeants around them, all looking out at the ground and the sky. Midnight Visitors – the black-clad servants of Monday's Dusk – drifted through the air overhead as well, their long whips trailing by their sides. They too looked out, constantly turning their heads to cover all angles.

'What are they looking for?' Arthur asked Dame Primus.

'Assassins,' snapped Dame Primus. 'That is one of the developments. Both the former Mister Monday and the former Grim Tuesday have been slain – by sorcery.'

CHAPTER TWO

'Slain by sorcery?' Arthur asked as they hurried into the elevator. He wanted to make sure he'd heard properly because it was very hard to kill Denizens. 'You mean killed? Really dead?'

Dame Primus gestured at Monday's Noon, who moved to Arthur's side and gave a rather foreshortened and cramped bow. They were in a very large elevator, a cube sixty feet a side, but it was completely full of various guards, clerks and hangers-on. In one corner, there was a seated string quartet, playing a soft tune Arthur almost recognised.

'Really dead,' replied Monday's Noon, his silver tongue flashing. Apart from his tongue, he hadn't changed much since he'd been promoted by Arthur from Dusk to Noon. Though he no longer wore black, he still seemed to Arthur to embody the quiet and failing light of the evening in his speech and measured movement. 'The former Mister Monday was stabbed through the head and heart with a sorcerous blade, and was not found quickly enough to remedy the damage. The former Grim Tuesday was pushed or thrown into the Pit from the top level.'

'Are you sure he's dead? I mean *really* sure?' asked Arthur. He was having real trouble accepting this news. 'Did you find his body?'

'We found bits of it,' said Noon. 'He landed in a pool of Nothing. More than a score of artisans who were working on filling in the Pit saw the impact. It is likely that he too was assaulted by some kind of sorcery before he fell, so he could not cry out or attempt to save himself.'

'Do you know who killed them?'

'We do not know,' Dame Primus said. 'We can only assume that both knew something about the Morrow Days and their plans that the Morrow Days do not want us to know. It is puzzling that they should do it now, when I have already questioned both the former Trustees at length without uncovering anything of note. It is possible that it is an attempt to cover up some very disturbing news that has come to light from other quarters. We will speak of this in our council.'

'I want to know about the Spirit-eater,' said Arthur anxiously. 'I mean, it's stopping me from going home, but what else is it going to do? Will it do anything to my family?'

'I don't know,' said Dame Primus. 'We . . . that is, I am not a House Sorcerer as such. I have called your newly appointed Wednesday's Dusk, Dr Scamandros, to the Dayroom to tell us about Spirit-eaters. It appears that he is now the sole Upper House-trained sorcerer to be found anywhere in the Lower House, the Far Reaches and the Border Sea.'

A bell jangled and the quartet's strings shivered into silence. But the elevator door didn't open.

'Secure the Dayroom,' Dame Primus ordered Noon. He bowed and touched the door, which opened just enough to let him lead out a dozen Commissionaire Sergeants and ordinary Commissionaires. Another dozen remained around Arthur, Leaf, Suzy and Dame Primus.

'We must be wary,' said Dame Primus. 'We can't let you be assassinated, Arthur.'

'Me?' Arthur tapped the small trident that was thrust through his belt. 'Isn't the Third Key supposed to protect me from harm?'

'It is,' agreed Dame Primus. 'But whatever killed the two former Trustees was House sorcery of a very high order. Grim Tuesday, in particular, though he had lost most of his power, would not be easy to overcome. So the assassin or assassins might be able to bypass or negate the Key's protection. And you mortals are very fragile.'

'Fragile.' Hearing it made Arthur think of eggshells, and then the terrible image of his own head being broken like an eggshell, smashed to pieces by a sorcerous assassin who had crept up behind him –

Arthur forced this mind picture away with an effort of will, though he couldn't help looking behind him. All he saw were his own guards but he still felt a tremor of fear flick through his stomach.

Aloud, he tried to make light of the situation.

'Great,' he said. 'Things just keep getting better, don't they?'

'There is more to fear,' said Dame Primus. 'We will speak of it soon.'

'All clear,' Noon reported from outside and the elevator door slid silently open to reveal the entrance hall of Monday's Dayroom. Architecturally, it looked pretty much like it had last time Arthur had seen it, after the steaming mud pits and iron platforms had been transformed into old-fashioned rooms that reminded him of a museum. But there was a major difference: now there were thousands of bundles of paper tied up with red ribbon and stacked from floor to ceiling all along the walls of the hall. Every ten feet or so these piles would have a Denizen-sized gap, each occupied by a Commissionaire Sergeant standing at attention.

'What's with all the paper?' Leaf asked as they walked down the hall.

No one answered until Arthur repeated the question.

'The Middle and Upper Houses are bombarding us with paperwork,' said Dame Primus. 'It is an effective effort to tie up our resources and impede our reorganisation. Take the next door on the left, Arthur. Sneezer should have everything ready for our council.'

The next door on the left was also completely surrounded by stacked bundles of paper. It looked ordinary enough, just a simple wooden door with a solid bronze doorknob. Arthur turned the knob and pushed the door open.

A vast chamber lay on the other side, a room four or five times the size of the gym at Arthur's school, with a ceiling ten times as high. The floor, walls and ceiling were lined with white marble veined in gold, so that Arthur's first impression was that he had walked into some giant's tacky bathroom.

In the middle of this huge room sat a round table about a hundred feet in diameter. It appeared to be made of cast iron, painted deep red. It was hollow in the middle and around the outside there were a hundred or more tall-backed chairs, also made of wrought iron, this time painted white. One chair had a much higher back and it was either made of solid gold or gilded iron. The chair next to it was also taller, but not quite so much, and it slowly changed colour from red to white to gold and back again.

Sneezer the butler stood in the open centre of the table, a white cloth over one arm of his now immaculate coat. His once untidy hair was combed back, tied with a gold ribbon and powdered white. He held a silver tray with three crystal tumblers of something orange (probably juice) and a tall wine glass full of a blood-coloured liquid Arthur hoped was actually wine.

There was no one sitting on the chairs, but there was a large crowd of Denizens behind the table, all standing quietly. Arthur recognised Dr Scamandros and waved, and then he waved again as he saw Sunscorch slightly behind him, looking very fine but somewhat uncomfortable in the admiral's uniform that was his right as the new Wednesday's Noon. Soon Arthur was waving all over the place as he recognised Japeth the

34

Thesaurus and Matthias the Supply Clerk standing together, and Monday's Dawn and Wednesday's Dawn, and others from his previous adventures – as Leaf might call them – in the House.

'Take your seats,' bellowed Dame Primus, her voice going all gravelly and low, startling Leaf. 'Let this council be in session. Suzanna, you can return the Transfer Plates to the china cabinet before you join us, please.'

Suzy grimaced, gave a clattering curtsey and ran out, pausing to stick out her tongue at Dame Primus as the Will turned and gestured at the golden chair.

'That is your throne, Lord Arthur. Everyone else is arranged in order of precedence.'

'Where do I sit then?' asked Leaf.

'You may stand behind Arthur,' said Dame Primus coldly.

'Actually, I think Leaf had better have a chair next to me,' said Arthur firmly. 'As an honoured guest.'

'Very good, sir,' said Sneezer, making Arthur jump. The butler was somehow behind him now, offering him an orange juice. 'I shall place a chair for Miss Leaf.'

'I have prepared an agenda for this council,' announced Dame Primus as she sat down. Her chair swirled through red, white and gold, and Arthur noticed it grew a few inches at the back, almost matching his own chair's height.

Dame Primus tapped a large hard-bound book of at least three or four hundred pages that was sitting in front of her on the table. Arthur had a copy in front of his seat too. He sat down, dragged the book over, flipped the cover open and read, *Being an Agenda for a Council to Discuss Various Troublesome Matters Pertaining to the House, the Release of the Will of the Architect, the Assumption of the Rightful Heir and other Divers Matters.*

The next page had a list of items numbered from one to thirty. The page after that had thirty-one to sixty. Arthur turned to the end and saw that there were over six thousand Agenda items.

'I suggest we begin with Item One,' said Dame Primus, 'and work our way through.'

Arthur looked at Item One.

Arbitration Between Demesnes, Article One: The Dispute concerning Record Filing and Transport of Records between the Middle and Lower House.

'The Agenda is arranged alphabetically,' said Dame Primus helpfully. 'All the Arbitration matters are first.'

'I haven't got time for this,' said Arthur. He shut the Agenda book with a loud clap. 'What I want to know is what that Spirit-eater is, what it's going to do to my family and how to get rid of it. Dr Scamandros, do you know?'

'This is quite improper,' Dame Primus complained. 'I must protest, Lord Arthur. How can we properly come to conclusions and act effectively if we don't follow our Agenda?'

'Why don't you put the Agenda in order of importance, and while you're doing that, we'll talk about the Spirit-eater,' said Arthur, not daring to look at Dame Primus as he spoke. There was something about her that made him want to quietly sit and do as he was told. She reminded him of the scariest teacher he'd ever had, who could stun a classroom into silence just by appearing in the doorway. But like that teacher, Arthur found that if he didn't meet her gaze, she was easier to confront. 'Dr Scamandros?'

'Ah, well, I haven't had much time to look into things,' said Scamandros with a jittery glance at Dame Primus. The tattoos of palm trees on his cheeks suddenly shook and half a dozen nervous monkeys fell out and slid down to his chin, before the palm trees disappeared and were replaced by clock faces with swiftly moving hands. 'I mean, I barely had time for a glass of revitalising tonic at Port Wednesday before I was hustled here. But nevertheless, I do have some information, collected with the aid of Monday's Noon, who while not trained in the Upper House is nevertheless a capable sorcerer . . .'

He paused to bow to Monday's Noon, who bowed back. Arthur gripped his orange juice and tried not to look too impatient. Out of the corner of his eye he saw Suzy slink back in and sit on the floor, hidden behind Monday's Noon.

'As far as we can ascertain,' Scamandros continued, 'Spirit-eaters have only been raised on a handful of occasions in the whole history of the House. A Spirit-eater is a potent and unpleasant type of Nithling created to assume the identity of someone, either Denizen or mortal. Its chief power is to cloak itself in an exact likeness of its target, and it also has the ability to extrude its mentality into those around it, whether they be mortal or Denizen –'

'What?' interrupted Arthur. 'What does "extrude its mentality" mean?'

'I'm not too certain … apparently once a Spirit-eater has done it though, it is able to control its victims' minds and read their recent thoughts and memories. It does this in order to further its deception. Initially, it will have only the usual, exterior knowledge of its target, so it seeks to learn more from the target's confidantes and fellows.'

'You mean it's going to mentally take over my family?' Arthur spilled his orange juice as he stood up in agitation. 'How long will it take to do that?'

'Yes, that is . . . I suppose that is what it will do,' said Scamandros. 'Though I don't know how.'

'How much time would it need?' asked Arthur. This was the worst thing, his family being in danger. He remembered the two Grim's Grotesques breathing their foul breath of forgetting over his father, how he had felt in that awful second as that fog had rolled over his dad. Now his whole family were threatened again and he was stuck in the House. They would be defenceless.

I have to help them, Arthur thought desperately. *There has to be something . . . someone . . .*

'A few days, I think. But I cannot say for certain,' said Scamandros.

Arthur looked at Leaf. She met his gaze.

'I guess you're thinking what I'm thinking,' she said. 'You can't go back or the whole world goes *kapow*. But I could go back and try to get rid of this Spirit-eater.'

'I don't know,' said Arthur. 'It sounds very dangerous. Maybe Monday's Noon could –'

'No interference!' boomed Dame Primus. 'Remember the Original Law! The mortal may return to whence she came, but no others may sully the Architect's work.'

'I think it's more than a bit sullied already,' said Arthur crossly. 'How come it's all right for the bad guys to do whatever they want, and whenever I want to do

39

something it's "forget about it"? What's the good of being the Rightful Heir anyway? All I get is trouble!'

Nobody answered Arthur's question and he noticed everyone was not quite looking at him – and no one was telling him to behave himself. He felt suddenly weird and wished that somebody would just say, 'Shut up, Arthur, we've got work to do.'

'Is it possible?' asked Leaf. 'To get rid of the Spirit-eater, I mean.'

Arthur and Leaf both looked at Scamandros. The tattoos on his face showed some anxiety, picturing shaky towers that were being built up stone by stone, only to fall down as the last course was laid.

'I think so. But it would require finding the item used to create the Spirit-eater in the first place. That will be something personal from its target, overlaid with spells. In this case, something of yours, Arthur, that was close to you for quite a while. A favourite book, or a spoon, or perhaps some piece of clothing. Something of that order.'

Arthur frowned in puzzlement. What could he have lost that could be used in this way?

'When would this have happened?' he asked.

'It would have taken more than a year of House time for the Spirit-eater to be grown from Nothing,' replied Dr Scamandros.

'A year . . . How long has it been since I was given the minute hand by Mister Monday?' Arthur asked. It was only the previous week for him, but much longer in the House. 'In House Time, I mean?'

'A year and a half,' replied Dame Primus stiffly. She had the Agenda open and was tapping it with a gold pencil. Every time she tapped, one of the items on the list moved up or down, or to some unseen page deeper in the volume.

'It must have been Monday's Fetchers,' said Arthur. 'Or maybe one of Grim Tuesday's Grotesques. But I can't think of anything really personal that I've missed.'

'You could enquire of the Atlas,' said Dame Primus. 'You still hold the Third Key, so the Atlas will answer.'

Arthur took the Atlas out of his pocket, set it on the table and held the small trident that was the Third Key with his right hand. But he didn't start concentrating on a question to ask the Atlas. After a moment, he put the Third Key down, the trident's tines pointing to the hollow centre of the table.

'I have to be careful how much I use the Keys,' he said slowly. 'I already used this one quite a lot back in the Border Sea and I don't want to turn into a Denizen. Then I could never go back home.'

'How close are you?' Leaf asked curiously. 'Like, do you get to use the Key a hundred times or something and then *wham*, you're suddenly seven feet tall and a lot better-looking?'

'I don't know,' said Arthur. 'That's part of the problem.'

Dr Scamandros gave a slight and rather fake-sounding cough and raised his hand. Dame Primus stopped tapping her Agenda for a moment and stared at him, then continued with her rearranging.

'You may care to know, Lord Arthur,' said Dr Scamandros, 'that there is a little student project of mine that could be of use to you. It measures the sorcerous contamination of things, including, of course, persons.'

Scamandros started rummaging around inside his yellow greatcoat and pulled out a peacock feather fan, several enamelled snuff boxes, a scrimshaw letter opener and a brass piccolo, all of which he laid distractedly on the table.

'Here somewhere,' he said, and then triumphantly pulled out a two-inch square velvet box that was very worn on the edges. Opening it, he passed it to Sunscorch, who passed it to Leaf, who looked curiously at the item inside before she gave it to Arthur. It was a slim silver crocodile coiled into a ring, its tail in its jaws. It had bright pink diamonds for eyes, and its body was scored with lines that divided it into ten sections, each marked with a tiny engraved Roman numeral.

'Is this relevant?' asked Dame Primus impatiently. 'I am ready to proceed with the reordered Agenda.'

Arthur ignored her and took the ring out of the box.

'What does this do?' he asked. 'Do I put it on?'

'Yes, do put it on,' replied Dr Scamandros. 'In essence, it will tell you the degree to which you have been . . . ah . . . tainted with sorcery. It is not exact, of course, and in the case of a mortal, the calibration is uncertain. I would say that if the ring turns more than six parts gold then you will have become irretrievably transformed into a –'

'Can we move on?' snapped Dame Primus, as Dr Scamandros said, 'Denizen.'

Arthur put on the ring and watched with fascination and growing horror as each silver segment of the crocodile slowly turned from silver to gold.

One . . . two . . . three . . .

If he was transformed into a Denizen, he could never go back home. But he needed to use the Keys and the Atlas against the Morrow Days, and that meant more sorcerous contamination.

Unless it was all too late already.

Arthur stared at the ring as the tide of gold continued on, flowing into the fourth segment without slowing at all.

CHAPTER THREE

Arthur kept staring at the ring with dread fascination. After the fourth segment the gold suddenly stopped spreading and then it slowly ebbed back a little.

'It's almost up to the fourth line,' Arthur reported.

'It is not exact,' said Dr Scamandros, 'but that would concur with my previous examination. Your flesh, blood and bone are some four-tenths contaminated with sorcery.'

'And past six-tenths I become a Denizen?'

'Irrevocably.'

'Can I get rid of the contamination?' Arthur tried to keep his voice calm. 'Does it wear off?'

'It will reduce with time,' Scamandros replied. 'Provided you don't add to it. I would expect that degree of contamination to lessen in about a century.'

'A century! It might as well be permanent. But how much would using the Atlas add to the contamination?'

'Without careful experimentation and observation I should not like to say. Considerably less than the interventions to heal your ailments or to undo misdirected application of the Keys' power. Anything not focused on your own body will be less harmful.'

'It is not harmful to become a Denizen,' said Dame Primus. 'It is to become a higher order of being. I cannot understand your reluctance to shed your mortality, Arthur. After all, you are the Rightful Heir of the Architect of Everything. Now can we please return to the Agenda?'

'I was only chosen because I was about to die and happened to be handy,' said Arthur. 'I bet you've got a stack of Rightful Heirs noted down somewhere if something happens to me.'

There was silence in the vast room for a few seconds, until Dame Primus cleared her throat. Before she could speak, Arthur raised his voice.

'We will go back to the Agenda! After we've worked out what to do about the Spirit-eater. I just wish I could remember what might have been taken.'

'Try to work your way back through everything you did,' Leaf suggested. 'Did you drop your inhaler on the oval? Maybe they picked that up? Or did you have something at school when they burned the library?'

Arthur shook his head. 'I don't think so . . . Hey, wait a second!'

He turned to look at Monday's Dusk. He was slightly shorter than he had been as Noon and looked rather less severe, though no less handsome. He wore the night-black, undertaker-like costume of Dusk, though he'd taken off his top hat with the long black silk scarf wound around its crown.

'You sent the Fetchers, when you were Noon. Did one of them bring something back or were they banished straight into Nothing?'

'They did not return to me,' said Dusk, his once-silver tongue now a shiny ebony and his voice much softer. 'But then I did not raise them in the first place. Mister Monday assigned them to me. I presume he bought them from Grim Tuesday, for he would not have been energetic enough to create them himself. You may recall that I was forced to return to the House when the Fetchers and I cornered you at your school.'

'At the school,' Arthur said slowly, revisiting that scene in his memory. 'They took the Atlas! I'd forgotten because the Atlas came back here and I just picked it up again. A Fetcher ripped the pocket off my shirt and it got the Atlas with it –'

'A pocket!' interrupted Scamandros, scattering the things he'd put on the table with an excited wave of his arms, and the tower tattoos on his cheeks grew sturdier and sprouted fancy battlements. 'That must be it. That will be the source of this Spirit-eater. A scrap of material that has lain next to your heart, overlaid with charms and planted in Nothing to grow a Cocigrue! Find that and we might be able to do something about the Spirit-eater!'

'Right,' said Leaf. 'That sounds really easy.'

'You don't have to try,' said Arthur. 'I . . . I understand if you want to stay out of all this.'

'I don't think there's much choice,' said Leaf. 'I can't just let an evil clone of you go around taking over people's minds, can I?'

'You could,' said Arthur. Though Leaf was trying to make light of the situation, he could tell she was afraid. 'I know people who wouldn't do anything unless it directly affected them.'

'Yeah, well, I don't want to be one of those people. And if Ed's out of quarantine, he can help . . . though I guess if it's still Wednesday when I get back he'll be stuck in hospital . . .'

Leaf pulled a face at the thought of her brother Ed still being stuck in hospital. Her parents, aunt and brother had all suffered from the Sleepy Plague and been quarantined.

'Anyway, Doc, is there anything particular that I can do to this Spirit-eater, you know, like salt gets rid of Fetchers and silver dissolved that Scoucher?'

Dr Scamandros pursed his lips and wooden scaffolding appeared around the tower tattoos on his cheeks, propping them up.

'I don't know. A silver spear or sword would annoy it, I suspect, and like all Nithlings it would not eat salt *voluntarily*, but only the lesser Nithlings suffer much from silver or may be banished with salt.'

'Does it sleep?' Leaf asked. 'And will it have Arthur's pocket on it or will it keep that somewhere else?'

'Good questions, excellent questions,' muttered Scamandros. 'I'm afraid my sources don't say anything about it sleeping, but it is quite possible that it does. I suspect it will hide the pocket somewhere near its lair – but again, my information is sadly lacking.'

'And do you have any idea where its lair will be?' Leaf continued to question. 'Arthur's house?' Two small clouds of dust on Scamandros's cheeks whirled into miniature tornadoes that threatened a house tattooed across the bridge of his nose.

'My sources are incomplete. One of the references refers to the "Spirit-eater's Lair" but is not more forthcoming.'

'I guess if it's imitating Arthur, it will leave the house *some time*,' Leaf pointed out. 'I can sneak in the back door or something. Is there a back door?'

'The best way would be through the garage,' Arthur volunteered. 'There's a remote control switch for it under a blue rock in the drive. I suppose it would probably be in my bedroom, up on the top floor, if it's being me. But I think we'd better get more information about it before we say for sure.'

He picked up the Third Key again and laid his other hand on the Atlas. Its green leather binding quivered under his hand.

'Wait a second!' said Leaf. 'You don't have to –'

'I can't let you take on something like a Spirit-eater without being prepared,' said Arthur. 'Besides, it will be a good test to see how much more I get contaminated.'

'Arthur –' Leaf started to say, but Arthur was already focusing on his questions for the Atlas.

What is a Spirit-eater? How can the one that has copied me be defeated? Where is its lair?

The questions had hardly formed in his mind before the Atlas burst open, expanding to become a much larger book, it pages fluttering like a wind-caught fan. When it reached its full size, the pages settled down and an invisible hand began to write. The first few letters were in a strange alphabet of straight lines and dots, but they shimmered as Arthur watched, turning into the stylish English characters of a fine calligrapher.

Everyone watched Arthur as he stared down at the Atlas. Suzy chose this moment to sneak across the room from one of the side doors where she'd been listening.

For the benefit of the others, Arthur read the entry aloud, with some difficulty because he wasn't used to reading the old-fashioned writing. Many of the words were not ones he'd used before.

'Spirit-eater' is a term often used to describe one of a type of Nithlings that are close to Denizen-class, known as Near Creations, for they utilise some of the technical sorcery used by the Architect Herself to create life from Nothing, while lacking Her artistry.

A Spirit-eater is always based upon one of the Architect's own creations, either directly, as in a copied Denizen, or indirectly, in the case of a copied mortal, the current end result of the Architect's ancient experiment with the evolution of life.

The purpose of a Spirit-eater, in either case, is to replace an original, usually for the purposes of espionage, treachery or other foul deeds. In order to do so, the Spirit-eater will, to most onlookers, appear to have the physical appearance of its target. Its true face and form may be seen by gazing at it through a veil of raindrops on a sunny day or by application of various sorceries.

Initially, the Spirit-eater will have limited knowledge of its subject, no more than it has been told by its creator. However, part of the spell used to grow a Spirit-eater in Nothing also develops other powers within the Nithling. It is able to extrude its mentality into any sentient mind that it has physical contact with, by the use of a mentally conductive mould that is symbiotic with the Spirit-eater. The mould, derived from a semi-intelligent life form from a world in the Secondary Realms (House Name: Avraxyn; Local Name: ꓳCxV♂*)

'I can't read the local name –'

Leaf was shaking her head, but it wasn't at Arthur's inability to read the alien name.

'A mentally conductive *what*? What did you say? It grows *mould* on people?'

'That's . . . that's what it says here,' said Arthur, who had only just realised what he was reading. He'd been concentrating so hard on getting the words right.

51

'I don't like the sound of that,' said Leaf, with a shudder. 'How do you stop it from doing that?'

'I'll . . . I'll see what the Atlas says,' said Arthur. He continued reading.

The mould enters its victim through skin, scales or hide once the Spirit-eater has provided a bridge by means of shaking hands, gripping a shoulder or such-like. Its spores are a grey colour, but they linger on the skin for only minutes, so the target is usually unaware it has been colonised. The mould travels through the blood, eventually lodging itself in the target's brain or other major sensorium. At this location it rapidly spreads, duplicating the nervous tissue until it is able to sift through the target's thoughts and memory, telepathically sharing them with the greater part of the mould that lies within the Spirit-eater's own secondary brain, usually located in its mid-section. The Spirit-eater uses these memories and thoughts to better mimic the target it has replaced. It is able to control the minds of those subjects where the mould is well-established, but not with great precision.

The influence of the mould is also felt in the behaviour of the Spirit-eater. In its natural state on Avraxyn, the mould always establishes a lair where it locates its primary host safe from harm. In the Spirit-eater, the mould is subordinate and must go where the Spirit-eater wills, but it will always influence the Spirit-eater to establish a lair. This will be dark and as deep in the ground as is practical for the Spirit-eater to easily access. It will be lined with soft materials, and somewhere in it will be the original seed item from which the Spirit-eater has been grown. This is usually a bone, piece of flesh, item of clothing, treasured personal possession or long-term pet or companion of the victim.

'That's really foul,' said Leaf.

'I've known worse,' muttered a voice from somewhere under the table. Dr Scamandros looked round, but either no one else heard Suzy's comment or they were well-practised at ignoring her.

'It's writing more,' said Arthur. The page cleared and the invisible hand wrote on.

The particular Spirit-eater that has duplicated Lord Arthur has chosen to call itself the Skinless Boy, perhaps because in its natural appearance it does not have very much skin, instead showing exposed bone. It may be defeated by taking its seed item, the pocket from Lord Arthur's school shirt. Lord Arthur must plunge that pocket back into Nothing.

At present, 10.20 a.m. local Earth Arthur time on Thursday, the Skinless Boy has established a temporary lair in the primary linen closet of East Area Hospital on Lower Ground Three. If the Spirit-eater moves to Arthur's home, it is most probable that it will establish its lair in the sump cavity beneath the house, which can be accessed by raising a concrete slab in the garden near the back fence.

'What was that about Thursday?' asked Leaf. 'What's Arthur time?'

Arthur read it again.

'It shouldn't be Thursday back home! We need to get back on Wednesday afternoon! How can it be Thursday?'

'Time is malleable between the House and the Secondary Realms,' said Dr Scamandros. 'But powerful personages such as yourself, Lord Arthur, affect and govern the relative flows. I can only surmise that the Spirit-eater, having something of your quality, has taken your place for chronological purposes. In ... ah ... other words, you are back.'

'But what about Leaf? Can she go back to Wednesday?'

'I would say not,' said Dr Scamandros. 'But I am no expert in these relativities. Perhaps Sneezer may know more, from the Seven Dials.'

'Without putting it to the test, sir, I cannot say,' said Sneezer. 'However, as a general rule the temporal relationship between a Secondary World and the House is set by the Front Door and defies explication. It presumably thought you had returned to your Earth and did not miss Miss Leaf, if you pardon me saying so. Therefore, the earliest Miss Leaf can return is twenty minutes past ten on Thursday. If it is still that time. More orange juice?'

'But that means I'll have been missing all night!' Leaf couldn't believe it. 'My parents will kill me!

CHAPTER FOUR

'Really?' asked Dr Scamandros. 'That seems rather harsh.'

'Oh, they won't actually kill me.' Leaf sighed. 'Even if they wanted to, they're in quarantine, so they can only shout at me through the intercom and pound on the interview window. It's just going to make life more difficult.'

Arthur was looking at the Atlas. Something had changed there, catching his eye. It took a second to work out what it was.

'Hey! The time back home's 10.21 now!'

'I have *got* to get back,' said Leaf. 'I'll try to do something about the Skinless Boy, I promise, but I really have to at least go and wave at my parents. So – how do I get home? And how do I get back here if . . . *once* I get hold of that pocket?'

'Sneezer can use Seven Dials to send you back to the hospital, I think,' said Arthur.

'Indeed, sir,' said Sneezer with a low bow.

'Coming back, I don't know . . .'

'The Skinless Boy went through the Front Door, so the House will have manifested itself on your world,' said Dame Primus with an airy wave of her hand. 'All you need to do is find it, knock on the Front Door and everything will be taken care of. Now, I must insist we return to the Agenda!'

'OK, OK,' said Arthur.

He turned to Leaf, but was suddenly unable to think of anything to say. He hadn't known her long but she already felt like an old friend, and he was asking her to do something really huge for him. He didn't know how to tell her how grateful he was for her friendship and help.

'I . . . I'm sorry I got you into this, Leaf. I mean I really appreciate it . . . you . . . uh . . . even my old friends back where I used to live wouldn't be as . . . anyway . . . I wish there was something . . . oh!'

He bent his hand back behind his neck and pulled off the string with the Mariner's medallion. It was the only thing he had that he could give.

'I don't know if it will be any use, but if things get really bad, try calling the Mariner. Maybe . . . not that he was very quick last time, but . . . well, good luck.'

Leaf dropped the string over her head, nodded firmly and turned away.

'Never gave me nuthin',' mumbled an unseen voice. Arthur looked down at the chair Leaf had just left and saw Suzy there, hunched over under the table. She was eyeing Dame Primus's foot and holding a large darning needle. She grinned at Arthur and stuck the needle in, but it had no effect. Tiny letters moved apart to allow the needle entry and then a savage red spark shot along the metal. Suzy dropped it and sucked her fingers as the needle became a small puddle of molten steel.

Arthur sighed and gestured at Suzy to come and sit next to him. She shook her head and stayed where she was.

Even though Leaf hadn't seen Sneezer move, he was already at the door when she reached it. She was about to go through when Dr Scamandros scurried over and put something in Leaf's hand as she went past.

'You'll need this,' he whispered. 'Won't be able to see the House without it, or find the Front Door. Dame Primus is a bit impatient – not intentionally, I'm sure.'

Leaf looked at what he'd given her: an open leather case that contained a pair of gold wire-rimmed spectacles, with thin lenses that were heavily cracked and crazed with tiny lines. She snapped the case shut and slipped it into the tight waistband of her breeches.

'This way please, Miss Leaf,' said Sneezer, as Scamandros ran back to his place at the table. 'Will you be requiring clothes more suitable to your own Secondary Realm and era?'

'If you've got something, that'd be great,' said Leaf, who was wearing a wide-sleeved cotton shirt and blue canvas breeches, the basic uniform of a ship's boy from the *Flying Mantis*. She hadn't even started to think about how to explain her clothes. Explaining why she hadn't been to see her parents, aunt and brother in quarantine for at least sixteen hours was going to be hard enough.

As she left, Leaf heard Dame Primus say something to Dr Scamandros and then launch into a speech. She sounded like a politician in a televised debate, wary of her opponent's delaying tactics.

'I trust, Lord Arthur, that we may now proceed as you have requested, with the Agenda rearranged in order of importance.'

'Sure,' said Arthur wearily, but he couldn't stop thinking about the Spirit-eater, this 'Skinless Boy' who was pretending to be him. What was the creature going to do? His parents would have no idea. They'd be helpless and so would his sisters and brothers. The thing would take over their minds and then . . . even if the Spirit-eater was destroyed and Arthur could go back, he might not have a family any more.

Something penetrated Arthur's thoughts. Dame Primus had just said something. Something very important.

'What was that?' he asked. 'What did you just say?'

'I said, Lord Arthur, we now suspect that the Morrow Days' misgovernance is no accident. They have been influenced or induced to behave as they do, with the ultimate aim being the complete and utter destruction of the House – and with it, the entirety of creation.'

'What?'

Arthur jumped out of his chair. Everyone looked at him and he slowly sat back down again, taking a deep breath to try to slow his suddenly speeding heart.

'Really, Lord Arthur, must I repeat myself again? If the Morrow Days are allowed to continue as they are, there is a great risk the entire House will be destroyed.'

'Are you sure?' asked Arthur nervously. 'I mean, Mister Monday was really lazy, and Grim Tuesday wanted to make lots of stuff and own it, and Wednesday . . . she couldn't help being a total pig. That doesn't mean they wanted to destroy the House.'

'In every case, the Trustees have put the House at risk,' said Dame Primus stiffly. 'Mister Monday's sloth meant the Lower House did not properly transport or store records, so it is even now impossible to ascertain what has happened to numerous Denizens, parts of the House, important objects, millions or possibly trillions of sentient mortals and even entire worlds in the Secondary Realms. There has also been considerable interference with the Secondary Realms, most of it via the Lower House.

'Grim Tuesday's case is even worse, for in his avarice, he mined so much Nothing that the Far Reaches of the House were in danger of inundation by Nothing. If the Far Reaches had fallen into Nothing, it is quite possible the rest of the House would have collapsed as well.

'Drowned Wednesday failed to stop the Border Sea breaking its bounds and now it extends to many places it should not, allowing passage to and from the House for those able to pass the Line of Storms, and impinging on areas of Nothing, again weakening the fabric of the House.'

She paused to sip her blood-red wine.

'All of this together suggests that the Trustees, knowingly or not, are part of a plan to demolish the House and reduce it and everything else the Architect created into Nothing!'

'The whole universe?' asked Arthur.

'*The whole universe*,' said Dame Primus. 'Though as yet we do not know who is behind this plot or what they can possibly hope to gain. Lord Sunday or Superior Saturday are the obvious candidates ... but then they too would be destroyed. Unless they have found a way to destroy only part of the House ... it is a curious puzzle. Being only three parts of the Will, I lack significant knowledge. In any case, it matters not, for our strategy does not differ, whether we oppose the Trustees or some force behind them.'

'What is "our" strategy?' asked Arthur.

'As it has been,' said Dame Primus. 'You will wrest the Fourth Key from Sir Thursday, the Fifth from Lady Friday, the Sixth from Superior Saturday and the Seventh from Lord Sunday.'

'That's it?' asked Arthur. 'You call that a strategy?'

'What did you expect from a frog-bear-fish?' said Suzy under the table, just loud enough for only Arthur to hear her.

'It is the grand strategy,' replied Dame Primus stiffly. 'Naturally, there are details to be gone into. One of the first things that must be done is to restore the bounds of the Border Sea before it causes any more problems. Since you have decided to retain the Third Key, Arthur, this should be your next task.'

'What do I have to do?'

'Wednesday's Dawn has identified 37,462 places where the Border Sea has impinged on the Secondary

Realms or Nothing. In each case, you must use the power of the Key to force the sea back to its proper place. Fortunately, you do not need to visit each location, as the power of the Third Key can be directed from Port Wednesday.'

'But I'd have to use the Key thirty-seven thousand times,' said Arthur. He looked at the crocodile ring on his finger. It didn't appear to have changed at all since he'd used the Atlas. Then he lifted it really close and could see that the gold had spread by the width of a hair and was now right on the fourth band. 'I'd become a Denizen in no time. And I could never go home.'

'This sentimental attachment to your original world and mortality is a serious weakness, Arthur,' said Dame Primus. She leaned forward as she spoke and Arthur felt his eyes drawn to her gaze. Her own eyes grew brighter, infused with a golden glow, and though she was not wearing her wings, Arthur could sense them rearing up behind her, increasing her majesty. He felt an almost overpowering urge to bow before her because she was so beautiful and powerful.

'The Border Sea must be brought within its bounds and only the Third Key can do it.'

Arthur tried to force his chin up, resisting the pressure to bow before the Will. It would be so easy to give in, to agree with whatever she wanted. But if he did, that would be the end of a boy named Arthur Penhaligon. He would be something else, no longer human.

But it would be so easy . . . Arthur opened his mouth and then shut it again as something sharp pricked his knee. The momentary pain enabled him to break eye contact with Dame Primus and he quickly looked down.

'Let me think about it,' said Arthur. It cost him an effort to even say that, but it worked. Dame Primus leaned back and the almost visible aura of her wings diminished, and her face no longer seemed so unbearably beautiful.

Arthur took a sip of his orange juice and glanced under the table. Suzy was pushing another large needle through the lining of her outer coat, where it nestled with half a dozen others.

He took a deep breath and continued, 'What's your plan for me after the Border Sea is taken care of?'

'Sir Thursday holds the Fourth Key,' said Dame Primus. 'As he commands the Glorious Army of the Architect, and is a very powerful, volatile and excessively violent Denizen, it would not be wise to confront him directly. Instead, we think it best if we employ agents to discover where Part Four of the Will has been imprisoned by Sir Thursday. Once we have found and released Part Four, then we can consider our next move. In the mean time, because of the danger from assassins, it would be best if you go to Port Wednesday under guard and work to contain the Border Sea with the Third Key.'

'Right ...' said Arthur. He frowned and sipped his orange juice as he tried to figure out what he should do. The only thing he knew for sure was that if he wanted any chance of ever getting back to being normal, he had to avoid using the Keys. Obviously, the Third Key needed to be used right now to get the Border Sea back under control. But Dame Primus could do that.

And I'll just hide out here, thought Arthur bitterly. He felt powerless and trapped, but at the same time, he could not think of anything else he could do.

'If I use the Third Key that much then I will turn into a Denizen, full stop,' Arthur said finally. 'But I realise that the Border Sea must be contained. So I will give you the Third Key.'

'Good,' said Dame Primus. She smiled and tapped her Agenda a few times with satisfaction, then suddenly stopped as if struck by a sudden recollection. 'However, you are the Rightful Heir. You should not remain a weak mortal. It probably would be best for you to keep and use all three Keys and become a Denizen as quickly as possible.'

Arthur was irritated now. 'I've told you tons of times – I know I can't go home now, but at least there's a chance . . . a small chance that one day, if I don't become a Denizen . . . oh forget it!'

Arthur sat back down and slapped the table angrily, spoiling the effect by choking slightly on his own spit as he did so. To clear his throat, he picked up his orange juice and drank it down – until something hard rolled out of the cup and into his mouth, almost choking him for real.

Arthur spat whatever it was on to the table. The object rang like a bell as it hit the metal surface, rolled in ever-decreasing circles and quivered to a stop. It was a silver coin, about the size of a ten-pence piece.

'What the –' said Arthur. 'There was a coin in my drink!'

'No!' said Dame Primus. She dropped her gold pencil and a tortoiseshell fan appeared in her hand. As she resumed speaking, she fanned her face in agitation. 'Surely you wouldn't be eligible?'

'What are you talking about?' Arthur picked up the coin and looked at it. One side showed a knight's head, with the visor of his helmet up and ostrich plumes falling down one side. The letters around the side were initially just gobbledygook to Arthur, but they changed as he looked at them, to spell out *Sir Thursday, Defender of the House*. The other side showed the top third of a big old-fashioned sword, with a serpent wound around the hilt. Or perhaps the serpent *was* the hilt – Arthur couldn't be sure. The words around this side also shimmered and changed, to become *One Shilling*.

'It's just a coin,' said Arthur. He looked around at everyone. They were all staring at him and they all looked disturbed. 'Isn't it?'

'It's Sir Thursday's shilling,' Dame Primus explained. 'You've been tricked into taking it. One of the very oldest tricks, to make someone accept something they don't want or don't know about.'

'What does that mean?'

'It means you've been drafted,' said Dame Primus. 'Into the Glorious Army of the Architect. I expect the papers will arrive at any moment.'

'Drafted? Into the army? But how –'

'I suppose that technically you have a position within the House,' said Dame Primus. 'Which allows Sir Thursday to draft you. Every Denizen, at some time, must do their century of military service –'

'Century! I can't spend a *hundred years* in the army!'

'The question is whether this is an intentional plan on the part of Sir Thursday to bring you into his power or just some accident of the administrative process. If the latter, you will be quite safe until we can find out where Part Four of the Will is, and then with its help, we can –'

'*Safe?* I'll be in the Army! What if I get sent into a battle or something? What if Sir Thursday just kills me?'

Dame Primus shook her head.

'He can't just kill you. Once you've been recruited, he'll have to follow his own regulations. I suppose that he could make things very unpleasant for you. But they do that to the recruits anyway.'

'Fantastic. What about the assassins that killed Mister Monday and Grim Tuesday? What if they kill me?'

'Hmmm. In fact, this could work to your advantage, Arthur. No assassin from the Middle or Upper House would dare attack you among your comrades in the Great Maze, and a Denizen from the Incomparable Gardens would be very obvious and give you time to get away or think of something. You would be out of the way, and comparatively safe, while we get on with things.'

'I beg your pardon, Dame Primus, but there is one thing Sir Thursday could and probably will do if he knows Arthur is among his recruits,' Monday's Noon interrupted. 'My own service was long ago, but I have not forgotten it. Arthur will probably be safe enough during his first year of training. But after that, he could be posted to the Borderers or to the Mountain Fort, where there is always fighting with the Nithlings. As a mortal, he would stand in much more danger in battle than any Denizen.'

'What if I just don't go?' Arthur asked. It was seeming like the best choice. 'I mean, come on. There has to be some benefit to being Master of the Lower House and Duke of the Border Sea and all that. I mean, Sir Thursday couldn't draft Mister Monday or Grim Tuesday or Lady Wednesday, could he?'

'Yes, he could,' said Monday's Noon. 'If they had not already done their service.'

'But I refuse to –' Arthur began to say. He was interrupted by a loud knock on the door. A Commissionaire Sergeant poked his head in and cleared his throat.

'Excuse me, ma'am,' he said to Dame Primus. 'Lord Arthur, there's a recruiting sergeant here. Says he's on official business and he's got the right papers. He's not carrying any weapons. What should we do?'

'We have no choice,' said Dame Primus. 'Sir Thursday has the power to do this. Delay him for a few minutes, then let him in. Arthur, you had best give me the Third Key now.'

'You're just going to hand me over?' asked Arthur.

'We have no choice,' Dame Primus repeated. The Agenda flicked over a few pages and she ticked something with her pen, an action that made Arthur even more furious. He couldn't see it, but he knew it had to be an item that said something like, 'Keep Arthur safe and out of the way.'

'I'm keeping the Third Key,' he said loudly. 'I'll probably need it.'

'If you keep it then you will be giving it to Sir Thursday,' said Monday's Noon. 'Recruits aren't allowed to have any personal possessions. Everything you need is issued to you.'

Arthur stared at Noon. He couldn't believe what he was hearing. Everyone was just accepting that he was going off for a hundred years of service in the Army of the House.

'I'm not going,' he said. He held up the Third Key like a weapon. Sensing his mood, it grew longer and sharper, till he was holding a trident as long as he was tall, its tines as long as his forearms. 'And anyone who tries to make me is going to suffer.'

'Twice,' added the voice under the table.

CHAPTER FIVE

'I'm afraid that won't work, Lord Arthur,' said Dame Primus. She was still irritatingly annotating her Agenda and she didn't even look up at Arthur. 'The Keys are only sovereign in their own demesne, though they are of equal puissance in the Secondary Realms.'

'What does that mean?' asked Arthur.

'The Third Key only has its full powers in the Border Sea, the Second in the Far Reaches and the First in the Lower House,' explained Dr Scamandros. 'They all work in the Secondary Realms, where they are of equivalent power. Except, I believe for the Seventh Key, which is paramount –'

'Time is short, Lord Arthur,' interrupted Dame Primus. She shut the Agenda with a businesslike clap. 'If you are going to relinquish the Third Key to me, it must be done now.'

'But I don't want to go into the Army,' said Arthur. The anger was leaving him now and he just felt sad and alone, his only ally still hiding under the table. 'Especially not for a hundred years! There must be some way I can get out of it.'

'If you can find the Fourth Part of the Will and gain the Fourth Key, then you can take Sir Thursday's place as commander and release yourself,' said Monday's Noon.

'We will, of course, also continue to search for the Fourth Part of the Will ourselves,' said Dame Primus. 'Once we find it, we may be able to help you.'

'I'll come with you, Arthur,' said Suzy. She crawled out from under the table, sat down in Leaf's chair and drank what was left of the other girl's orange juice, before adding, 'It can't be that bad.'

'You shall do no such thing,' said Dame Primus. 'You have a job to do here, as Monday's Tierce.'

'No one ever volunteers for the Army,' said Monday's Noon. 'Everyone gets drafted. Besides the Denizens originally made to be soldiers, I mean. I'm not even sure it's possible to volunteer.'

'I reckon if Arthur wants me to go along then it is my job,' said Suzy. 'I kind of remember that I might have been in the Army before. I was probably drafted ages ago and did my time, only it's got washed out from between my ears. Maybe it'll come back. I can help Arthur find Part Four of the Will anyway.'

'Thanks, Suzy!' exclaimed Arthur. He felt enormously better. Having Suzy along would make all the difference. 'I do want you to come. You always cheer me up, not to mention helping me. I suppose . . . if I've got to go, I'd better get on with it.'

He got up, taking the Third Key, and went over to Dame Primus. She slid out of her chair and bowed to him. When she straightened up, Arthur was struck by just how much taller she was, now that she contained three parts of the Will. She was well over seven feet tall, perhaps even eight feet tall now, and up close he could see tiny words crawling everywhere over her skin and clothes. There were hundreds and thousands of tiny old-fashioned type letters in constant movement, changing colour as they shifted to become skin or clothes. Every now and then Arthur could just make out a word or a fraction of a phrase, things like, 'The Will is the Word and the Word is –' Looking at her was a bit like examining a banknote, where you could only see all the tiny engraved detail that made up the images if you were up close.

'Do you recall the words, Lord Arthur, to appoint me Steward of the Third Key?'

'No,' said Arthur. 'You start and I'll say them after you.'

'Very well. "I, Arthur, Duke of the Border Sea, Lord of the Far Reaches, Master of the Lower House, Wielder of the First, Second and Third Keys to the Kingdom, do grant my faithful servant, the combined First, Second and Third Parts of the Great Will of the Architect, all my powers . . ."'

Arthur repeated the words mechanically, his mind elsewhere. He was afraid of what the Skinless Boy was going to do and whether Leaf was just going into danger without any hope of success. He was also afraid of what was going to happen to him. After all, he was only a boy. He shouldn't be a recruit in any army, let alone one full of immortal Denizens who were much tougher and stronger than he was.

Dame Primus took the trident, and for the first time Arthur realised that the gloves she was wearing were in fact the gauntlets of the Second Key, transformed to be more ladylike. And the sword made of clock-hands that was the First Key was thrust through her belt, mostly concealed by the outer train of her long dress, which flowed around her like a cloak.

'Thank you, Arthur,' said Dame Primus. 'I had best take the Atlas too.'

'I suppose it's not much good to me without a Key,' said Arthur. He pulled the small green book out and slowly handed it over. He felt like he was losing everything that might help him.

'Excellent! I will begin to work on the Border Sea immediately,' announced Dame Primus. 'We will also spare no effort in trying to find the Fourth Part of ourself and will keep you informed of our progress.'

'Mail call only happens twice a year at recruit school,' said Monday's Noon. 'And the recruits are not permitted to telegraph or telephone.'

'We will find some means,' said Dame Primus. 'Now, we had best let the recruiting officer in. Good luck, Arthur.'

'I still don't like this,' said Arthur. 'I want you to find out any way I can be released from the army.'

'As you command, Lord Arthur,' said Dame Primus. She inclined her head but didn't bow, and Arthur once more had the feeling that it would suit the Will to have him trapped in the House for ages, and with the Skinless Boy taking his place back home . . . he might have nowhere to go after he got out of the Army, except to become a Denizen.

'I'll be back,' Arthur said fiercely. 'As myself, not as a Denizen. If I have to find Part Four of the Will myself and get the Fourth Key from Sir Thursday, I'll do it. And I expect everyone here to help Leaf however they can, particularly if . . . when . . . she gets back with the pocket.'

'Ah, Lord Arthur,' Dr Scamandros said nervously, with a sideways glance at Dame Primus. '*Expect* is such a . . . shall we say . . . inexact word –'

'Here is the recruiting officer!' interrupted Dame Primus. 'Welcome to Monday's Dayroom, Lieutenant.'

The officer in question stood at attention just inside the door and snapped a salute. To Arthur he looked like someone out of a history book. He wore a scarlet tunic with white lapels and white facings laden with many gold buttons. His legs were covered by black trousers with a broad gold stripe down each leg, his feet by black boots with spurs and he was made at least a foot taller by a towering black fur hat with blue and white plumes. He also had a hand-sized crescent of bronze hanging around his neck, which was engraved with curlicues and numbers.

He looked round the room and saw Dame Primus, clearly the tallest and most important Denizen.

'I do beg your pardon, ma'am,' said the Lieutenant. 'Crosshaw is my name, recruiting officer. I have a draft requisition for one Arthur Penhaligon, only I think there must be a mistake, as it gives this Arthur a precedence within the House of . . . well . . . six. I thought perhaps there might be a large number of zeros missing . . . Perhaps if there is someone among Mister Monday's staff called Arthur Penhaligon, I might test the draft document?'

'There is no mistake,' said Dame Primus. She indicated Arthur with a lofty wave of her hand. 'The person in question is Lord Arthur Penhaligon, Master of the Lower House, Lord of the Far Reaches, Duke of the Border Sea, sixth in precedence within the House. I am Dame Primus, Parts One, Two and Three of the Will of the Architect.'

Crosshaw gulped loudly, opened his mouth, shut it again, then looked at the papers in his hand. He seemed to find strength there, for he looked straight at Arthur and marched over, coming to a heel-stamping stop right in front of him.

'I do beg your pardon, ah . . . Lord Arthur. Having been at a remote outpost in the Great Maze up until yesterday when I assumed my new duties, I did not know that there had been changes, um, among the Trustees. The thing is . . . I don't quite know how to put it . . . As far as I know, if your name's on the draft form then you've been drafted. I have to give it to you.'

The lieutenant held out a large square of parchment, which had a lot of small type with Arthur's name written clearly in a space in the middle.

'What happens if I don't take it?' Arthur asked.

'I'm not entirely sure,' said Crosshaw. 'If you do take it, I escort you via elevator to the Great Maze, to the Recruit Camp. If you don't take it, I think the powers within the draft form take you to the Recruit Camp anyway, by more . . . unpleasant means.'

'If I might glance at the document?' asked Dr Scamandros, who had moved to stand at Arthur's shoulder. He set his crystal-lensed glasses on his forehead, not on his eyes, and peered at the document. 'Ah, yes, here we are. Most interesting. If you do not go willingly, Arthur, then you will be transformed into a shape, generally a small package of brown paper tied up with string, able to pass through the House's postal system . . . which given the problems still current in the Lower House would not be an . . . ah . . . efficient means of travel.'

'OK, I'll take it,' said Arthur. He reached out and took the paper then cried out in horror as it wrapped itself around his hand and started to shrug itself up his arm like a horrid slug consuming his flesh – though it didn't hurt.

'Don't be alarmed!' cried Crosshaw. 'It's just turning into a recruit uniform!'

Arthur looked away and tried to relax. The paper continued to move over him, rustling and billowing. When he looked down, his clothes had been transformed into a simple blue tunic with black buttons, blue breeches and short black boots. A white canvas belt with a brass buckle carried a white ammunition pouch and an empty bayonet loop (known as a frog) on his hip.

But the draft notice wasn't entirely finished. Arthur flinched as he felt it come out from under his tunic and swarm up the back of his neck. It climbed on to his head and transformed itself into a blue pillbox hat, with a tight and uncomfortable chin strap that buckled on under Arthur's lip instead of under his chin.

'Very good, recruit,' said Crosshaw. He was no longer nervous, and Arthur felt immediately smaller and more insignificant. 'Follow me.'

The lieutenant saluted Dame Primus then spun on his heel and took a step towards the door.

'Hang on!' said Suzy. 'I'm coming too!'

Crosshaw turned in surprise. 'I beg your pardon!'

'I'm volunteering,' said Suzy. 'I want to go along with Arthur.'

'We don't take volunteers,' said Crosshaw. 'Never know who we might get.'

'But I think I might have served before – I'm probably in some kind of Reserve.'

'We're not calling up reservists either,' Crosshaw sniffed. 'Particularly Piper's children who've had everything they ever knew washed out from between their ears.'

'I've got a piece of paper somewhere,' said Suzy as she rummaged through her pockets.

'I can't help you, miss,' Crosshaw dismissed her with finality. 'Come along, Recruit Penhaligon. Hold yourself a bit straighter. What's that on your leg?'

'Crab-armour,' said Arthur. Unlike the rest of his clothes, the crab-armour had remained, his new blue breeches forming under it. 'For a broken leg.'

'As prescribed by me,' said Dr Scamandros. 'Dr Scamandros, at your service. Major Scamandros, Army Sorcerer, retired. I did my draft service about three thousand years ago, before going on to advanced study in the Upper House.'

'Very good, sir,' said Crosshaw. 'If it's a prescribed medical necessity, it can remain.'

'Lord Arthur is a mortal,' added Scamandros. He got out a small notepad and hastily scrawled something on it with a peacock-feather quill that dripped silver ink. 'He needs the crab-armour and the ring on his finger for medical reasons. He should be given special consideration.'

Crosshaw took the proffered note, folded it and tucked it under his cuff.

'I'm still coming along,' said Suzy.

'No room for you in our elevator,' snapped Crosshaw. 'I suppose there's nothing to stop you petitioning Sir Thursday to re-enlist, if you actually are a reservist. Not something I'd do. But there's nothing to stop you. Come along, Recruit Penhaligon. By the left, quick march!'

Crosshaw led off with his left foot, boot-heels crashing on the marble floor as he marched towards the door. Arthur followed, doing his best to imitate the lieutenant's marching style and keep in step.

He felt suddenly incredibly alone, abandoned by everyone and extremely uncertain about what the future held.

Was he really going to disappear into the Army for a hundred years?

CHAPTER SIX

'Are the clothes satisfactory, Miss Leaf?' Sneezer asked Leaf as she came out from getting changed behind the central bookshelf in the middle of the library.

'I guess so,' she answered. She looked down at the band T-shirt that featured a group she'd never heard of. From the tie-dyed swirl of mythological creatures, she guessed it was from about 1970. She had jeans on below that, but they were not exactly denim though they looked like it, and the patch on the back pocket was a very sharply focused and impressive hologram featuring an animal that she was sure did not exist on Earth.

'If you would like to do so, we can try to take a look at your destination before you go through,' said Sneezer. He walked over to a row of bookshelves and pulled on the hanging rope at the end. A bell rang somewhere above Leaf's head and the entire wall of floor-to-ceiling bookshelves rolled back and then slid away to show a seven-sided room of dark walnut panelling. In the centre of the room, seven tall grandfather clocks were arranged in a circle, facing one another.

'What's that noise?' asked Leaf. She could feel as much as hear a weird, low humming noise, but there was no ticking sound coming from the clocks.

'The pendulums of the clocks,' said Sneezer. 'The heartbeat of time. These are the Seven Dials, miss.'

'I would like to have a look first,' said Leaf. 'Can you show me where the Skinless Boy is?'

'We can but try,' Sneezer replied. He tapped one long finger against his nose and smiled. In Monday's service that would have been a ghastly gesture made with a dirty, long-nailed hand against a nose covered in boils, but now Sneezer's hand was clean and manicured and his nose, though long and hooked, was healthy. Even the long white hair that grew from the back of his head was neat and tied back with a dark blue velvet bow, matching his long, tailed coat. 'Please stay out of the circle of clocks until I tell you otherwise, Miss Leaf.'

The butler took a deep breath then quickly strode in and started moving the hands of the nearest clock. That done, he raced to the next, and then the next, adjusting the time on each face. After changing the seventh clock, he quickly left the circle.

'We should see something in a moment,' Sneezer explained. 'Then I shall tweak the setting a little and send you back. I'm afraid it is clear that I am unable to return you any earlier than twenty-one minutes past ten on the Thursday after the Wednesday you left. Ah – it is beginning.'

A slowly spinning tornado of white fog began to swirl up out of the floor, getting slower and spreading wider as it rose. In a few seconds, it had completely filled the circle between the grandfather clocks. As Leaf watched, a silver sheen spread through the cloud, becoming so bright that she had to squint.

Then the silver paled and the cloud became transparent. Leaf found herself looking down on a hospital room, as if she were a fly on the ceiling. It was a typical hospital room with a single bed. Arthur was in the bed – or rather, Leaf reminded herself hastily, the Skinless Boy was in the bed. It looked exactly like Arthur and she shivered, thinking that if she hadn't been told, she would never have known it wasn't her friend.

The next thing she saw was the clock on the wall. It read 10.25, which was comforting. If it was still only Thursday . . .

The door opened and a doctor came in. Leaf started because she hadn't expected to hear anything. But the sound of the door opening and the doctor's footsteps were as clear as if she really was looking down from the ceiling.

'Hello, Arthur,' said the doctor. 'Remember me? Dr Naihan. I just need to take a look at your cast.'

'Help yourself,' said the Skinless Boy. Leaf shivered again, for the Nithling's voice was exactly the same as Arthur's.

The doctor smiled and folded back the bedclothes to take a look at the high-tech cast on the Skinless Boy's leg. He had hardly looked for more than a few seconds when he straightened up and scratched his head in surprise.

'This is . . . I don't understand . . . the cast appears to have merged with your leg . . . but that's impossible. I'd better call Professor Arden.'

'What's wrong with the cast?' asked the Skinless Boy. It sat up and slid off the bed as Dr Naihan picked up the bedside phone.

'No, you mustn't get up, Arthur,' exclaimed Naihan. 'I'll just call –'

Before the doctor could say anything else, the Skinless Boy struck him in the throat, so hard that the man was propelled against the oxygen outlets on the wall. He slid down the wall and lay on the floor, not moving.

The Skinless Boy laughed, a strange mixture of Arthur's laugh overlaid with something else, something inhuman. It bent down and laid one finger against Naihan's neck, clearly checking to see if he was dead. Then it picked up the body with one hand, something Arthur could never have managed, and casually slung the dead doctor in the closet.

Then it went to the door, opened it and looked out for a second before it went through. The door slowly swung shut behind the Nithling, closing with a final click that made Leaf shudder.

She had not realised just how awful it would be to see a monster that looked and sounded exactly like Arthur. A monster that killed people with careless ease.

'Now, Miss Leaf, it is time for you to return,' said Sneezer, making Leaf jump. As he spoke, the hospital scene vanished and Leaf saw again only the wooden panelling of the walls and floor, and the humming clocks.

The butler stepped in and quickly changed the hands of just three of the clocks.

'Stand in the circle, quickly, before the clocks strike!'

He jumped out and Leaf stepped in. A second later, the clocks all began to strike at the same time, ringing out as the room shimmered around Leaf. She felt dizzy as everything went hazy and indistinct, and then a wave of nausea hit her as a white glow began to spread across the walls, floor and ceiling. Soon she could see nothing but white around her.

She was just about to scream or vomit – or both – when the light receded on one side and she could see a kind of corridor, bordered by white light but more comfortably dim in the middle.

Leaf staggered out and along this corridor, holding her stomach. She felt totally disoriented, with the white light pressing behind her and close to the sides. She couldn't hear her own footsteps, or her breath, or anything else.

Then, without warning, sound came back: a kind of roaring like wind in her ears, which quickly faded and was gone. A moment later, the white light vanished. Leaf, her eyes still screwed up, took a few loud steps on a hard floor and fell over, rolling on to her back. It took her disturbed mind a while to realise that the lights she was now staring at, though white, were simply fluorescent panels in a pale blue ceiling.

She sat up and looked around. She was in a hospital corridor. East Area Hospital. She recognised the pale blue and ghastly brown colour scheme. There was no one in the corridor, but there were lots of doors all the way along.

And there was a clock above the swing doors at the end of the corridor. According to it, the time was ten past twelve, which made her worry because when she'd been a fly on the wall looking down at the Skinless Boy, it had only been 10.25. If it remained Thursday then it was only a little more than an hour lost, but still . . .

She got up, wiped her mouth with the back of her hand and checked the nearest doors. They were all storerooms of some kind, which indicated that she was on one of the lower, non-public areas of the hospital. Which meant her first priority had to be to get out, before she was picked up by hospital security and had to explain what she was doing there or how she'd got in.

A few minutes later, leaving a shrieking exit door alarm behind her, Leaf stepped out of an elevator on to the quarantine reception floor. But it wasn't like when she'd left it. Then, the waiting area had been full of people who'd come to see their relatives in quarantine, who were still being kept in case the Sleepy Plague wasn't really gone. Now the waiting room was empty and there were huge sheets of plastic draped all over the chairs, and there was the tell-tale smell of recently sprayed disinfectant. Worse, from Leaf's point of view, instead of just the two usual security guards by the secure reception area, there were four hospital security guards, half a dozen police in full biohazard gear and a couple of soldiers in camouflage biosuits.

Before she could get back in the elevator, they all noticed her.

'Don't step forward!' boomed one of the hospital guards. 'This whole level is Q-zoned. How did you get here?'

'I just got in the elevator,' said Leaf, acting younger than she was and much more stupid.

'It's supposed to be locked off from the ground,' grumbled the guard. 'Just get back in and go down to Level One.'

'I won't catch anything, will I?' asked Leaf.

'Go back down!' ordered the guard.

Leaf stepped back in and pressed the button. Clearly, something had changed in the time she'd been away. The fact that this whole quarantine level had now been locked off did not sound good. But the Sleepy Plague had gone . . .

The elevator doors opened on the ground floor. Leaf stepped out, into pandemonium. There were people everywhere, filling the lobby, the corridors and the waiting areas. Most of the people sitting looked like hospital workers, not visitors, and as far as Leaf could tell from a quick scan, there were no patients.

She started walking through the crowd, her mind busy trying to work out what to do. The first thing would be to establish exactly what day it was, and what was going on. Then she'd have to work out how to get to the linen storeroom where the Skinless Boy had supposedly hidden Arthur's pocket. Then get that out of the hospital and find the manifestation of the House, which Arthur had told her ages ago had appeared near his house, taking up several streets . . .

Getting there was going to be very difficult, Leaf realised as she looked out of the main doors. They were shut, and taped with black and yellow biohazard tape. The windows were pasted with posters that even from a distance Leaf could see were headed with the words CREIGHTON ACT, the legal authority that allowed the government to establish a quarantine area and use lethal force to make sure everyone stayed in it.

Beyond the windows, out in the hospital car park, there were four or five armoured vehicles and lots and lots of soldiers in biohazard suits. Mixing with them were orange-suited figures with three bright fluoro-yellow letters on their backs: NBA, which stood for the National Biocontrol Authority.

Leaf looked around to see if she could see anyone she knew. But there were no familiar faces, until she finally spotted one of the nurses she'd talked to when Ed and the rest of her family were first taken away. He was sitting with his back to the wall, wearily sipping a cup of coffee, while two other nurses dozed to either side of him, heads slumped forward, abandoned coffee cups and half-eaten sandwiches on the floor.

Leaf threaded her way through the crowd and stood in front of the nurse.

'Hi,' she said. She couldn't remember his name and the nameplate on his shirt was tilted down.

The nurse looked up. His eyes didn't focus for a second. He shook his head, wiped a palm across his face and smiled.

'Oh, hi. You get caught here when we got Q-zoned?'

'Yeah,' said Leaf. 'Only I was asleep in the waiting room ... uh ... over there, and I just woke up and I don't know what's happened. Is it the Sleepy Plague back again?'

'No, it's something else,' said the nurse. He straightened up a little and Leaf saw his nameplate. Senior Nurse Adam Jamale. 'Maybe nothing even, but you know, no one wants to take a chance.'

'So what happened?'

'Beats me.' Jamale shook his head. 'It all came down an hour ago. I heard a rumour that they found signs of a bioweapon attack on one of the staff.'

'Yeah, that's right,' said one of the other nurses with a yawn. 'Dr Penhaligon herself, which kind of makes sense. I mean, if you're going to take out someone, you take out the best, right?'

'But who would do that?' asked Leaf, immediately worried for Arthur's mother. 'And what kind of bioweapon?'

'Maybe terrorists,' said the other nurse. 'We didn't get any details. Just that Dr Penhaligon noticed some symptom and reported herself straight away. She'll be in total exclusion on Level Twenty now.'

'I sure hope she beats whatever it is,' said Jamale. 'You know, she invented half the stuff we use to pinpoint viruses? Way back, from the Rapid-Lyse I to the new DNA deep-scanning PAG we got last month.'

'Yeah? I didn't know she was behind the Rapid-Lyse. She never mentioned it in that course we did on anti-viral –'

Leaf tuned out. The bioweapon attack Arthur's mum had noticed had to be the grey spores of the mould from the Skinless Boy. Since it was sorcerously created from some alien thing, it was extremely unlikely that human medical science would be able to

92

do anything about it. But perhaps they might be able to slow it down.

'Oh yeah, I forgot,' Leaf said, interrupting the two nurses. 'What day is it?'

'Thursday,' said Jamale. 'Maybe you should get some more sleep.'

'Not after seeing my family with the Sleepy Plague,' said Leaf. 'Sleep isn't so attractive now. But I have to go. Thanks!'

'No problem,' said Jamale. 'Take care, now.'

'I'll try.' Leaf waved and headed back through the crowds, thinking furiously. What would the Skinless Boy be doing? Did it have some objective other than to simply replace Arthur? The quarantine would make it harder for it to infect people with the mind-reading mould, but it was still a Nithling. There was nothing and no one on Earth who could stop it doing whatever it wanted.

No one except her. She had to find Arthur's pocket fast, somehow break out of the quarantine around the hospital and find the House.

She changed direction and headed to the cafeteria. Accordingly to the Atlas, the Skinless Boy had made a lair in a linen storeroom. Presumably there would be some way of getting towels and tablecloths and so on from the linen store to the cafeteria and back again.

Maybe a laundry chute or something. All Leaf had to do was find it and trace it backwards.

Leaf was weaving her way through the crowd, and nearly at the cafeteria entrance, when she caught a glimpse of a familiar face.

Arthur's face.

The Skinless Boy was just ahead of her, hobbling along with the help of a single crutch. As it passed through the crowd, it accepted hands to help it and often almost slipped, grabbing the nearest shoulder or elbow to steady itself.

It smiled and whispered 'Thank you' with each touch and helping hand.

CHAPTER SEVEN

Lieutenant Crosshaw didn't talk to Arthur in the elevator, at least not after issuing instructions on how Arthur was to stand at attention. They were in a very narrow, military-issue elevator not much larger than a phone box. There was a red line painted on the floor about two feet back from the doors. Arthur had to stand at attention with the toes of his new boots on the line.

Arthur had been only mildly surprised to find the elevator was behind one of the doors in the corridor outside the big meeting room. He knew there were elevators all over the place, belonging to different demesnes of the House or designated for particular uses or passengers. He imagined it was a bit like all the tunnels and conduits for water, power and transport under a modern city, criss-crossing all over each other, clustering close together in parts and very spread out in others. Somewhere there must be a map or a guide to all the House's elevator networks. The Atlas would have such a thing of course . . .

Arthur's musings on elevators were interrupted as he and Crosshaw arrived at their destination. Unlike the other elevators Arthur had been in, this one had neither operator nor bell. It had a horn, which blew a single sharp note as the doors sprang open.

Beyond the doors was a windswept plain of very short, very brown grass. The wind was hot and Arthur saw a sun, or at least the kind of artificial sun that parts of the House had, high in the sky. Perhaps half a mile away, across the plain, he could see a very planned, orderly-looking town of twenty to thirty houses and other larger buildings. Beyond the town, to what was notionally the west, he was rather surprised to see a tropical jungle. To the north there was an area of sharp granite hills, stark and yellow, and to the east there was a high ridge, covered in a forest of cold-climate firs and pines, complete with scatterings of snow.

'Ten paces forward, quick march!' shouted Lieutenant Crosshaw.

Surprised by the command, Arthur stepped forward and was immediately unsure how many steps he'd taken. Was it one or two? Anxiety rose as he counted out the remaining steps. What would happen if he got it wrong?

'That's ten paces! Can't you count, Recruit?' bellowed a new and highly unpleasant voice behind him. Even though he'd only counted nine, Arthur stopped and started to turn around.

'Face front!' screamed the voice, from what felt like two inches behind Arthur's left ear. 'Don't move!'

'Ah, Sergeant Helve, if I may have a word,' interrupted Crosshaw tentatively, as Arthur felt an intake of breath behind his neck, indicating another vocal explosion was about to take place.

'Yes, sir!' bellowed the voice, which Arthur presumed belonged to Sergeant Helve. He didn't dare look around or move, though he badly needed to scratch his nose as the heat had already sent a bead of perspiration sliding down towards his left nostril.

Lieutenant Crosshaw and Sergeant Helve spoke quietly behind Arthur for about thirty seconds. He couldn't hear what Crosshaw said, but even Helve's whisper was louder than a normal voice, so he caught the sergeant's half of the conversation.

'Who?'

'I don't give a raised rat's whisker who he is.'

'Bad for morale, sir. Can't be done. Is that all, sir?'

'I accept delivery of one Recruit Penhaligon, sir. With medical advice.'

Arthur heard footsteps then the sound of the elevator doors closing. But he still didn't dare to move, though now the itching sensation on the bridge of his nose was almost unbearable.

'Stand at ease, Recruit!' barked Helve.

Arthur relaxed, but he still didn't scratch his nose. He had a vague memory of his much older brother Erazmuz – who was a major in the army – talking about the things that movies always got wrong about military service. One of them was the difference between 'stand at ease' and 'stand easy'. Unfortunately, Arthur couldn't remember exactly what the difference was. Staying still seemed to be the best option.

'Feet this far apart, hands behind your back, thumbs crossed, head straight, eyes straight ahead,' shouted Helve. He suddenly marched in front of Arthur and stood at ease himself. 'Say "Yes, Sergeant!"'

'Yes, Sergeant!' shouted Arthur, putting all his strength into his voice. He knew about the need to yell ridiculously loudly from Erazmus as well.

'Good!' shouted Helve. He stood at attention and leaned in towards Arthur. He wasn't the tallest Denizen

Arthur had seen – no more than six and a half feet high – but he had the broadest shoulders the boy had seen outside one of Grim Tuesday's Grotesques. His face was not handsome, as was usual for Denizens, but it might once have been. Now it was marred by a Nothing-burn that stretched from his left ear to his chin. If he had ever had any hair, it had been shaved off.

Like the lieutenant, Helve was wearing a scarlet tunic, but his had three broad gold stripes on each sleeve. He also had three medals pinned on his left breast, all of dull gunmetal, with multicoloured ribbons attached. One of the medals had five small clasps attached to the ribbon, and another had a score of tiny silver star pins on its ribbon arranged in a pattern that left space for several more.

'Lieutenant Crosshaw says you are a special case!' bellowed Helve. 'I do not like special cases! Special cases do not make good soldiers! Special cases do not help other recruits become good soldiers! Therefore, you will not be a special case! You understand me!'

'I think so –'

'Shut up! That was not a question!'

Sergeant Helve suddenly leaned back then scratched the back of his head and looked around. Arthur didn't dare follow his gaze, but whatever he saw or didn't see reassured the sergeant.

'Stand easy, Recruit. For the next two minutes I'm going to talk to you Denizen to Piper's child, not sergeant to recruit. But you will never mention it to me and you will not ever speak of it to anyone else. Do you understand?'

'Yes, Sergeant,' said Arthur cautiously.

Sergeant Helve reached into his belt pouch and pulled out a flat tin from which he took a cigarillo, which he didn't light. Instead, he bit the end off and started chewing. He held out the soggy end to Arthur, who shook his head and took the opportunity to rapidly scratch his nose.

'It's like this, Penhaligon. You shouldn't be here. There's something political going on, isn't there?'

Arthur nodded.

'I hate politics!' said Helve. He spat out a disgusting gob of chewed tobacco for emphasis. 'So here's what I want to do. It's not strictly legal, so you'll have to agree. I want to change your name. Just while you're here. That way, you can get on with the course, the other recruits won't be distracted and we won't have any trouble. It'll only be on the local record here, nothing permanent. You'll graduate under your own name. If you make it.'

'OK,' said Arthur. If he had to be here, it would make sense to hide under another name. 'I mean, yes, Sergeant.'

'What'll we call you?' Helve took another bite of his cigarillo and chewed thoughtfully. Arthur tried not to breathe in. The smell of chewed tobacco was revolting, worse than he'd have imagined. If it was tobacco and not some close equivalent from another world out in the Secondary Realms.

'How about Ruhtra?' Helve suggested. 'That's Arthur backwards.'

'Roottra . . . ah . . . maybe something that sounds better . . . or less obvious,' suggested Arthur. He looked across at the horizon, wrinkling his eyes against the harsh sunlight, so much in contrast to the lush green jungle to the west. 'How about Ray? Ray . . . um . . . Green? I could be an Ink-Filler from the Lower House.'

Helve nodded and spat again. He carefully restored the half-masticated cigarillo to the tin and slid it back into his belt pouch. Then he drew out a clipboard that was five times larger than the pouch, took a pencil from behind his ear, though one had not been there before, and made some quick amendments to the papers on the board.

'Hide that ring,' Helve said as he wrote. 'The crab armour can be explained for a hurt Piper's child, but no recruit has a personal item like that ring.'

Arthur twisted off the crocodile ring and slipped it into his own belt pouch. As far as his questing fingers could tell, it was the same size inside as out, though the sergeant's pouch was obviously transdimensional.

'Recruit Ray Green, we never had this conversation,' said Helve, quietly for once, as he stuffed the clipboard back in the pouch, both board and papers twisting bizarrely as they went in.

'No, Sergeant,' agreed Arthur.

'Atten-hut!' screamed Helve. The sudden intensity and volume of his voice made Arthur leap into the air. He came down quivering at attention.

'You see those buildings, Recruit! That is Fort Transformation where we take Denizens and make them into soldiers. We are going to march there and you are going to do me proud! Back straight! Fists clenched, thumbs down, by the left, quick march!'

Arthur started marching towards the buildings. Helve followed a few steps to the left and behind him, bellowing corrections to his posture, his step, how he swung his arms and his timing. In between these practical comments, Helve lamented what he had done to deserve such a sickly-looking specimen, even for one of the Piper's children.

By the time he got to the buildings, Arthur was wondering whether he would ever learn how to march properly, or at least up to Helve's standards. He was also wondering where everybody else was. As far as he could tell from the position of the rather rickety but extremely hot sun that was crossing the horizon, it was late afternoon, so he would have expected lots of recruits and training staff to be out doing . . . military stuff.

'Halt!' yelled Sergeant Helve, once Arthur had passed the first row of buildings and was about to step on to a large area of beaten earth ringed with white-painted rocks that was clearly the parade ground. 'When I give the command "Recruit, dismiss" you will smartly pivot on your left foot, raise your right foot and bring it crashing down next to your left foot, stand at attention for precisely one second and then you will march briskly to Barracks Block A which you will see in front of you unless you are Nothing-rotted blind as well as stupid! You will report there to Corporal Axeforth. Recruit! Waaaait foooor it! Dismiss!'

Arthur pivoted on his left foot, brought his right down and then marched clumsily rather than briskly forward. There was only one building directly in front of him, so he headed straight for that. It was a long single-storey whitewashed wooden building, raised on stilts about four feet high. Steps led up to a door, which had a red plaque on it with black-stencilled type that said: BARRACKS BLOCK A, SECOND RECRUIT PLATOON, CORPORAL AXEFORTH.

Arthur marched up the steps, pushed the door open and marched in.

The room was bigger inside than it should have been, but Arthur hardly even noticed this sort of thing any more. It was common in the House. The room was about the size of a football field, with a ceiling twenty feet up. What light there was was provided by about twenty large hurricane lamps that swung from the rafters. There were windows on each side, but they were all shuttered.

In the pools of light from the hurricane lamps, Arthur saw that one side of the huge room was entirely lined with stretcher beds and large wooden wardrobes, rather like Captain Catapillow's aboard the *Moth*. There had to be a hundred beds, each with a wardrobe next to it.

The other side of the room was more open, with thirty or so racks arranged in rows of three. The racks were ten feet high and thirty feet long, and they were hung with all kinds of weapons and armour, all of it to Arthur's eye very old and some of it very strange. The rack closest to him held a variety of straight and curved swords, small round shields, large kite-shaped shields, blue uniform coats, large unwieldy-looking pistols, and grappling irons and rope. The next one along was entirely given over to fifty or sixty muskets, with strange stovepipe hats of stretched white cloth arranged above the weapons.

At first Arthur thought no one was there, but as he marched further into the room, he saw a group of Denizens in blue recruit uniforms standing down the other end. As he drew closer, he saw a scarlet-uniformed instructor in front of them, demonstrating some kind of weapon. From the two gold stripes on the instructor's scarlet sleeve, Arthur guessed he was Corporal Axeforth.

The Denizens looked like a typical bunch. An even mix of men and women, they were all very good-looking, but none was over six feet tall, so they were presumably not important in their civilian positions. None of them turned round as Arthur marched up.

Corporal Axeforth glanced up though. He was also about six foot tall and stocky, and like Sergeant Helve, disfigured by scars from Nothing-injuries. In his case, his entire ear and nose had been dissolved and he wore a carved wooden ear and a silver nose, both of which appeared to be glued on as Arthur could see no other means of attachment.

'You're late, Recruit!' barked Axeforth. 'You'll have to pick up as we go along.'

'Yes, Corporal!' shouted Arthur. He took a few steps to the left and joined the semi-circle. As he marched round the end, he saw that there was a very small Denizen opposite, partly obscured by a weapons rack. Not even a Denizen, but a Piper's child. A boy who looked about the same age as Arthur, though he had probably lived for hundreds or even thousands of years in the House. He had short black hair and looked friendly, his mouth turned up with the hint of a smile. He winked surreptitiously at Arthur, but otherwise maintained his interest in the corporal's weapon demonstration.

If it *was* a weapon. Arthur found his place and looked on. The corporal was holding a large rectangular block of grey iron by its wooden handle. There was a regular pattern of holes in the iron block and as the corporal lowered it to the table, steam jetted out.

'This here iron is the section iron,' said the corporal, pressing down on a white collar. 'It's always hot and it will burn your clothes if you leave it face down. I will demonstrate the correct procedure for pressing your number two Regimental dress uniform collars. Watch carefully!'

The Denizens all leaned in as the corporal carefully moved the iron over the collar from right to left six times. Then he sat the iron up on its end, flipped the collar over and repeated the process.

'Everybody get that?'

Everyone nodded, except for one Denizen who raised his hand. He was the most handsome of them all, with finely chiselled features and bright blue eyes. Unfortunately, those eyes were rather vacant.

'Could you do it again, Corporal?'

Arthur rocked back on his heels very slightly and suppressed a sigh. It looked like it was going to be a long ironing lesson.

CHAPTER EIGHT

'Hey, isn't that Emily's kid? He's supposed to be in Exclusion on Level Twenty!'

It was a doctor who shouted, pointing at the Skinless Boy, who ignored him and disappeared through the cafeteria doors. Leaf hesitated then hurried after the Nithling. Behind her, the doctor shouted again and hospital security guards started to move through the crowd. But they were on the far side of the main atrium and it would take them minutes to get through the throng.

The cafeteria's serving bays were shuttered, but the room was full of people sitting around or slumped over the tables. They were nearly all hospital staff too. The Q-zone must have been clamped down just as the shift changed, Leaf realised. So all the staff going off-shift had been trapped here and were trying to rest in the public areas. There were few non-staff because visiting hours were in the afternoon.

The Skinless Boy was already on the far side of the cafeteria, not using the crutch, walking faster than any human could with a broken leg in a cast. It still touched people on shoulders or backs as it went by.

Every touch would be spreading the mould, Leaf thought. In a matter of hours, or however long it took, the Skinless Boy would control the minds of hundreds of hospital workers. It would have a brainwashed army under its control.

The Skinless Boy turned left past the serving counters and pushed open a door. It didn't bother to look behind, but Leaf slid sideways to put some people between her and the Nithling, just in case. When the door closed behind the Nithling, she ran the rest of the way across the room, listened for a second then opened the door and went through.

Even though she'd heard receding footsteps, Leaf still feared the Skinless Boy would be there, waiting, its hand out-stretched, to strike her as it had struck the doctor, or simply to infect her with its mind-mould. But it wasn't. Only an askew door at the other end of the corridor showed which way it had gone.

The door was more than askew, Leaf found when she got there. It was still electronically locked on one side, but the Skinless Boy had peeled back the other side, ripping the hinges from the wall. No alarm had been triggered and the door would appear locked in the hospital's security centre. It was an ingenious way to evade security.

That probably meant the Skinless Boy already had access to the thoughts of some of the hospital staff, Leaf figured. Otherwise, it wouldn't have known to be careful. As it had been on Earth since at least five past seven the night before, it could already have spread the mould to lots of people.

There was another twisted door further along, and then two more on the fire stairs. Leaf followed the Skinless Boy very cautiously, listening for its footsteps. At the peeled-back door that led to the Lower Ground Three floor, she stopped and peeked around, rather than going right through.

The Skinless Boy was in the corridor, outside a door that she felt must be close to the linen store the Atlas had recorded as being its lair.

The Nithling stopped and suddenly looked back towards the stairs. Leaf froze, hoping it hadn't seen her.

For a moment, she thought she was safe. Then the Skinless Boy hissed – a sound Arthur would never make – spun on its heel and came sprinting down the corridor towards her.

Without thinking, Leaf ran down the fire stairs because that would be quicker than going up. She'd only jumped down four or five steps when she realised her mistake. All the doors going down would be locked. There would be nowhere to go.

She was trapped and in seconds the Skinless Boy would be on the stairs behind her. Panicked, Leaf tried to go even faster, tried to jump too many steps at once – and fell.

She fell headfirst, hit a step hard and slid down to the next landing.

The Skinless Boy stopped five steps above her and looked down. It saw Leaf lying still, blood trickling from under her hair. But her chest still rose and fell, indicating that she was breathing. The Nithling hesitated, then it slowly walked down the remaining steps and extended its hand, brushing its palm against the back of her outstretched hand. Satisfied, the Skinless Boy returned back up the stairs, eager to commune once more with the sorcerous scrap of material that was the source of its identity.

Leaf returned to a consciousness dominated by pain. Her head really hurt and there were aches and pains all down her left side, from ribs to ankle. She was disoriented, for a few seconds thinking she was back aboard the *Flying Mantis*.

Have I fallen from the rigging? she thought. But it wasn't the deck beneath her, it was a concrete floor. And it wasn't Pannikin shouting at her. It was ... a loudspeaker.

Leaf rolled over and sat up very gingerly. A voice was booming through the stairwell, coming out of the emergency speakers that dotted the ceilings of each landing.

'... check for indications of the bioweapon code-name Greyspot. The indications are grey spots on the hands, neck, face or other exposed areas of flesh. If you have the grey spots, do not approach anyone else. Move immediately to Level Three for treatment. If you had the grey spots but they are now gone, move immediately to Level Five for treatment. If you do not have the grey spots and did not notice them previously, stay where you are. Avoid skin contact with all persons. Do not attempt to leave the hospital. This hospital is now zoned as a Red Biohazard Area under the Creighton Act and anyone attempting to leave will be shot and flamed.'

The voice was followed by a loud pulsing tone then the same message started again.

Leaf touched the sorest part of her head, at the back. Her skull was intact as far as she could tell, but when she looked at her fingers, there was partially dried blood all over them.

She rolled her hand, looking at the blood and feeling sick. Then she froze, staring not at the blood, but at a small patch of skin behind her knuckles. The skin was brown, like every other part of her that had been exposed to various suns aboard the *Flying Mantis*. But right in the middle there were three small grey dots.

Suddenly, everything came rushing back. The Skinless Boy turning to chase her. Her fall down the stairs. Then . . . while she was unconsciousness, the Nithling must have infected her with the spores. It would only be a matter of time before the Skinless Boy would be able to read her mind and make her do whatever it wanted.

It would learn everything. It would totally control her.

Leaf struggled shakily to her feet and started climbing the stairs, only managing to keep her balance by gripping the hand-rail. The warning message kept repeating, echoing around the stairwell, making it even harder for Leaf to think.

She had to get the pocket and find the House. Dr Scamandros would . . . might be able to cure her.

By sheer force of will Leaf managed to get her pain-racked self back up to Lower Ground Three, arriving at the same time the recorded message stopped blaring out through the loudspeakers. She rested for a few minutes on the landing there, gathering her strength and her thoughts. But she couldn't think of anything to do other than to go to the linen store and try to find the pocket. This would be hopeless if the Skinless Boy was there. But if he wasn't, and she could get the pocket, then . . .

Leaf shook her head, wincing as pain shot down into her neck. She didn't know what she would do if she got the pocket, but it was the first step. *One step at a time*, she told herself. *One step at a time.*

She took that step, slowly walking down the corridor to the linen room, her hand trailing along the wall for support. She passed the door that she had thought the Skinless Boy had been about to enter, but it had no sign, so she kept going. The next door said it led to a stationery storage area, so she kept going to the next. This said it was an electronic parts storeroom. Leaf was about to keep going to the next door when she suddenly wondered why the first door had no sign. Every door in the hospital had a sign. Why not that one? She turned around and went back. Sure enough, there were faint marks of glue where the sign had been ripped off the front of the door. But why would the Skinless Boy bother to do that?

Leaf put her head to the door, holding back a gasp as she misjudged slightly and sent yet another stab of pain through her neck. That also triggered a moment of panic as she wondered if she had a cracked vertebra or something. But her head moved well enough, and the pain felt like it was in the muscles that ran up the side of her neck to the chin. She ignored it and listened again.

She could hear something, but it didn't sound like the Skinless Boy. It sounded like a woman talking quietly. Leaf kept listening, and didn't hear anyone answer. It sounded like the woman was talking to herself.

Leaf turned the handle and pushed the door open just a crack. Looking in, she saw shelves and shelves of folded sheets, pillowcases and other linen. There was also a trolley and, leaning back on it, a nurse who was holding a long whippy piece of plastic that Leaf recognised as the sign from the door.

'You can't come in here,' said the nurse.

'Why not?' asked Leaf. She made no move to open the door wider or to shut it. The woman didn't look entirely normal. There was something about the way she was slouched against the trolley. As if some of the muscles in her arms and legs weren't working together.

'He told me not to let anyone in,' said the nurse. 'And to find a sword. Only I couldn't find a sword. Just this.'

She brandished the sign.

'I just want –' Leaf started to say, but the nurse held up her hand.

'Wait, he's telling me something . . .'

The nurse's head went back and Leaf saw something else that wasn't right at all. The woman's eyes didn't have any white in them any more, or any colour in her irises. The white had become a pale grey, and her irises and pupils were entirely black.

Leaf didn't wait. She threw the door open, charged the nurse and pushed her back on to the trolley. It crashed back into a shelf, which partly toppled over, burying the nurse under a cascade of blue-striped towels.

As the woman struggled to get out from under the avalanche of linens, Leaf dragged more things off the shelves and threw them on top of her. Pillows, blankets, towels – everything that came to hand. At the same time, she was desperately looking around. How could she find a small square of cloth in a room full of linen?

She would only have a minute or perhaps seconds. The nurse was bigger and stronger than her, particularly with Leaf in her injured state. Since the Skinless Boy knew what the nurse knew and could see what she saw and heard, there would probably be more of its mental slaves coming. Or the Skinless Boy itself.

The glasses. I could use Dr Scamandros's glasses.

Leaf frantically checked her pockets. For a terrible second she thought she'd lost the glasses case, but it was just the unfamiliar arrangement of the pockets in her alien jeans that confused her. The case was in a narrow pocket almost behind her thigh and not much above her knee. She got it out, snapped it open and flung on the glasses.

The linen room looked quite different through the crazed lenses, but not because the view was all blurry and cracked. In fact, to Leaf the glasses were perfectly clear, but she could see strange fuzzy colours in things that hadn't had them before. Sorcerous auras, she supposed, or something like that.

Quickly, she scanned the shelves and was immediately rewarded. Most of the colours overlaid on the various items of linen were cool greens and blues. But one shelf stood out like a beacon. It was lit inside by a deep, fierce red.

Leaf sprang at it, pulling away a rampart of pillowcases. There, behind this linen wall, was a clear plastic box the size of her palm, that had formerly been used to store sterile bandages. Now it had a single square of white cloth in it, but with the aid of the glasses, Leaf could see rows and rows of tiny letters across the cloth, each letter burning with an internal fire.

She snatched the box and backed away, pausing to tip another shelf-full of towels over the nurse, who was staggering to her feet.

Leaf was out the door and in the corridor when the nurse got her head free and shouted after her, her voice a strange mixture of a woman's and a boy's. Whatever she said – or the Skinless Boy said through her – was lost as the door slammed shut on Leaf's heels.

Though Leaf couldn't hear the exact words, she caught the tone. The Skinless Boy knew she was infected with the mould. Sooner or later, it would control her mind and she would have no choice but to bring the box and the pocket back.

After all, there was nowhere for her to go.

CHAPTER NINE

After the ironing lesson, Corporal Axeforth tediously demonstrated how to smear a kind of white clay over the recruits' belts, preferably without getting it anywhere else. This was followed by painting their boots with a hideous tarry mixture and then sanding the very black but rough result back to a smooth finish before applying a glossy varnish that was the stickiest substance Arthur had ever encountered.

Following the demonstrations, when they got to practise what they'd been shown, Arthur talked quietly with the Piper's child, whose name was Fred Initial Numbers Gold. He was a Manuscript-Gilder from the Middle House and had been drafted the day before.

Fred was optimistic about their future Army service and even welcomed it as a change from his nitpicking job of applying gold leaf to the numbers in important House documents. He'd heard – or he remembered, he wasn't sure which – that Piper's children were usually employed in the Army as drummers or other musicians, or as personal aides to senior officers. This didn't sound too bad to him.

After the final lesson on preparing their recruit uniforms, the section was dismissed for dinner. Only there wasn't any – and there wouldn't be any, Corporal Axeforth explained, for six months. Food was a privilege and an honour to be earned by good behaviour and exemplary duty. Until they had earned it, the dinner break was merely an hour to be used to prepare for the evening lessons and the next day's training.

Arthur missed the food, though like everyone else in the House he knew he didn't actually need to eat. He spent the hour going through all his equipment and the uniforms that were laid ready on his bed and in his locker. The most useful item of the lot was a thick illustrated book called *The Recruit's Companion* which, among its many sections, listed and illustrated every item and had short notes on where and how each would be used, though Arthur still had to ask Fred to explain some of its contents.

'How come we have so many different uniforms?' he asked.

Fred looked down at the segmented armour and kilt, the scarlet tunic and black trousers, the buff coat and reinforced leather trousers, the forest green jerkin and leggings, the long mail hauberk and coif and the bewildering array of boots, pieces of joint-armour, bracers and leather reinforcements.

'The Army's made up of different units and they all wear different uniforms,' Fred explained. 'So we got to learn the lot, case we get sent to the Legion, the Horde or the Regiment . . . or one of the other ones. I forget what they're all called. That armour there, the long, narrow pieces that slide together and you do up with the laces, that's Legionary wear. Scarlet's for the Regiment, and the Horde wear the knee-length ironmongery. They've all got different weapons too. We'll learn 'em all, Ray.'

'I guess I'd better sort them out according to this plan,' said Arthur. He put *The Recruit's Companion* down on the bed, and unfolded the poster-sized diagram out of it that showed the correct placement of every one of the 226 items Arthur was now personally responsible for. 'Though I don't see anyone else putting their stuff away.'

'They're ordinary-grade Denizens,' said Fred, whose bed and locker were patterns of military order. He said this as if it explained everything.

'What do you mean?' Arthur asked, since it didn't really explain anything to him.

'They won't do anything until they're told to,' said Fred with a puzzled glance at Arthur. 'Are the ordinary

Denizens different in the Lower House? All this lot are from the Middle. Paper-Cutters, most of them, though Florimel over there, she was a Binder, Second Class. Have to watch out for her. She thinks she ought to be Recruit Lance-Corporal because she's got the highest precedence in the House of the lot of us. I guess she'll find out that doesn't matter here. All of us recruits are equal in the eyes of the Army: low as you can go. The only way from here is up. I reckon I might be able to make general by the time my hitch is up.'

Fred liked to talk. Arthur listened to him as he packed away his equipment, a process that was much more difficult than the illustration indicated. Though Fred had only been at Fort Transformation for a day longer than Arthur, he had already found out a lot about their training, the training staff – or training cadre, as they were supposed to be called – and everything else.

'The first week is all getting to know how to look right and some marching about and suchlike,' Fred explained. 'At least, that's what's on the schedule. Over there.'

He pointed at the door. It was so far away, and the light from the hurricane lights so dim, that Arthur couldn't tell what he was pointing at.

'On the noticeboard, next to the door,' continued Fred. 'Let's go take a look. We've got five minutes till dinner's over and we'll need to be over there anyway.'

'How do you know?' asked Arthur. His watch had disappeared when the recruit uniform had swarmed up his arm.

'Axeforth just went out the back door. He'll march around to the front, come in and shout at us to line up there like he did before. It's called "falling in". Don't ask me why. You need your hat on.'

Arthur picked up his pillbox hat and put it back on, grimacing at the feel of the chinstrap under his mouth rather than on his chin, which he felt was the proper place for something called a chinstrap. But everyone else wore theirs the same way, under the bottom lip, and the strap wasn't long enough to do anything else.

'Ready?' Fred stood at attention next to Arthur. 'We have to march everywhere or we'll get shouted at.'

'Who by?' asked Arthur. The other twenty Denizens in the platoon were all lying down on their beds, staring at the ceiling.

'Sergeants, corporals . . . non-commissioned officers they're called,' said Fred. 'NCOs. They appear mysteriously. Best not to risk it.'

Arthur shrugged and when Fred marched off, fell into step with him. After the first dozen paces, he felt like he was getting the hang of it and stopped worrying about his feet and concentrated on swinging his arms.

Stopping in the right way – or *halting*, as Sergeant Helve called it and had explained to him at length – was somewhat more difficult.

'I'll give the command, shall I?' asked Fred as they approached the wall and the noticeboard. 'Got to give it as the right foot comes down, we take one step with the left, hang on . . . no . . . oops. Halt!'

Fred had waited too long and both of them did funny little steps to avoid hitting the wall, which made them halt completely out of time. Arthur turned to laugh at Fred, only to freeze his smile into a grimace as Sergeant Helve loomed up out of the shadows.

'What misbegotten disgrace of a movement do you call that?' screamed the sergeant. A brass-tipped wooden pace-stick appeared in his hand and whistled through the air to point back towards the beds. 'Double back to your bunks like soldiers, not like some prissy paper-pushing puppets!'

Fred spun round and was off like a shot, still marching but at a much faster rate. Arthur followed him more slowly, till he was suddenly accelerated by Sergeant Helve's voice bellowing so close and so loud that it felt like it was inside his ear.

'Double! When I say double, I mean at the double. Twice as fast as normal marching, Recruit Green!'

Arthur doubled, Sergeant Helve running backwards in front of him at a rate that Arthur supposed must be triple or quadruple time, or some other measure only possible to sergeants.

'Back straight, chin just so, swing those arms! Not that high!'

When Arthur was halfway back, Helve spun forwards and out of the pool of light from the hurricane lamp overhead. Before Arthur could take more than two steps, the sergeant appeared next to the closest bed, striking his pace-stick on the boot-soles of the resting Denizen and yelling something that sounded like a single word: 'Standfastforinspectionyoudopydozy-disgracefullumpofleftoverNothing!'

The Denizen stood extremely fast, spare equipment cascading off the bed. His movement was like the first in a line of dominoes as every Denizen along leaped from their bed.

'Fall in on this line in order of height!' commanded Sergeant Helve. He gestured with his pace-stick and a glowing white line appeared on the floor. 'You will not be seen on the parade ground of Fort Transformation until I am sure you will not disgrace me! You will parade inside here instead! Every evening after dinner and every morning at one hour before sunrise, dressed and equipped as per the training schedule which you will find posted by the south door. Atten-hut!'

Arthur barely managed to reach the end of the line in time to brace at attention. Since Fred was slightly taller, he fell in on Arthur's right. Both boys stared at a spot in space ahead of them as Helve marched along, pausing to pull Denizens out and rearrange them. When he got to Arthur, Helve looked down his nose at him then marched out to the front, did an about turn that seemed to Arthur as if it relied on him being suspended by invisible wires from the ceiling and shouted, 'Stand at ease!'

Only half the Denizens moved, the other half remaining at attention. Of those that moved, most moved the wrong leg, or waved their arms or otherwise did things that attracted the displeasure of Sergeant Helve, who proceeded to tell them what they had done wrong and just how displeased this made him.

Two hours later, after hundreds of commands of 'Atten-hut' and 'Stand at ease,' Arthur fell over from sheer exhaustion. Though his crab-armoured leg had stood up well, his entire body could not cope with the constant activity.

Helve marched over and looked down at him. When Fred bent to help Arthur up, the sergeant ordered him to stand fast.

'You are a weak reed, Recruit Green!' Helve shouted. 'Weak reeds make for badly woven baskets! This platoon will not be a badly woven basket!'

What? thought Arthur. Grimly, he struggled to his feet and tried to straighten up. Helve stared at him, his jaw thrust out aggressively. Then the sergeant spun about and resumed his place in front of the platoon.

'Reveille is one hour before dawn,' he announced. 'You will parade in Number Two Recruit Field Uniform at that time, unless detailed for a special parade, in which case you will wear Number One Recruit Dress Uniform. Platoon! Dismiss!'

Arthur turned to the left, stamped his foot and marched off, as did Fred and eight of the platoon. The others turned right or completely about and crashed into their neighbours and fell over.

'You all right?' asked Fred. 'I wouldn't have thought a bit of foot-thumping would knock you out. Not like we're proper mortals any more.'

'That's the problem,' said Arthur, very wearily. 'I . . . I got kind of . . . a bit affected by sorcery. So I am more mortal now than most of the Piper's children.'

'Cripes!' exclaimed Fred with extreme interest. 'How did that happen?'

'I'm not allowed to talk about it.'

'I knew there's been something going on in the Lower House,' said Fred, 'what with the mail being cut off and all. But we never heard what happened. Has Mister Monday been doing something he shouldn't?'

'Mister Monday?' asked Arthur. 'Then you haven't heard –'

'Heard what?' Fred seemed eager for news. 'I haven't heard anything, that's for sure. No mail for two years and no newspaper neither. All the fault of the Lower House, least that's what my boss said.'

Arthur didn't reply. Fred was a good guy and he thought they would be friends. But Arthur couldn't afford for his real identity to get out and he didn't want to tell Fred too much too soon.

'Heard what?' Fred repeated.

'I can't talk about it,' Arthur replied. 'Sorry. If . . . if I get permission, I'll tell you.'

'Permission from who?'

'Look, I really can't talk about it. I just want to get to sleep. We've got to get up . . . I don't know . . . *soon*.'

Arthur clutched at Fred's shoulder as the ground shifted under his feet. He was so tired it took him several seconds to process that it wasn't the ground moving. He was swaying where he stood, so exhausted he couldn't even stand still.

'We'd better check the schedule first,' said Fred patiently. 'I don't like the sound of "special parades".'

'You go,' Arthur groaned. 'I don't think I can march that far.'

'Yes, you can,' said Fred. He removed Arthur's hand and pushed on his shoulders to turn him around. 'Do you good. Bit of a stretch.'

Arthur groaned and tried to turn back towards the beds, but Fred nudged him onward.

'Oh, all right,' said Arthur. He shook his head to try to clear it. 'Let's go then. By the left, quiiiiiick march!'

This time, with Arthur carefully giving the command, they managed to halt properly. After a nervous look around for a jack-in-the-box sergeant, they studied the schedule papers on the noticeboard.

Fred was the first to notice that their names appeared, all on their own, under a single heading on a separate piece of paper.

'Oh no,' he said, tapping his finger on the paper. 'That is really bad luck.'

Arthur read the notice. In his weary state it took him several seconds to even focus on the words and they didn't mean anything to him.

'*Recruits R Green and F Gold Report to Bathroom Attendants in Administration Building Blue at 0600.* What's bad about that?'

Fred looked at him, his eyes wide in disbelief.

'Bathroom Attendants, Ray. From the Upper House.'

Arthur still looked puzzled.

'Cleaning between the ears, Ray! They're here to clean between our ears! Tomorrow morning!'

CHAPTER TEN

Leaf hesitated in the corridor, uncertain whether to go back to the fire stairs or explore more of the Lower Ground Three floor. She had no time to think, but through the cracked lenses of her glasses the fire stairs looked ominously red-tinged, so Leaf decided to check out what was on her current level.

Clutching the box with the precious pocket in it, she hobbled off down the corridor, pushing through the swinging doors that led deeper into the hospital.

The nurse might or might not come after her, but if she didn't, Leaf knew other mind-slaves of the Skinless Boy would. She had to find somewhere to hide and rest and work out what to do next. But that was easier said than done. Particularly since every door she tried along the corridor was locked.

Leaf forced herself to move faster, though it hurt, as her options grew more and more limited. The corridor was turning out to be like the fire stairs: if she couldn't open any of the doors, she'd be cornered at the end.

She had a moment of relief when she saw a utility door open in the wall, with orange safety cones around it and a sign that said CAUTION WET FLOOR. But when she looked inside it was just a tiny room, not much bigger than a cupboard, with a big red vertical pipe marked FB WET RISER, whatever that was.

Finally, with the end of the corridor in sight, Leaf found a door that opened. She slid through it then shut and locked it before even looking around. The room was a laundry room, a big open area dominated by four huge washing machines on one side and four equally large driers on the other. They were all off, though there was washing in wheelie baskets in front of them.

There was also a desk with a phone on it. As soon as Leaf saw it, she had an idea. She couldn't think of what to do next, but she could phone a friend. Or, in this case, her brother Ed. He was almost never without his mobile phone, and since he'd been recovering from the Sleepy Plague he'd been sitting up there in quarantine texting his friends.

Leaf picked up the phone and dialled. She could hear her brother's phone ringing, but he didn't pick up straight away.

'Come on!' Leaf urged. She couldn't believe she was going to get diverted to voice mail.

'Hello?'

'Ed, it's me, Leaf.'

'Leaf? Where are you? Mum and Dad are going crazy in here!'

'I'm in the hospital downstairs. Look, this is going to sound weird, but I've been somewhere else . . . I mean like a whole other planet . . . with Arthur Penhaligon. It's complicated, but there's an enemy of his here and it's trying to get me and I've got to get out –'

'Leaf! Have you hit your head or something?'

'Well, yes . . . but no! I know it sounds strange. Remember the dogfaces we saw?'

'Yeah . . .'

'They're part of it. And this new bioweapon, the Greyspot thing. That's part of it too. Oh, and the Arthur that's here now isn't the real Arthur. I don't suppose he . . . it . . . will get into the closed quarantine areas, but if it does, don't let it touch you. Not even a handshake or anything.'

'Leaf, you're freaking me out! What do I tell Mum and Dad? They thought you must have been hurt in that water explosion and no one's found you yet.'

'What water explosion?'

'On the fifth floor. Some kind of big pipe called a firefighting riser exploded and flooded a whole bunch of rooms. It was all over the net until this Greyspot thing.'

'The Border Sea ...' whispered Leaf. Ed had to be talking about the wave that had carried her and Arthur and his bed out of this Secondary Realm.

'What?'

'It doesn't matter,' Leaf quickly covered. 'I need to work out some way of getting out of the hospital. Past the quarantine line.'

'Leaf! They'll shoot you! Just ... I don't know ... relax. You sound really stressed out.'

'I am stressed out! Look, can you think of anything or not? I haven't got much time.'

'Hang on, Dad wants to talk to you –'

'Leaf?'

Leaf's father sounded very anxious.

'Dad, look I know it sounds weird, but I'm caught up in something –'

'Leaf, we're just relieved to hear from you. Stay where you are and stay on the phone. I'll arrange for the police to come to you –'

'Dad, I don't need the police. This isn't ... it's not something ... look, I can't explain. Love you!'

133

Leaf dropped the phone on its cradle, collapsed on to the chair and pressed her fingers into her forehead. That reminded her she was still wearing the glasses. She thought about taking them off for a moment because it was a bit distracting seeing the coloured auras. But she left them on since they might help her see things that would help.

'There must be some way out,' she whispered to herself.

I can't go out any of the main doors, or the staff exits or anything like that on the ground floor. There's no point going higher because there's no way out from there, unless I got picked up by a helicopter or something off the roof, and that's not going to happen. But lower down ... there are the car parks. But those entrances will be guarded too. All the entrances for people or cars will be guarded.

The door handle suddenly rattled. Leaf jumped in her seat. She heard male voices on the other side and tensed, waiting for the door to be unlocked or broken down.

'Locked,' she heard a man say. 'Try the next one.'

Leaf listened intently. She heard footsteps, then someone else talking, though she couldn't make out the words. Then more footsteps, going away.

The search had begun. It could be either hospital security, catching her on a surveillance camera, or mind-slaves of the Skinless Boy. Or they could be both, Leaf realised.

I can't go out at ground level. No point going up. But there must be other ways out. A laundry chute . . .

Leaf got up and carefully looked around, but there was only the door she'd come in. Still, an idea lurked at the back of her mind. She just couldn't tease it out of her bruised and numbed head. Something had flashed up when she was talking to Ed . . .

The firefighting riser that burst. FB Wet Riser. The big red pipe. Caution wet floor. Maybe the pipe went somewhere . . .

Leaf went to the door, listened, opened it and slid out into the corridor. There was no one visible on this side of the swing doors. Quickly, she ran to the utility door and went in, shutting it after her.

She had only just started to inspect the pipe when she heard running footsteps move past her, then a man shouting.

'She's in 3G104 – she called from there two minutes ago!'

Leaf turned to the pipe again. It was only a few inches wider in diameter than her shoulders and extended through the floor and the ceiling. At first it looked like there was no way in, but when Leaf walked around, she found a panel had been unbolted from the back, the eight nuts laid out neatly on the floor. There was a long wrench next to them and an open lunch box next to it, with a half-eaten sandwich and an apple indicating the workers had been forced to leave quickly, presumably to join everyone else waiting upstairs.

Leaf looked inside the pipe. There were beads of moisture all over the steel lining, but it wasn't full of water. Looking up, she could see that other panels had been removed and cold white fluorescent light was shining in.

Looking down, it was dark and the pipe was blocked. But as Leaf's eyes adjusted, she saw that the blockage was a big box mounted on a swivelling ring that had little wheels all round its edge. The box had probe-arms that touched the sides of the pipe, and there were warning stickers on it that Leaf couldn't quite make out in the dim light.

It was some sort of remote-controlled device for inspecting the pipe. It had electric motors too, driving the four biggest wheels, as well as a whole bunch of electric and other cables hanging below it.

'Not here!' shouted the voice down the corridor. 'Check all the rooms.'

Leaf hesitated, tucked the box with the pocket into her waistband and wriggled into the pipe, standing on the inspection unit. It rocked within its ring then started to slowly slide down into darkness, taking Leaf with it.

Alone, pressed in on all sides, accompanied only by the sound of her beating heart and the faint whirr of the inspection unit's wheels, Leaf felt the sides of the pipe get wetter and wetter, triggering an instant of total panic.

What if there is water down below and I go straight into it?

Rational thought fled. Leaf clawed the sides of the pipe and pressed her back against the metal, trying to slow her descent. But the metal was too water-slick and the inspection unit kept going down, taking Leaf with it.

A light swept down from above. Leaf looked up, but the flashlight beam fell short of her.

'Nothing!'

The guard's voice echoed down the pipe from at least fifty feet above. Leaf stared up at the light, choked with panic, desperately trying to draw a breath so she could scream for help, fear now overriding her desire to escape with the pocket.

The scream suddenly became a stifled grunt as a dim red light spilled in from the side. Leaf just had time to throw herself against an open inspection port and grab hold of the lip before the wheeled unit continued on its way down.

As Leaf hung there panting, she heard a splash below and then a *glug-glug-glug* as the inspection unit continued down the riser, into deep water.

Two seconds later, the weary but relieved girl pulled herself up and slithered out on to the floor of a narrow tunnel filled with pipes, cables and all the other circulatory systems of a major modern building. She lay there for several minutes, gathering her strength, then sat up and looked around.

As above, the inspection panel here had been unbolted. In this case the nuts had been put in a plastic bag taped to the panel.

The tunnel stretched off as far as she could see to the left and right, but that wasn't far because there were only the small, dim red lights in the ceiling every fifteen yards or so. It was also extremely cluttered, with only just enough space between all the pipes and cables for a small adult to crawl along.

That was plenty of room for Leaf. She chose a direction at random, checked that she still had the box with the pocket and started crawling.

CHAPTER ELEVEN

'I can't let them wash me between the ears,' said Arthur.

'There's not much choice,' said Fred gloomily. 'Even if you hide, they always find you. We'd better start getting ready.'

'There must be a way to avoid it,' Arthur insisted. 'And what do you mean, "start getting ready"?'

'Start writing down the important stuff,' said Fred. 'You know, name, friends, favourite colour. Sometimes it's enough to bring some memories back. Of course, if we had some silver coins and some salt . . .'

'We could even forget our names?' In Arthur's weary state it was only just beginning to hit home that cleaning between the ears could be even worse than he'd thought. He'd been worried about forgetting some details about his life on Earth, or his family, or the Morrow Days and the Keys . . . not that he might entirely forget who he was.

'You must have been cleaned quite recently if you can't even remember *that*,' said Fred. 'If they do a complete job you'll forget everything about yourself. And they don't care if you were only done yesterday, they just do you again.'

'What was that about silver coins and salt?'

'A silver coin under the tongue is supposed to help resist the washing,' said Fred. 'And salt in the nose. But we've got neither, so we'd better start writing. I really hope I don't forget how to read this time. It's going to set back our training too. I'll never make general if I get washed between the ears too often. Come on.'

He marched back to the beds, Arthur following more slowly and out of step. But no NCOs appeared to berate him. As far as he could tell, it was the middle of the night and their appointed wake-up time would be in only three or four hours.

Despite his weariness, Arthur followed Fred's lead and got out a service notebook and scarlet pencil with the platoon name on it in gold type. But while Fred wrote busily, Arthur wondered about what he should put down. If he wrote his real name and other important stuff, someone might see it.

In the end, he compromised by starting his list with *Ray Green* and then putting underneath it *Real name?* and then *AP*. After that, he put down his favourite colour, which was blue, his parents' first names, *Bob* and *Emily*, and his brothers' and sisters', *Erazmuz*, *Staria*, *Patrick*, *Suzanne*, *Michaeli* and *Eric*. Arthur thought for a while then added *Suzy TB*, *Leaf*, and *Mister Monday*, *Grim Tuesday* and *Drowned Wednesday*. If those names didn't trigger memories he'd be in a really bad state.

He wanted to write more, but he felt faint. The paper was swimming around . . . or maybe his vision was. He managed to lose a few seconds in between writing *Drowned* and *Wednesday*, waking with a start as his chin hit his chest. So he closed the notebook, slid the pencil into its pocket and lay back on his bed. He told himself he'd just sleep for a little while, maybe half an hour, and then he'd wake up and write some more.

The next thing he knew, he was being shaken awake by Fred. Groggily, Arthur swung his legs out of bed and stood up. There were trumpets blasting out long, irritating notes, and only half of the hurricane lanterns were lit. Fred thrust a towel and a leather case into Arthur's hands.

'Come on! We have to wash and shave.'

'But I don't shave . . .'

'Neither does anyone else really. Hair doesn't grow much in the House. But we have to try. Regulations.'

Arthur stumbled after Fred. In a dim, more-asleep-than-awake way, he was surprised that they were walking, rather than marching, and heading for a door he hadn't seen before, on the east side of the barracks.

The door shone slightly with a faint greenish light. When Arthur stepped through it into a narrow, dark corridor, he almost lost his balance, the floor wobbling under his feet like jelly. He threw out a hand to steady himself on the corridor wall, and that gave way under his fingers.

'This is a weirdway!' he protested.

'Yes,' Fred agreed. 'It leads to the washroom.'

A few steps later, though as far as he could tell he'd passed no other door, Arthur came out into a truly vast washroom that had no roof. The night sky above was brilliant, with strange constellations of stars that looked too close and a rather unsteady crescent moon that cast a pale green light. Arthur stopped where he was, momentarily stunned by the unexpected night sky and the sight of endless lines of Denizen soldiers stretching out as far as he could see in the moonlight, standing in front of equally endless lines of mirrors and washbasins, each one lit by a naked gas flame above the mirror.

The Denizens were mostly stripped to their under-vests, but even these varied with their units. The uniforms' trousers, kilts or leggings included every kind Arthur had in his cupboard, plus a few more he hadn't seen before.

'We share the washroom with the whole Army,' said Fred. 'Come on, let's find our spot. You need to get some cold water on your face, I think.'

He set out on a diagonal path, walking right through a couple of Legionary Denizens and their washbasins and mirrors as if none of them were there and they were all just ghostly images. The Legionaries ignored Fred, but Arthur saw them talk to one another, though he heard no sound.

'Hold on!' Arthur yelled. 'Where are we? How come you just walked through them?'

'Oh, they're not real to us or us to them,' said Fred. 'Corporal Axeforth explained yesterday morning. We just have to find our washbasins. They won't be far away.'

He kept walking. Reluctantly, Arthur followed, flinching as he stepped through the Legionaries. Fred was still ahead, passing through a couple of buff-coated Artillery Denizens. On the other side, there was a row of vacant wash basins, and to either side of them, some other Recruit Denizens. They turned to look as Arthur and Fred arrived, and Arthur heard the gurgle of the water in their basins and the chink of razors laid down on the porcelain.

'But how does this work?' asked Arthur. 'Are they all here or not?'

'The corp wasn't all that informational,' Fred said as he opened his leather case and removed a cut-throat razor, brush, soap and lathering bowl. 'Something about weirdways leading to lots of different washrooms that coexist in the same place within the House but offset in time. Saves on hot water or some such.'

Fred started to whip up a lather in his bowl. Arthur shook his head then splashed his face with the water from the basin, which was warm and filled up again immediately, though there were no visible taps or spout.

Fred applied the lather to his face and began to shave, at the same time whispering to himself. Arthur wondered if it was some kind of prayer that Fred might not cut his own throat. He'd just taken his own razor out and it was incredibly sharp and dangerous. Then he saw that Fred was using the blunt back instead of the blade.

'What're you whispering?' Arthur enquired.

'My name,' said Fred, as he carefully scraped some lathered soap off his chin. 'And my favourite colour.'

'Oh,' said Arthur. 'I forgot . . .'

He stared at the mirror, looking at his familiar – though not very satisfying – face. He couldn't believe he might not know himself soon.

'You'd better shave or you'll get put on defaulters,' Fred warned. 'That means get punished.'

'Even though my skin is perfectly smooth?' Arthur ran his hand over his chin. 'I won't have to shave for years.'

'They'll know you haven't shaved,' said Fred despondently. 'Just because we're going to get washed between the ears doesn't mean they'll let us off shaving or anything else.'

'OK,' said Arthur. 'OK!'

He put some soap in his lathering bowl and started to whisk it with the brush, as he'd seen Fred do. Then, following the other boy's lead, he slapped the frothy soap on his face and shaved with the back of the razor. It was completely pointless, just putting on soap and scraping it off. Arthur thought about what he was going to do as he scraped, flicked and rinsed.

'Let's not go back,' he said as they were washing their necks and under their arms. 'Let's stay here.'

'Here?' squeaked Fred. He was obviously unnerved by the idea. 'I'm not sure this place even *exists* after morning ablution time. The weirdway closes . . .'

'If we stay by these basins, I reckon we'll be OK,' said Arthur. 'They're real to us, so they must be somewhere.'

'But we'll be absent without leave,' mumbled Fred. 'Not on parade. The Bathroom Attendants will come looking for us.'

'If the weirdway's closed till tomorrow morning, they won't be able to find us, will they?' asked Arthur. 'How long do they hang around?'

'They come, do the washing and go,' said Fred. 'Just as long as it takes to do all the Piper's children in the area.'

'So we wait here then go back tomorrow morning,' said Arthur. 'Take our punishment and get on with the training.'

'You'll do no such thing,' said the recruit who'd just finished packing up next to them. Arthur vaguely recognised her as being from his platoon. Florimel – the one Fred had said to watch out for. 'You will report as ordered.'

'No, we won't,' said Fred, all his despair of a moment ago vanishing. Apparently, all it took to encourage him was someone like Florimel telling him he couldn't do something.

'I'm ordering you back to the barracks!'

'Who made you High Lady Muckamuck?' asked Fred. 'You're just a recruit, same as us. We'll do what we want and you keep your mouth shut.'

'I'll report you,' said Florimel, drawing herself up to her full height.

'No, you won't,' said Arthur sternly. 'You won't say a word.'

Though Florimel was tall, for a moment Arthur appeared taller still, and his hair suddenly moved as if it had been swept by the beat of unseen wings. There was something of Dame Primus in Arthur's stance and voice, for an instant. Then he was just a boy again, but Florimel had already looked down and backed away.

'Yes, sir,' said Florimel. 'Whatever you say, sir.'

She half-saluted, did a clumsy right-turn and marched away through a couple of green-clad Borderers who were also leaving, but in the opposite direction.

'How did you do that?' asked Fred, open-mouthed. 'I thought for sure she'd put us in the pickle. Someone like that . . .'

He stopped talking as the moon above their heads suddenly lurched towards the horizon. At the same time, a rosy glow fell on them from the east. Arthur turned to look. He couldn't see the sun, but the light was the first hint of the dawn.

With that hint, the remaining soldiers hurriedly left in all directions, evidently disappearing back through their own weirdways to their respective places in the Great Maze. Within a few minutes, Arthur and Fred were alone in the vast, lonely washroom, with nothing but mirrors and basins to see in all directions, the mirrors beginning to reflect the morning light.

'I hope this turns out to be a good idea,' said Arthur.

'So do I,' said Fred with a shiver.

He shivered again as some of the further mirrors began to fade away, as if they had dissolved in sunshine.

He backed up to his own basin. Arthur found that he too had unconsciously backed up to make contact with the solid porcelain.

Slowly, as the sun rose and became an identifiable disk above the horizon, the sinks and mirrors around them faded away. Arthur and Fred drew closer together till they were standing shoulder to shoulder. They could see nothing around them save sunlight, but their own basins remained solid and their mirrors shone.

'Maybe it's going to be all right,' Fred whispered.

'Maybe,' Arthur said.

That was when everything went black. Just for an instant. Arthur and Fred blinked and saw that while they were still shoulder-to-shoulder they were no longer leaning against a basin, nor were they surrounded by sunlight.

They were back in the barracks, leaning against Arthur's wardrobe, and the only light came from the hurricane lantern above their heads and the others like it, all of them now lit.

In the dim light, Arthur saw three shapes standing ten feet in front of him. They were Denizen-sized and shaped, but clad in all-concealing daisy-yellow robes with long pointed hoods. Their hands were gloved in flexible steel mesh and their faces too were hidden – this time behind masks of beaten bronze.

One mask had a smiling mouth. One had a mouth turned down in sombre reflection. The third mask had a mouth twisted in agony.

There was no sign of anyone ... or anything ... behind the mouths or the eyes of the masks. There was only darkness.

'B-B-Bathroom Attendants,' whispered Fred. 'Fred Inital Numbers Gold, Manuscript-Gilder's Assistant Sixth Class, favourite colour green, tea with milk and one sugar, shortbread but not caraway biscuits ...'

The Bathroom Attendants glided forward, robes whispering on the floor. Two of them reached into their broad sleeves and pulled out strange crowns of sculpted blue ice, all spikes and shards that crackled and sparkled with dancing light. The third produced a length of golden rope that moved in his hand like a spitting cobra, rearing up to spit its venom.

But it did not spit poison. Instead, the golden rope leaped through the air and fastened itself around Arthur's ankles, bringing him down even as he turned to run away.

Arthur hit the floor hard. The golden rope swarmed over his legs, wrapping them tight, then the loose end fastened itself on his left wrist, and started to draw it behind his back. Arthur resisted as hard as he could and scrabbled desperately in his pouch with his right hand, trying to get the silver crocodile ring. It wasn't a coin, but it was silver and Arthur wanted it under his tongue.

He had it in his grasp and was bringing it up to his mouth when a coil of the rope lashed itself around his right wrist and pulled it back. Arthur snapped his head forward, got his fingers in his mouth and pushed the ring under his tongue, cutting his lip in the process.

Blood trickled down his chin as he was hauled up on to his knees, the golden rope securing his arms behind him and his ankles together.

Arthur looked up and saw the fizzing, sparkling crown coming down.

I'm Arthur Penhaligon, he thought desperately. *Arthur Penhaligon, my parents are Bob and Emily. I'm the Master of the Lower House, the Far Reaches, the Border Sea –*

The crown was wedged tight upon his head – and Arthur fell silently screaming into darkness.

CHAPTER TWELVE

Leaf got herself in a good position near the top of the ladder and pushed up the manhole cover. It was steel-reinforced concrete and very heavy, but she got it up far enough to admit sunlight, and then with an additional heave managed to slide it half off the manhole.

Peering up, Leaf could see the sky and the tops of some buildings. Strangely, she couldn't hear any traffic, though the manhole had to be in the middle of a road and, as far as she could work out, about a mile from the hospital. It was the third ladder she'd come to, crawling down the tunnel – she had decided not to climb the earlier ones in case they were still inside the quarantine perimeter. Since she had no idea which direction the tunnel went in, she wouldn't know for sure where she was until she climbed out and had a look.

Hoping that the lack of traffic noise meant she wouldn't be run over as soon as she popped her head out, Leaf hauled herself up and quickly looked around. As she'd thought, she was in the middle of a city street. There were rows of old terraced houses on either side, behind a line of parked cars. But there were no moving cars, or other traffic. The street was unnaturally quiet.

Leaf took a deep breath and pulled herself out. That took most of her strength, so it was a few seconds before she could crouch and then stand up. She had an idea of where she was, but to check she looked back towards where the hospital ought to be.

It was there all right, but that wasn't what made Leaf gasp and sit back down as if she'd been punched in the guts.

Looking over the rim of her special glasses, she didn't just see the white bulk of the hospital's three towers, all concrete and glass, about a mile and a half away. She could also see another building, hovering in the air directly above the hospital. A vast, crazy building of weird turrets and towers, houses and halls, outbuildings, underbuildings, overbuildings and battlements. One small part of it rested directly on top of the hospital and Leaf could just make out a shining gate that she knew instinctively was the Front Door.

It was the House. Not manifested where Leaf had expected it to be, near Arthur's home, but above the hospital. She had just managed to escape from the only place where it might have been possible for her to reach the Front Door.

Leaf lowered her head and gripped her hair, ready to pull some of it out. How could she have assumed the House would manifest itself where Arthur said it had before? Clearly, it appeared wherever the last Denizen or Nithling to use the Front Door had got out – in this case, the hospital.

'Get off the road, girl! You'll get shot!' Leaf jumped at the voice and looked wildly around.

'Come on then! Get in here!'

It was a woman talking. An old woman, standing in the doorway of one of the terraces, gesturing at Leaf to come inside.

Leaf groaned, rolled over, pushed herself up with her hands and walked slowly over to the woman's door.

'Hurry up!' the woman called. She glanced up the street. 'I can hear something coming.'

Leaf heard it too: the low, ground-vibrating growl of very large vehicles. She quickened her step, getting into the house just as a tank came round the corner at the far end of the street, its left track locked, the right bringing it round. Leaf stared through the window in the door, surprised by how loud the tank was and how much the house around her shook as it passed.

Six more tanks followed the first, all of them fully buttoned up, no one sitting up out of the turret or peering out through open driving hatches. Leaf had never seen real tanks before. These were twice the size of the light armoured vehicles she'd seen the army and NBA using.

'What's your name then?'

Leaf turned round. The old woman was very old and quite hunched over, but she moved deftly and was very alert.

'I'm sorry,' said Leaf. 'I was distracted. Thanks . . . thanks for warning me. Oh, My name's Leaf.'

'And mine is Sylvie,' said the woman. 'You've been in the wars, haven't you? You'd best come into the kitchen and I'll clean up your head.'

'No, I have to . . . I have to . . .'

Leaf's voice trailed off. She didn't know what she had to do now. Get back into the hospital? Even with full-on tanks heading there now?

'A cup of peppermint tea, some cleaning up and a bandage are what you need,' said Sylvie firmly. 'Come on.'

'What's going on?' Leaf asked as she obediently followed Sylvie down the hall and into the kitchen. 'Those were tanks . . .'

'There's been some sort of biological attack at the hospital.' Sylvie got a first aid kit down from the top of the fridge and reached over to flick on an electric kettle. 'Though I haven't really been keeping up with all the developments. They re-established the city quarantine this morning. We can go and watch the television in the lounge, if you like. Just sit near the window so I can see what I'm doing with your head.'

'Thanks,' said Leaf. 'I would like to know what's happening. You said they re-established the city quarantine?'

'About two hours ago, dear. This way.'

'But you let me in,' Leaf pointed out as she followed Sylvie into a small but comfortable lounge room. There was a screen on the wall. Sylvie clicked her fingers and it came on, the sound too low to hear, but Leaf could read the scrolling type across the bottom. It said, *Red Level Quarantine Imposed on City. Army and NBA seal off East Area Hospital. Psychotropic Bioweapon believed to be behind first attempted breakout, another imminent.*

There was a picture of perhaps a dozen people coming out of the hospital doors. They weren't walking properly, with their legs trailing in weird ways and their arms flailing about. The camera panned away from them to the soldiers and NBA agents, who were shouting and waving their hands and then lowering their weapons, the turrets on their armoured vehicles traversing. Then they started shooting. It took Leaf a moment to realise that she could hear that shooting, the sound coming in distantly from outside, not on the television.

It was live coverage.

'Yes, I know I shouldn't have let you in,' said Sylvie, who wasn't watching the television. She lifted Leaf's hair and started swabbing the cut on her head with a stinging disinfectant. 'But I'm very old, you know, and I didn't want to see a young girl be shot in front of me. If you do have some nasty disease, I daresay I shall catch it and die quite quickly without causing much trouble to anyone.'

'I don't have anything,' said Leaf quickly. Then she looked at her hands.

Except that's a lie. I do have something. You can't catch it from me though. Only from the Skinless Boy. But soon he'll know what I know and I'll be a puppet. Like those poor people he must have sent out, the ones killed to keep the quarantine.

On the television, two NBA agents with flame-throwers were walking forward now. Leaf looked away as long jets of flame gushed out towards the people who had just been shot.

'Keep still,' admonished Sylvie. 'More of a bruise than a cut. You probably should have your head scanned. When did you do it?'

'About an hour ago, I think,' said Leaf. 'Maybe two hours. Ow!'

'I've put a little anaesthetic gel on,' said Sylvie. 'And a skin-seal to keep it clean. You should have that scan though.'

'Are you a doctor?' asked Leaf. 'Or a nurse?'

'I'm retired,' said Sylvie. 'But I was a pharmacist. Sit there. I'll get the peppermint tea.'

Leaf looked back at the television. A senior military officer was being interviewed. A general. Behind him, Leaf could see the tanks that had rolled past her. Now they were moving into positions facing the hospital and other troops preparing positions between the tanks. Leaf held out her hand, palm up, waited for the television to calibrate on her, then lifted her finger. The volume came up and she could hear what the general was saying.

'We don't know what it is. It may be related to enFury, the water-borne psychotrope that caused so much trouble worldwide two years ago. But it's clearly widespread in the hospital and, as we have just seen, some of the infected are no longer capable of rational thought and are highly dangerous. Our task is to contain this outbreak. We will carry out our task, by whatever means are necessary.'

'Has there been any further communication from Dr Emily Penhaligon?' asked the unseen interviewer.

'Dr Penhaligon and her team are trying to slow the effect of the bioweapon by various means, and are profiling it and computer-modelling agents that will counter it. We are doing what we can with our people, and the NBA's inside the hospital to ensure that the labs and the upper isolation wards remain sealed from the rest of the hospital where the infection is widespread.'

'General, is there any information on how the bioweapon was deployed and by whom?'

'It's clearly a terrorist action,' replied the general. 'I have no further comment at this stage.'

'A number of commentators have said that it is most likely to be –'

The sound suddenly went down again. Leaf turned her head to see Sylvie wiggling her fingers. She'd just put down two steaming cups.

'The television noise annoys me so,' said Sylvie. 'Drink up your tea, dear. We must have a little talk.'

'Thanks,' said Leaf. 'But I don't want to –'

'Oh, I don't want to know what you were doing climbing out of the underworld,' said Sylvie, 'but I think we should call your parents. You do have parents? Well then, we should call them and let them know that you are here, and will be sitting out this quarantine with me.'

'I can't do that.' Leaf had just realised what she did have to do. Or rather, had thought of something that might offer a way back to the House. 'I have to go somewhere.'

'You can't go anywhere,' said Sylvie. 'Not by foot and not by car, even if I was silly enough to drive you. No civilian traffic of any kind allowed.'

'I have to get to a house in Denister,' said Leaf. She told Sylvie the address. 'As quickly as I can.'

It was Arthur's home she wanted to go to. The House might be above the hospital and essentially unreachable, but Leaf remembered something else Arthur had told her, long ago in his hospital room. It was only yesterday to everyone else, but Leaf had been months at sea in that time. Even so, she clearly remembered Arthur talking about his phone. A phone in a velvet box that could be used to call Denizens in the House.

'That's out of the question,' said Sylvie rather severely.

'It's incredibly important,' Leaf insisted.

'Why?'

Leaf was silent. She couldn't tell Sylvie the truth. The old woman wouldn't believe her and it would only make things worse.

I can't tell her, she thought suddenly. *But perhaps I can show her.*

'Do you have a window that looks towards the hospital?' Leaf asked.

'Yes, upstairs,' said Sylvie. 'What's that got to do with anything?'

Leaf hesitated for a moment. Sylvie was very old and a shock might kill her. But Leaf needed the old woman's help. Arthur was depending on Leaf to get the pocket back to the House so it could be destroyed. Not just Arthur, but everyone else too. What if the Skinless Boy kept spreading its mind-control mould everywhere? There might be other things the Nithling could do as well . . .

'I want us to go upstairs, then I want you to look at the hospital through these glasses. It'll be a shock, I warn you. But after you take a look, I'll tell you everything.'

Sylvie looked cross, but then a smile slowly undid her frown.

'You are being very mysterious and I'm sure you're also wasting my time. But what do I have to waste but time? Come on.'

The window that faced the hospital was in Sylvie's bedroom, a spare, tidy room with nothing personal about it. The old woman crossed it quickly and pulled back a curtain.

'There's the hospital,' said Sylvie. 'Complete with helicopter gunships, I fear.'

Leaf looked through the window. There were three sharp-nosed helicopter gunships doing slow orbits around the hospital buildings, about six hundred feet up. She pushed the glasses further up on her nose then quickly took them off. It made her head hurt to see the helicopters apparently flying into the solid buildings of the House and then come out again.

'Please look through these,' said Leaf. 'But be prepared.'

'I doubt I'll see anything,' said Sylvie as she took the glasses. 'These are cracked!'

'You will see something and then I'll explain.' Leaf frowned as a pain shot through her head again. It was different to the pain she'd experienced before. It felt like there was an odd pressure building up inside her skull. Like a sinus pain but in the wrong places.

The mould! It must have got into my head already!

'I really can't see a thing,' said Sylvie. She had the glasses on, but was not looking out of the window.

'The window!' urged Leaf, but she suddenly felt desperate and uncertain.

What if Dr Scamandros's glasses only worked for her?

CHAPTER THIRTEEN

Lieutenant Corbie lowered his perspective glass and rubbed his right eye. It was sore from looking through the telescope for so long. For a whole afternoon, he and his troop of Borderers had been watching and counting the enemy column as it advanced through the pass below them.

'Add another five thousand to the tally,' said Corbie to his sergeant, who was keeping count in his notebook. 'More of the regular Nithlings, arrayed in units of one thousand.'

'That's more than twenty-six thousand today, sir,' said the sergeant. 'All on the one tile.'

'It's scheduled to go east and north at sundown,' said Corbie, tapping the Ephemeris in its pouch at his side. 'Shift a few more of them out of the way.'

'There must be a million of them in the Maze by now,' said the sergeant quietly. 'What happens when every tile is full up with Nithlings? No point moving them around then.'

'That's defeatist talk, Sergeant, and I won't have it,' snapped Corbie. 'Anyway, there are still plenty of empty tiles and the Nithling invasion is being broken up very successfully. Tectonic strategy, as always, is working. And I heard the Second Battalion of the Regiment won another battle yesterday.'

Corbie did not mention the fact that the XIXth Cohort of the Legion had almost lost a battle the day before yesterday. While the Nithling forces were being broken up every sundown when the tiles shifted them away, there were many tiles where there were very large numbers of Nithlings. Sometimes these tiles had to be cleared or retaken because they were scheduled to come close to GHQ or one of the other fixed positions.

It was six weeks since Corbie and his troops had left the Boundary Fort. That was in Nithling hands now. Though Colonel Nage had been killed with his entire garrison, he had managed to hold the switch room for twelve hours and the gates had been closed. But not before four to five hundred thousand Nithlings had come through. And then, a month later, the gates had somehow been opened again, even though this was supposed to be impossible. Tens of thousands more Nithlings had marched in.

Still, as Corbie had reassured the sergeant, the time-honoured tectonic strategy was working. With the tiles moving every sundown and the enemy unable to concentrate their forces, the Army was able to battle the Nithlings piecemeal, winning most of its direct confrontations.

Not that this was enough for Sir Thursday, Corbie had heard. Never very even-tempered at the best of times, Sir Thursday was supposed to have become even angrier than usual. Apparently, he had even lost his temper with Marshal Dawn and had seriously injured her, after Dawn had questioned some aspect of the Army's response to this unprecedented invasion and the wisdom of changing the campaign in the first place, so radically and so late.

Corbie reflected that Dawn had been right of course. It was very strange that the plan had been changed only hours before it commenced. Colonel Pravuil had been an odd messenger too. He hadn't seemed quite right to Corbie, like he held some kind of special commission and wasn't a regular officer at all. It all stank of politics and interference from higher up.

Corbie hated politics.

'More movement near the tile border,' called one of the Borderers. 'And I reckon we've been spotted. There's an officer ... superior Nithling, or whatever we're supposed to call it ... directing a squad our way.'

Corbie peered down from the hill. He and his fellow Borderers were concealed among the tumbled rocks at the top, but some movement might have given them away. Or the reflection from his own perspective glass.

Instinctively, he looked to the sun. It was near the horizon, making its rickety way down, but there was still half an hour at least till sundown. The tile border, visible to his trained eye as a slightly different tone of colour in the earth, was a hundred yards below them. If the Nithlings did attack, they'd have to make it past that border before dusk, when the tiles moved. Which was possible, Corbie estimated.

He wasn't that troubled though. His forces were in the corner of their current tile and a quick sprint in any one of two directions would get them on tiles that were moving to fairly safe areas.

'Something strange about that column,' muttered the sergeant. 'Looks like they're transporting something. They've got a whole chain of Not-Horses.'

Corbie raised his perspective glass. Not-Horses were valuable livestock, creatures that had been copied from Earth horses and then half-bred and half-manufactured in the Pit by Grim Tuesday. Since Grim Tuesday's fall, there had been no new supplies of Not-Horses, much to the annoyance of the Moderately Honourable Artillery Company and the Horde.

But down below, the Nithlings had more than two hundred Not-Horses harnessed up to a giant twenty-wheeled wagon that was at least sixty feet long. On the wagon was . . .

Corbie lowered his glass, rubbed his eye again and took another look.

'What is it?' asked the sergeant.

'It looks like a giant spike,' said Corbie. 'A sixty-foot-long spike made out of something very strange. It's dark and it doesn't reflect light at all. It must be some kind of –'

'Nothing?'

'Yes, I think so. Sorcerously fixed Nothing. But why transport it into the Maze? What would be the point, since they're never going to know where it will end up –'

Corbie stopped talking, put the telescope on a rock and quickly opened his Ephemeris, flicking through the pages till he found the appropriate table, cross-indexing the day with the tile the Nithling Not-Horse train was on.

'That tile moves right to the centre of the Maze tonight,' said Corbie. 'Grid 500/500.'

'There's nothing special there,' commented the sergeant.

'Not that we know of. But I've heard mention of a famous problem they set at Staff College called "The 500/500" . . . The Nithlings must know where that tile is going. And they must have known where all the other tiles have been going to get that thing this far.'

'But they couldn't get hold of an Ephemeris without it exploding,' said the sergeant. 'Could they?'

'We never thought they could be organised either,' said Corbie. 'But they are and they're being led by someone who knows the business. Here, take this and see if you can see anything else.'

He handed the perspective glass to the sergeant and took out a small ivory stand and a lead soldier from the pocket of his quiver. The figure was of a colonel in the Regiment, all scarlet and gold. As Corbie put the model colonel in position on the stand, its colours grew brighter and lines sharper, and then it was like a tiny living version of the real officer, far away at GHQ.

'Colonel Repton!'

'Hello, Corbie! Another informal report?'

'Yes, sir. I'll be reporting to Captain Farouk, but it'll take time for this news to get from him through official channels, so I thought you'd better hear this and try to get it to Sir Thursday directly –'

The little model colonel grimaced when he heard this, but nodded for Corbie to continue.

'We've spotted a major Nithling column at Tile 72/899, which is escorting an enormous wagon drawn by over a hundred Not-Horses. On the wagon is a sixty-foot-long, ten-foot diameter object pointed at one end that appears to be made from Nothing, though its shape is consistent. I can only describe it as a giant spike, sir. The thing is, that tile will move at sundown to tile 500/500 and I –'

'Did you say tile 500/500?' Colonel Repton sounded alarmed. 'Would you describe the spike as obviously sorcerous?'

'Yes, sir!'

The figurine visibly paled.

'I must inform Sir Thursday at once! Wish me luck, Corbie!'

The figure stiffened and was once more merely lead.

'Better wish ourselves luck,' said the sergeant, handing the glass back to Corbie and picking up his bow. 'There's another three squads moving out towards us. They're definitely going to attack.'

CHAPTER FOURTEEN

'I think I just remembered something,' said Fred. 'About my old job. I remember separating the flakes of gold!'

'That's good,' said his friend Ray Green. 'I still don't remember much. I dream about it though, and it's on the edge of my mind as I wake up. Then I open my eyes and it's gone.'

'It'll come back,' said Fred. 'It usually does eventually. Most of it.'

Ray frowned. 'The thing is, I have this feeling that I need to remember quickly. That there's something really important I have to do.'

'It'll come back,' said Fred. 'It can't be that important, anyway. Not when we're stuck here for the rest of the year. Not to mention the other ninety-nine years stuck in the Army.'

'You wanted to be a general,' said Ray suddenly. 'I remember you telling me that some time.'

'Did I?' asked Fred. 'Really? Hmmm. That's not such a bad idea.'

It was six weeks since Ray and Fred had been washed between the ears. They'd each woken later that same day, on their beds, with pieces of paper pinned to their tunics. The pieces of paper had their names on them and nothing else. When they first woke they couldn't even read, but fortunately their reading and writing abilities had come quickly back to them, along with various skills and background knowledge.

But very few specifics about their previous lives had returned. They'd found their notebooks, but those hadn't helped much. Fred had relearned his favourite colour and how he took his tea, but Ray found his own notes very cryptic. After reading them, he did feel that Ray probably wasn't his real name, but he didn't know what his real name was. Or the significance of the Trustees' names.

Ray couldn't even remember anything about being an Ink-Filler. Fred had remembered quite a lot about his civilian life in the Middle House. Ray's was a mystery. Try and try as he might, he could not summon up any memories. Sometimes he would feel as if there was an important memory on the very edge of his consciousness, but whenever he reached for it, it would be gone. It felt almost like a physical pain, a dull ache of lost life.

Fred told Ray at least some of his memories would come back in time, but that was small comfort. When the platoon got together in their rare time off, conversation would invariably come around to everyone's previous lives. Ray would sit there, silent and still, but listening intently in the hope that a detail from someone else's life might spark some memory of his own.

The pain of listening to the others reminisce was lessened as their time off got scarcer and scarcer every day. For some reason, soon after they'd been washed between the ears, the normal training schedule had been accelerated and it got accelerated again. In the beginning, the recruits were given six hours off a night and two hours free during the day. That had been cut back to a mere five hours a night and then four, and even that was prone to interruption.

The training had been intense. Ray and Fred now knew how to march moderately well by themselves, with their platoon or with larger formations. They could march unarmed, or march and do basic drill with a variety of weapons, including clockwork-action pole-axes, Nothing-powder muskets, explosive pikes, muscle-fibre longbows, savage-swords and bucklers, power-spears and lightning-charged tulwars. They knew the seventeen forms of salute and the thirty-eight honorifics used in the Army.

They could also use the weapons they drilled with and look after them without injuring their companions. They could manage to present themselves in the basic uniforms of the Army's main units, though never completely to the satisfaction of Sergeant Helve. They had learned to follow orders first and think about them afterwards.

They were becoming soldiers.

'You should have remembered more straight-away,' said Fred, 'with that silver ring and all.'

Ray dug the ring out of his pocket and looked at it again. He'd woken with it under his tongue and asked Fred about it. But Fred couldn't remember ever seeing it before and it was a week before he recalled that a silver coin under the tongue was meant to prevent against washing between the ears.

'It's not all silver,' said Ray. 'Part of it has turned gold. I think that mean something . . . but –'

'I can't remember,' finished Fred. He looked over at the scrubby desert to the west. 'Almost sunset. Maybe Helve'll let us off when it gets dark.'

'I doubt it,' said Ray. He didn't want time off. Time off meant time trying to remember. He preferred to be busy, to have no time to think at all.

The section was on clean-up detail. The tiles to the southwest, west and northwest had changed a lot in the last week, and the wind had been westerly, blowing bits of vegetation into the camp. Unsightly leaves had lodged themselves under the buildings and in various corners, upsetting the cadre stuff. So the recruits had been unleashed and ordered to clean everything up, the penalty for the survival of a single leaf or whirly-thorn being a fourteen-mile route march that night in Horde armour (good when riding Not-Horses, but terrible for marching) with Legion weapons and Borderer boots (as Horde boots would render the whole recruit battalion lame if they marched fourteen miles in them).

'What's that over in the desert?' asked Fred. 'Is one of the other recruit companies doing an assault exercise?'

Ray looked where Fred was pointing. A line of figures was marching across the desert, less than a mile away. The late afternoon sun glistened on the points of their long spears and their helmets, and reflected very brightly from the metallic thread of the banner that flew above the knot of four or five Denizens on the left flank who were riding Not-Horses.

'They aren't recruits,' said Ray. 'Or any unit I've ever read about.'

To try to make up for not remembering his earlier life, Ray had read all the way through *The Recruit's Companion* and had memorised large sections of it.

'Maybe we should tell Sergeant Helve,' said Ray thoughtfully. He turned around to march to the orderly office, but jerked to attention instead. Sergeant Helve was right there, staring at the desert. He was panting very slightly, which surprised Ray and Fred. They'd never seen Helve out of breath.

'Stand to!' shouted Helve, at a volume they'd also never heard before, despite some truly stupendous vocal performances when they'd inadequately polished their brass or whitened their belts. 'All recruits Legion dress, savage swords and power-spears, on the double! This is not a drill! We are under attack!'

'Who are they?' asked Fred as he and Ray sprinted to the barracks, without any NCOs telling them off. There was a torrent of corporals and sergeants going the other way, but they were not concerned with petty infringements like sprinting instead of marching today. 'Can't be Nithlings.'

'Why not?' asked Ray, as they burst inside and rushed to their lockers.

'That lot out there are organised. Disciplined. Uniforms and banners and the same kind of weapon and everything,' said Fred a minute later. 'Here, help tie this up will you?'

Ray tied the leather laces on Fred's segmented armour and stood still while Fred returned the favour. They strapped on their savage-swords, with the blades that twirled when you twisted the hilt, swung on their rectangular shields and picked up their power-spears. The long metal points of these spears started to glow as they were lifted up and wisps of black smoke coiled towards the ceiling. Many a roof or a companion's uniform had been set alight by recruits with power-spears.

'What do we do, Ray?' asked Florimel. She and the rest of the section were just finishing their preparations. Though no formal recruit-corporal had ever been appointed, and both Sergeant Helve and Corporal Axeforth said none ever would be because none of the recruits were good enough, the rest of the section all looked to Ray to explain orders or to tell them what to do. If Ray was unavailable for some reason, they looked to Fred as his deputy.

Ray wondered if it was something to do with his past. He had a vague inkling that he had been someone in authority which, though unusual for a Piper's child in the House, was not unheard of.

'We're under attack,' explained Ray. 'So we'll fall in here and march out and just follow orders and everything will be fine. Everyone got everything? Theodouric! Where's your savage-sword? Grab it and catch up with us. Everyone else, fall in! By the left, quick march! Left . . . left . . . left, right, left!'

They were just marching out of the barracks when a panting Corporal Axeforth met them. He wasn't in full Legionary rig-out, having just swapped his hat for a helmet and thrown a cuirass over his scarlet tunic, and he had a clockwork poleaxe instead of a savage-sword. But he was calm enough as he quickly fell in step next to the line of recruits.

'Good work, Recruit Green. We're assembling on the parade ground. Recruit Rannifer, march towards that gap to the left of Two Platoon. We'll be forming up on them.'

Rannifer was the tallest of the Denizens, by a hair over Florimel, so he was always the right marker, the one whom the others formed up on and who consequently was first in line when the rest marched in twos as they were doing now. This was not a very good thing as Rannifer was more easily confused than most of the other Denizens.

This time, Axeforth marched very close to Rannifer, to make sure there was no error. The corporal also marched faster than normal, Ray noticed, though it was not double time. Making sure they got in place quickly, he guessed, while not appearing to be panicked or hurried.

The other recruit platoons were all marching on to the parade ground as well. Some were already formed up, with their sergeants bellowing and shouting. There were even officers present, conferring together nearby. Ray automatically assessed the plumes on their helmets, for all were in Legionary uniform. Four lieutenants, a major and even a colonel. Ray was impressed. He'd seen the lieutenants, but never anyone of higher rank.

'I've just remembered something,' whispered Fred as they halted, in the centre of the front line. 'About Piper's children.'

'What?' Ray whispered back. The enemy were only five hundred yards distant now, advancing at a steady march. They had a whole lot of big bass drums for keeping the time, their low pounding rhythm punctuated every ten steps or so by all the enemy making a sound that was more like an animal snarl than a shout.

There were also a lot more of them then he'd first thought. Many hundreds at least. Not that Ray was counting. It was just the impression he got, that there were an awful lot of them, approaching very quickly.

'We aren't so good with getting hurt as Denizens,' said Fred. 'I mean, if our heads get cut off, that's it. And our arms and legs probably won't grow back either.'

'Silence in the ranks!' shouted Sergeant Helve. He walked slowly along the front line, not even looking at the onrushing enemy. 'This will be just like a drill! The enemy are Nithlings. They are inferior! We are the Army of the Architect! The Architect! Let me hear you say it! The Architect!'

'*The Architect!*' boomed out six hundred Denizen mouths. It sounded incredibly loud and solid and confident, and Ray started to feel a bit better, despite what Fred had just said.

'We will not give ground!' shouted Sergeant Helve. 'The Architect!'

'*The Architect!*' boomed out the massed recruits. Ray noticed that Sergeant Helve was timing it so they shouted at the same time the enemy made their creepy snarling noise, the shout almost completely drowning out that and the enemy's drums.

'Colonel Huwiti is going to tell you the plan!' shouted Sergeant Helve. 'Just remember to stand by your comrades! Remember your drill!'

Colonel Huwiti strolled out in front of what was now four ranks of recruits spread in lines right across the parade ground. He casually saluted Sergeant Helve, who returned the salute with absolute precision. Neither Denizen seemed to even notice that there was a solid dark mass of humanoid Nithlings in dark lacquered armour with short, spark-tipped spears tramping straight towards them, and now only three hundred yards away.

'This will be very simple,' said the Colonel in a quiet but carrying voice. 'First rank, if you would be so good as to lock your shields, set your power-spears and draw swords. Second rank, ready your power-spears to throw. On the command "throw", you will throw and retire to the rear. As the second rank retires, third rank will march forward and on the command "throw" and then retire as fourth rank marches forward and throws on command. As each rank reaches the rear, it will turn to face front again and draw swords. Listen for your sergeants' and corporals' commands and all will be well.'

'Yes, sir!' bellowed Helve, the kind of 'yes, sir' that drew everybody else to empty their lungs yelling 'Yes, sir!' as well.

'I feel a bit small,' muttered Fred as he locked his shield with Ray's and the Denizen to his right, and set the butt of his power-spear in the ground.

'So do I,' said Ray. They were both at least a foot shorter than the Denizens to either side of them, and even when they held their shields high, the line suddenly dipped when it came to them.

They could hear the beat of the enemy's footsteps vibrating up through the ground now, and their snarls and even the crackle of their weapons, all too like the sound of lightning-charged tulwars, the favoured weapon of the Horde.

'You two Piper's children, retire at once to the fourth rank!' snapped someone in front of them.

Ray automatically obeyed the voice of command, unlocking his shield and turning on the spot to march back, Fred at his side. Behind him the line shuffled together and in front of him, Denizens stood aside.

They were just about to go through the third rank when the enemy all screamed at once, and the pounding of their feet got much louder and faster, with the drums suddenly booming twice as fast and horns blaring as well. At the same time, Helve and some other sergeants were shouting, 'Second rank! Throw!' though even their legendary voices were almost lost in the din.

Ray knew the enemy had charged, and two seconds later, he almost felt the shock wave of sound and movement as the Nithling's front rank crashed into the locked shields of his comrades, and the air was filled with screams and cries and curses, the hiss of super-heated spears and the ratcheting screech of savage-swords meeting Nithling armour.

'Third rank, throw! Fourth rank, advance!' Ray had only just reached the fourth rank. He swivelled round as the whole line advanced, and he and Fred wedged themselves in, raising their power-spears as they did so.

As he saw as well as heard the indescribable pandemomium, with the Nithling and the Denizen front ranks intermixed in violent battle, Ray Green was totally in the present. There was no part of his mind trying to remember anything of his past, but as his body obeyed without thought, the power-spear soaring out of his hand and into the rear ranks of the enemy, he had a sudden flash of memory. He was throwing something – a white ball – and someone else was shouting at him, 'Way to go, Arthur Penhaligon!'

The name resonated in Ray's mind so powerfully that for an instant he wasn't even aware of the incredible tumult of the battle.

'I'm not Ray Green!' he shouted. 'I'm Arthur Penhaligon!'

CHAPTER FIFTEEN

Sylvie looked out of the window. Leaf watched her, her heart sinking as the old lady did not react as she expected. She just stood there, fiddling with the left arm of the spectacles.

'Very interesting,' she said at last.

'Did you see it?' asked Leaf. 'The House? Above and around the hospital?'

'Yes, I did, dear,' said Sylvie in a very matter-of-fact way. 'Is it real or some sort of 3D projection from these glasses?'

'It's real,' said Leaf grimly. 'Very real. The glasses are not some sort of technology. A sorcerer made them.'

Sylvie took them off and looked at the wire frames and the cracked lenses. Then she put them on again and stared out of the window once more.

'I haven't got much time,' said Leaf. 'That disease, the one they think is a bioagent, it's actually caused by a ... a creature from that House, a Nithling. You can only get the ... virus ... if that one Nithling touches you. I've got it and when it kicks in the Nithling will see what I see, know what I know and will be able to control my mind.'

'Even from this distance?' asked Sylvie. She was still staring out the window.

'Um ... I don't know,' said Leaf. 'I can't take that risk. I have to get over to Arthur's ... my friend's house. He's got a phone that can call Denizens ... the people in the House. I was thinking that if you called the police – no, no, that's too risky. If you called an ambulance then I could hijack it and get them to drive me.'

'You are an adventurer!' exclaimed Sylvie. She tore herself away from the window and handed the glasses back to her. 'But I suppose that could work. Only what will happen afterwards?'

'I was planning to worry about afterwards when there is an afterwards,' replied Leaf. 'And I'm *not* an adventurer. At least not by choice. I've done that once and learned my lesson. No more adventures without knowing what I'm getting into.'

'They wouldn't be adventures then,' said Sylvie. 'You know, I was never adventurous. Perhaps it is not too late. I have a medi-alert here. Shall I activate it now? It's a subscription service, not public health, so we can be assured an ambulance will come quickly.'

'Activate it!' Leaf agreed. She started downstairs. 'Can I borrow a knife from your kitchen? And some salt?'

'If you so wish.' Sylvie opened her bedside drawer and took out a small electronic device, flipped open the cover and pressed the red button within. It started to beep and a synthesised voice said, 'Stay calm. Help is on the way. Stay calm. Help is on the way.' Then the device started to play a Vivaldi piece for lute and bassoon.

Sylvie threw it back in the drawer and followed Leaf downstairs, finding her in the kitchen eating spoonfuls of salt, washed down with orange juice.

'What on Earth are you doing?'

Leaf coughed – a cough that was nearly a vomit. Then she wiped her mouth with a tissue and said, 'I'm not sure, really, but salt might put off the Nithling's control. They don't like salt . . . or silver.'

'I have a silver bangle,' said Sylvie. 'I'll fetch it.'

'Thanks,' said Leaf through the corner of her mouth. She felt extremely nauseous, more than she would have thought possible just from half a dozen spoons of salt. Perhaps the mould didn't like salt either. Just in case, she quickly gargled with some more dissolved in water, and then snorted salty water up her nose, as if she were irrigating her sinuses. Perhaps it would help.

By the time Sylvie returned with not just the silver bangle but a necklace of tiny silver acorns as well, they could hear a siren approaching and then the sound of the ambulance pulling up outside.

'I've got my allergy injector,' said Sylvie, showing Leaf an auto-injector she had hidden under her shawl, the brand-name on the cartridge blacked out with pen. 'I'll tell them it's got something nasty in it which they'll get if they don't do what I say. But not till we're in the ambulance. First I'll sit here and we'll tell them I blacked out. You can be my granddaughter.'

'Thanks,' said Leaf, with surprise. She hadn't expected Sylvie to get so involved. 'Uh, I don't want to actually hurt them . . .'

'I know, I know,' said Sylvie. She sat back in a kitchen chair and started making noises like a small sick cat. They were so realistic that Leaf was worried for a second, till she saw Sylvie wink.

Leaf opened the door. There were two paramedics, both in full quarantine gear, only their eyes visible behind their face masks.

'It's my grandma!' said Leaf. 'In the kitchen!' The paramedics hustled past her, the second one noticing her bandaged head as he went past.

'What happened?' asked the first paramedic.

'She blacked out,' said Leaf. 'It's her heart, I think.'

'Oh, oh, oh, oh,' mumbled Sylvie.

'We'd better take her in,' said the first paramedic as he ripped the plastic covering off a diagnostic unit and attached it to Sylvie's wrist. The second paramedic nodded and went back out. 'Yeah, pulse very elevated, blood pressure OK. Could be some kind of heart episode. You'll be all right, ma'am. My name's Ron and I'll be taking care of you. Just relax and we'll have you in the ambulance very soon.'

Sylvie's pathetic mewing quieted as the paramedic patted the back of her hand. Her other hand lay hidden under her shawl, holding the auto-injector.

'Can I come too?' asked Leaf.

'You understand that, with the quarantine, if we take you to a hospital you may end up having to stay there? And we'll have to spray you first.'

'Sure,' said Leaf. 'Long as we don't go to East Area.'

'Uh, No way,' said Ron. 'There's some serious s—stuff going on there. We're working out of Lark Valley Private now. OK, stand back. We're going to lift you now, on to the stretcher.'

The second paramedic had returned, pushing a rolling stretcher. The two of them expertly picked Sylvie up and put her on it, lightly strapping her in. The diagnostic unit beeped as they did so.

'Pulse spike,' said Ron. 'We'll have you hooked up to a couple of our miracle machines in a few minutes. You'll be fine.'

Leaf had been worried that some neighbours might ask who she was when they got outside, but she had nothing to fear. Though there were faces at various windows, no one came outside. They were probably all wondering if Sylvie was a victim of the new bioweapon.

They would not be reassured by the sight of the second paramedic handing Leaf a pair of goggles and a face mask and then liberally spraying her all over with something that looked bright blue when it came out but was colourless when dry. It did have a faint odour, though, of wet newspaper. Fortunately, it didn't leave any residue Leaf could feel.

After the spraying, the paramedic went to the front and got behind the wheel. Leaf climbed in the back, where Ron was bringing online a device that swung out above the stretcher and had half a dozen hanging tubes, leads and sensors.

Leaf shut the door behind her and the ambulance took off, the siren coming on once more. As they rounded the corner, she bent over and undid the straps around Sylvie's arms, just as the paramedic on the other side was unscrewing the lid of a tube of conductive gel.

'What are you –'

'Don't move!' hissed Sylvie, rearing up and pressing the auto-injector hard against Ron's thigh, where the needle would easily strike through his protective suit. 'This is a 250 milligram dose of Rapyrox. Tell your partner not to radio or hit an alarm either.'

The paramedic froze, then slowly turned his head to the front. Leaf didn't know what Rapyrox was, but Ron certainly did and he was afraid of it.

'Jules, the old lady's got an injection unit of Rapyrox against my leg. Don't do anything . . . I mean anything.'

'What?'

'I've got 250 milligrams of Rapyrox here and I'm not afraid to use it!' screeched Sylvie, scaring Leaf almost as much as Ron. 'I want you to drive me somewhere. And you keep quiet, young lady!' Leaf nodded, suddenly unsure how much of this was an act.

'Anything you want, lady,' said Jules. Leaf could see his eyes in the rear-view mirror, flicking nervously from that to the road ahead. 'Where do you want to go?'

Sylvie gave an address two doors down from Arthur's house. Leaf looked at her when the old lady said the wrong street number, then slowly nodded.

'I read a lot of detective stories,' said Sylvie, apparently without reference to anything.

'Great, great,' muttered the paramedic in the back. 'Why not? I read a few myself. Uh, why do you want to go to –'

'Did I say you could talk?' yelled Sylvie.

The rest of the journey occurred without conversation. Jules in the front kept glancing back in the rear-view mirror, but he didn't try anything. Ron closed his eyes and took very regular, very controlled breaths. Sylvie watched him like a hawk, her eyes brighter than they should have been for someone so old.

Leaf sat and worried. She could still feel the pressure in her head, but it hadn't got any worse. She still couldn't think of anything else to do but try to call Dame Primus and hope that the Will would help in some way. Preferably by taking the pocket and getting to Arthur so he could destroy the Skinless Boy. Though even that might not help those already affected by the mould.

Even if there was something that Dame Primus or Dr Scamandros could do about the mould, Leaf knew she was going to be in a whole lot of trouble – but hopefully not the kind that ended with her being one more drooling zombie in the slave army of the Skinless Boy.

'We're almost there,' said Jules from the front. 'Do you want me to pull over?'

'Yes,' said Sylvie. 'Girl, look out of the window. See if we've got any company. If we have . . .'

'I haven't done a thing!' protested Jules. Ron took an even deeper, more measured breath, but didn't open his eyes.

Leaf looked out of the tinted windows in the back of the ambulance. She couldn't see anyone or any other vehicles on the street. But she could see the house numbers. There was Arthur's house a couple of doors down from where they were parked.

'There's no one there.'

'Good,' said Sylvie. 'Go and pick me some flowers, girl. I'll wait here.'

'But I don't –' Leaf got into the act.

'I said, go get me some flowers!' ordered Sylvie with a maniacal giggle.

'Whatever you say,' said Leaf.

She climbed out the back, missing the sight of Ron trying to blink an SOS at her.

'Stop that!' ordered Sylvie. 'You just get flowers, girl. Nothing else! And shut the door!'

Leaf shut the door and quickly walked up to Arthur's house. It was pretty big, but the front door was very visible across the lawn. Leaf ignored that and walked on till she came to the drive. Ten feet from the garage door, she knelt down and pressed the button on the remote control wired in place under a rock, exactly as Arthur had told her.

The remote control opened the side door of the garage. Leaf crossed the drive, looking up at the house's windows as she did, but she didn't see anyone looking out.

Once inside the garage, it was quick work to get into the house proper and up the stairs. There were three levels above the garage, Leaf knew, and Arthur's bedroom was right at the top.

She felt a bit weird breaking into someone's house, and very nervous as well. More nervous than in the ambulance for some reason, though hijacking and kidnapping the paramedics was a really serious crime. Every time she took a step and it sounded louder on the stairs than she'd thought it would, she freaked out, anticipating a sudden meeting with Arthur's dad or one of his sisters or brothers.

They're probably all at the hospital, Leaf tried to reassure herself. *Or staying with friends or something. The house is really quiet. Only one more floor to go . . .*

She arrived on the third-floor landing. There were three bedroom doors and a bathroom door. Arthur's was the first on the left . . .

Or was it the first on the right?

Leaf suddenly doubted her memory. Surely Arthur had said first on the left?

Leaf quietly opened the door on the left and peered in. Then she shut it again as quietly as she could and backed away.

There was a girl in there, with her back to the door and earphones in, listening to music – or maybe the news – while she did something complicated with a light pen and a big flat-panel display.

Leaf swallowed and opened the right-hand door, trying to be just as quiet. It was Arthur's room, exactly as described, though tidier. And on the bookshelf was a red velvet box.

Leaf hurried over to the box, picked it up and put it on the bed, taking off the lid at the same time. There was a phone inside. An old-fashioned phone, like a candlestick with the mouthpiece on that and an earpiece on a cord. Leaf took the phone out and held it in front of her mouth, sat on the bed and pressed the earpiece against her ear.

Even though the telephone was not visibly connected to anything, Leaf heard an old-fashioned, crackly dial tone, which was quickly replaced by a voice.

'This is the Operator. What number please?'

'Dame Primus,' said Leaf urgently. 'I don't know the number.'

'Who is calling please?' asked the Operator.

'Leaf,' said Leaf. 'Arthur's friend Leaf.'

'Hold, please.'

The voice went away and the crackling increased in volume. Leaf tapped her feet anxiously, and gripped the main part of the phone even tighter.

'Dame Primus is not available,' said the Operator after at least a minute. 'Can I take a message?'

CHAPTER SIXTEEN

The power-spear had hardly left Arthur's hand when he was carried forwards by the sheer press of bodies around him, as the Denizen ranks pushed ahead to replace the losses in the shield-wall of the front rank. It was incredibly loud, frightening and confusing. At times Arthur wasn't even sure which way was forwards as the lines shifted and moved, and he had to move with the Denizens at either side or be trampled underfoot.

He'd automatically unsheathed his savage-sword, again without thinking, and he used it several times, moments of intense fear when he was either hacking at a Nithling that suddenly appeared in front of him or desperately blocking a lightning-tipped spear that came straight at him, apparently out of the blue.

Once he stood alone for several seconds, in a six-foot-wide circle of clear space in the middle of battle. Badly wounded recruits and Nithlings gasped and gurgled around his feet, small sounds that were drowned out again as Arthur was swept up once more by his companions. But he would remember them always, for they were the sounds of terror, bewilderment and finality.

There was always noise. Metal screeched on metal. Weapons thudded into armour and flesh and bone. The drums kept banging. Denizens and Nithlings shouted and screamed and howled. Lightning crackled and sparked and fizzed. Smoke and hideous burning smells drifted through the mêlée, wafting up from burning power-spears.

Arthur's mind overloaded on fear and adrenaline. He became like a robot, his body moving according to training and orders, with no real intelligence directing it. He felt like his conscious self had retreated into a bunker, letting his eyes, ears and nose record what was going on. He would look at it later and think about what his senses reported. He could not handle it now.

The battle lines surged backwards and forwards for a time that Arthur could not measure, for it was composed of seconds of total fright and sudden action, but those seconds also stretched on so long that he felt exhausted, as if he had been running and fighting for hours and hours.

Then, like a natural turning of the tide, the Nithlings were pushed back. The recruits began to surge after them, but were restrained by yelled commands and directed to re-form ten yards ahead of the front rank's previous position. They obeyed, trampling over dead enemies and their own fallen comrades. Against this flow of forward movement, there was also a steady stream of badly wounded Denizens heading to the rear, many supporting each other, though no able recruit left the lines.

The sun had almost set when the Nithling's withdrawal became a full retreat. They fled back to the tile border, trying to get across it before the last thin segment of the sun dipped below the horizon and the desert tile moved somewhere else.

Arthur stood with Fred on one side and an unknown Denizen on the other, dumbly obeying the commands that were being shouted around them. It was still too much for him to take in. There were too many horrible details everywhere, from the awful feel of blue Denizen and oil-black Nithling blood underfoot to the croaking cries of the Nithlings that were too hurt to flee.

Refuge could be had in looking straight ahead, and trying not to think about anything other than following the shouted commands. The first of these was to march, so they tramped forward, steadily pursuing the Nithling force back to the tile border.

Twice, groups of Nithlings turned to fight, and then the order was given to charge, but it was not a wild, every-which-way run. The recruits kept roughly in their ranks, double-timing, shouting the war cry as they charged.

These charges were exhilarating and exhausting and dangerous, and Arthur found that it took all his energy and attention to make sure he wasn't knocked over and trampled by his own side. He wasn't sure which rank he was in now, as there were many more behind him, the Denizen force shrinking its front line and turning more into a broad column, harangued into shape by shouting sergeants relaying and amplifying commands from Colonel Huwiti.

Finally, it was too dark to continue, the green moonlight and pallid starshine insufficient to track down the small groups of Nithlings that were all that remained. Many of the attacking force were dead or wounded and captured, but a significant proportion had crossed the tile boundary just before sunset and had disappeared as that tile moved on, the desert instantaneously replaced by a square mile of lush, rolling grassland. Tall grass that was helpful to the

Nithlings who crossed a few minutes too late to be carried away with the tile change.

Several platoons of recruits with additional NCOs and some of the officers were posted as pickets, but the rest of the force marched back to Fort Transformation. There was some attempt to sing at first, but this faded away as they crossed the field of battle and its remains. There were dead Denizens and Nithlings sprawled amid still-sparking weapons and blackened bits of ground, and there was blood everywhere, blue and black mixed together.

'I thought Nithlings dissolved when they died,' whispered Fred. Even at a whisper, his voice sounded strangely loud and dissonant, sharp above the sound of the marching and the occasional rattle of weapons or armour. 'Went back into Nothing.'

'They do,' said the Denizen next to Arthur. Arthur looked at her properly for the first time and saw she was a corporal, the one in charge of one of the other recruit platoons. Urmink was her name.

'What about these ones then, Corporal?' asked Fred.

'Near Creations,' said Urmink. 'Originally made from Nothing, but close to being Denizens. They're flesh and blood, of a kind. Very tough flesh and blood. Much closer to Denizens than mortals, and not at all like your normal Nithling.'

She spoke in a conversational tone, not the barking order-voice Arthur and Fred were used to. Her candour was unexpected, but they didn't want to push it, choosing to remain silent. Both were surprised when the corporal spoke again, just as the column wheeled to avoid the worst remnants of battle, in the middle of the parade ground.

'There's going to be a lot more fighting with that lot. This current campaign is not like any other. You all did well, but this was an easy battle. We outnumbered them and they were already tired.'

We have to fight again? Arthur thought. He felt a stab of fear rise up from his stomach, so strong that it almost made him throw up. He fought it down. *Of course, we're soldiers, but that was so horrible . . . how can we do it again . . . How can I do it again . . .*

The recruits were not dismissed when the force was halted at the clear, rear part of the parade ground. Instead, each platoon was sent on particular duties. Most were to pick up the dead, salvage useable equipment and clear up. Arthur and Fred stood at attention, waiting for their platoon to get its orders. After Corporal Urmink left, they also talked to each other quietly out of the sides of their mouths.

'We were lucky to be ordered out of the front line,' said Arthur.

'We were,' Fred agreed. 'I wonder . . . I wonder if everyone else got through all right.'

They were silent for a while, thinking about that, as platoons turned and marched off around them. There were only sixty or seventy recruits left on the parade ground now, and none at all around Fred and Arthur, unless there were more behind where they couldn't see.

Finally, they recognised the voice of Sergeant Helve, ordering Two Platoon to form up in front of their barracks.

'What was that you shouted when the battle started?' asked Fred, as they marched towards their barracks.

'My real name,' said Arthur. 'It's . . . well . . . I think I'm supposed to keep it secret for some reason. It came back to me, just as the enemy attacked. Only I can't remember anything more. Just the name.'

'Is that *everyone*?' asked Fred as they approached the barracks. There was a very short line in front of the door. Half of the platoon was missing. It took Arthur several seconds to work out that this meant they were probably dead or at the least wounded badly enough to require treatment.

'That can't be everyone,' whispered Fred as they got closer. 'Denizens are too hard to kill . . .'

'Green and Gold, fall in!' ordered Helve, but he didn't scream like he normally did.

Arthur and Fred quickly joined the end of the line. Rannifer wasn't at the other end. Florimel was there instead, now the tallest.

'You fought well,' said Helve, again in an almost conversational tone. 'As I expected you to. We've got the plum assignment now. Colonel Huwiti has ordered that as a reward, there will be a special mail call tonight. So you won't have to wait another three months. And since you've fought today as soldiers, there's going to be a rum ration as well – though not for you Piper's children, I'm sorry to say. Don't know why not, but it's expressly ordered so.

'We've been detailed to pick up the mail and take it to the Mess Hall. As there is still some danger of Nithling attack, we will stack shields here but keep savage-swords. That doesn't mean you get out of cleaning them or your other weapons or yourselves. We'll do a quick clean now and finish up properly later.'

The cleaning took fifteen minutes. Arthur was glad to remove at least some of the visible evidence of battle, though in his mind he could still picture Nithling blood on the blade of his savage-sword.

Helve did not leave them time to think after the immediate cleaning was done.

'Platoon, by the left, quick march! Left wheel! Keep in step, Lanven!'

'He didn't mention what happened to the others,' whispered Fred to Arthur. They were fairly safe talking, as they were right at the back, with Helve marching at the front.

Helve directed the platoon to a building Arthur hadn't been to before. There were a lot of buildings at Fort Transformation he hadn't been into. Like the Mess Hall. He hadn't even known there was one. This building had the ubiquitous red and black sign on the door, which said POST POST OFFICE.

Like the barracks, the Post Post Office was larger inside than it was outside. It appeared to be completely empty, save for a long wooden counter which had a bell on it. Helve halted the platoon then marched up and smacked the bell with his palm.

This had an immediate response. A Denizen in a dark green uniform Arthur recognised as Commissary field dress leaped up from behind the counter.

'We're closed!' he said, with a sniff. Arthur was amazed that a mere Commissary Corporal would dare to speak to Sergeant Helve in such a manner. Particularly as the Sergeant's cuirass was dented in several places and smeared with Nithling blood. 'Come back in three months!'

Helve's hand shot across the counter and gripped the Commissary Corporal by the top button of his tunic, preventing him from sliding back down again.

'The CO's ordered a special mail call, Corporal. Don't you read your orders?'

203

'That's different then,' said the corporal. 'Mail for the entire recruit battalion?'

'That's right,' said Helve. He let the corporal go with a twang that threatened to separate button from tunic. 'The whole battalion.'

'Coming up,' said the corporal. He retrieved a piece of paper from under the counter, got out a quill pen and ink well and quickly wrote on it. He then marched out from behind the counter to the empty space beyond and threw the paper into the air.

An instant later, there was a deafening rumble. The corporal jumped back as a dozen six-foot-tall canvas mailbags thudded down out of nowhere.

'That's it,' said the corporal. 'Help yourself.'

With those words, he sank behind the counter again.

'Grab those bags,' said Helve. 'One each. Green and Gold, you take one between you.'

The sergeant picked up two of the bags, one under each arm, without apparent difficulty. Arthur and Fred found it hard to even lift one off the ground, but once they got it balanced it wasn't as immovable as they'd feared.

'Stay in line and look orderly,' said Helve. 'We'll stay off the parade ground. Round the back to the Mess Hall.'

Arthur was not all that surprised to discover that he'd never seen the Mess Hall because it was not a building at Fort Transformation. It was like the washroom, reached by a weirdway in the outside wall of an armoury.

Lugging their mailbags, the platoon lumbered along the weirdway, eventually emerging in a room so large that Arthur couldn't see the walls, though there was a ceiling fifty or sixty feet up. Like the washroom, the Mess Hall was populated by ghostly images of thousands of other soldiers, most of them sitting on benches alongside trestle tables laden with food and drink.

Unlike the washroom, these tables were labelled, each one having a sign on it for a particular unit.

Fort Transformation Recruit Battalion was about fifty tables directly in from the weirdway entrance. As they marched through, Arthur noticed that a lot of the ghostly soldiers were visibly wounded. There were many bandages, crutches, eye-patches and very new scars. And most of the unit tables were considerably less than fully occupied.

It was not the picture painted by *The Recruit's Companion*, Arthur thought with a sinking heart. In the book everything was clean and spotless, and the illustrated soldiers positively radiated health, fitness and contentment.

Fred and Arthur were very weary by the time they got to their own spot, and they almost didn't have the strength to haul their bag on to a table.

'Open them up,' said Helve. 'We don't have to go back immediately. We might as well get our mail before the rush.'

The bags were opened, cascades of mail pouring out on to the tables. Then suddenly a letter left the cascade, flew through the air and struck one of the recruits sharply on her helmet. She reached up and caught it, exclaiming in delight, 'I got a letter!'

Ten seconds later, a brown paper parcel ricocheted off Florimel's armour and into her hands. It was followed by an envelope for Fred, and soon everyone except Arthur had something. Even Sergeant Helve had received a small pink envelope decorated with flowers.

'I won't get anything,' said Arthur. He didn't know why he knew that, but he did.

Even as he spoke, a large buff-coloured envelope smacked him in the face. Arthur reeled back on to a bench and found himself sitting down with the envelope in his hands.

It was addressed to Arthur Penhaligon, which confirmed the name he had remembered.

Arthur opened it. The letter was written on the inside of the envelope, so he had to crack the seams and smooth it out, which was quite difficult. It was very heavy paper. The letter was handwritten in pale silver ink.

Dear Arthur.

An agent of ours has your parents under its control. Unless you immediately relinquish the Keys to Us and give up all claims to being the Rightful Heir, we will have our agent cleanse their minds of all knowledge of you. Our agent will also do this to your brothers and sisters and your friends. It will be as if you were never born. Your home will continue to physically exist, but you will have no place in it. As we believe that you desire to return to a merely mortal existence, you should consider this as an opportunity. Simply sign on the dotted line below and everything will be taken care of.

Saturday, Most Superior Denizen of the Upper House

Arthur read the letter again, but he couldn't make sense of it. He was a Piper's child. Whatever parents or family he might have had were long dead, somewhere in the

Secondary Realms. And as far as he knew, he had no desire to return to some kind of mortal existence.

'This is good,' said Fred, tapping his own letter. 'From my old mates back in Gilding Workshop Seventeen. Bringing back lots of memories. Who's your letter from, Ray?'

'I'm not sure,' said Arthur. 'I think it's a hoax. Only . . . I do feel as if it's triggered some memory just out of reach. Something about keys . . .'

'Right, that's enough loafing,' ordered Sergeant Helve. 'There's more cleaning to be done. And preparation for tomorrow's lessons.'

Arthur stuffed his letter into his pouch and stood up. He was just in time as Helve suddenly snapped, 'Stand fast!', swivelled on the spot and saluted an officer whom Arthur had seen coming but had dismissed as one of the ghostly figures of another unit.

'Thank you, Sergeant,' said the officer. Close up, it was easy to see he was one of the lieutenants that had talked with Colonel Huwiti before the battle. His helmet plume was rather ragged now and he'd been cut down the arm. Blue blood had dried in a line from shoulder to wrist, surrounded by scorch marks. On a mortal, it would have been an incapacitating injury. The lieutenant seemed little bothered by it, returning Helve's salute with only a slight stiffness.

'I'm taking your two Piper's children,' said the lieutenant. 'Orders came in just before the battle. From the very top. All Piper's children to report to GHQ immediately. Have they had their Not-Horse riding lessons yet?'

No, we haven't, thought Arthur with a sinking heart.

CHAPTER SEVENTEEN

'N o!' Leaf cried out. 'No message – but hey! Don't hang up! Put me through to Suzy Turquoise Blue, please.'

'Please hold,' said the Operator.

A stab of pain hit Leaf behind the right eye as the Operator spoke, and her left hand wriggled without any conscious direction. It was horrible, as if the hand itself had become imbued with a life of its own. But Leaf knew what was happening.

The mould was established inside her brain and now it was checking its control. The Skinless Boy might already be able to see through Leaf's eyes, hear through her ears, feel what she felt.

'Hello. Suzy here.'

'Suzy! It's Leaf. I've got the pocket, but the mould . . . the Skinless Boy's mental mould is in my head! And I can't get back to the House!'

'Well done!' said Suzy. Her voice faded and Leaf heard her say, 'She has got it, Sneezer. Set the dials!'

'I need help,' said Leaf. 'I know you're not supposed –'

Her left hand was flopping about like a stranded fish, but so far it was the only limb affected. The pain behind her eye was no worse . . . but it wasn't getting any better either.

'Who cares about that!' exclaimed Suzy, talking away from the receiver and then into it again. 'I'm coming through. Hurry, Sneezer!'

The phone abruptly hung up, the dial tone returning. Leaf dropped it back in the box then used her right hand to restrain her flailing left arm before she hurt herself. Her arm didn't fight against her, as Leaf had half-feared, but the strange sensation she'd first felt in that limb was starting to occur in her right leg as well.

'Come on, Suzy!' Leaf whispered. She had an idea what to do to save herself, but first she had to get rid of the pocket. The mould was taking over so fast!

The door opened and Leaf choked on a gasp because it wasn't Suzy. It was a teenage girl, maybe sixteen or seventeen. Arthur's sister. The youngest one. Michaeli.

'What the – are you doing here?' asked Michaeli. 'Who are you?'

'Friend of Arthur's!' said Leaf, but her mouth wasn't working properly because her lips and tongue were suddenly partially numb so it came out as, 'Fiend up Arfloor.'

'What?' asked the girl. She had a mobile phone in her hand, thumb poised over what was probably a speed-dial button for the police.

'Arthur!' burst out Leaf, speaking slower so she could be understood. 'I'm a friend of Arthur's!'

'What are you doing here?' repeated Michaeli. She hadn't pressed the button. 'And what's wrong with you?'

'Arthur sent me,' said Leaf. 'Got Greyspot.'

Michaeli recoiled in horror, backing out the door so fast she ended up against the corridor wall on the other side.

'Not contagious,' said Leaf, spoiling her words by losing control of her leg and falling on the floor, where she writhed around in a desperate struggle with her own body.

Michaeli screamed then, but it wasn't because of Leaf's contortions. Suzy Turquoise Blue had material- ised in the corridor, and she was wearing pale yellow wings which were fully extended, tip-feathers touching the ceiling and walls. She also had a Metal Commissionaire's truncheon in her hand, an apparently wooden club that was covered in crawling blue sparks.

'What's going on?!' screamed Michaeli. She had dropped her phone, Leaf was pleased to see.

'I'm a friend of Arthur's,' said Suzy. She folded her wings and bent over Leaf, gesturing with the truncheon in her hand. 'Do I need to knock you out with this, Leaf?'

'Not yet,' chattered Leaf. Her jaw was moving of its own accord, but her right arm was still her own. She made contact with her jeans and tried to pull out the box with the sorcerous pocket, but her legs kept thrashing away. 'Thanks . . . coming . . . so quick.'

'I've been watching through Seven Dials,' said Suzy. 'Off and on, after the Army nobs knocked me back. Got to do something useful, even if old Primey objects.'

She suddenly transferred the truncheon to her belt and put her booted foot on Leaf's thigh, stopping her spasms. Then she reached down and took the plastic box.

Leaf's arms whipped around to try to snatch the box back as Suzy took the sorcerous pocket, confirming Leaf's worst fears. The Skinless Boy could see what she saw. It would probably only be minutes before it had total control of her body.

'Take . . . to House,' she said. 'Quickly.'

'What about you?' asked Suzy.

'Knock me out,' whispered Leaf. Her right hand was starting to crawl across the floor to Suzy's foot. 'Tell Sylvie in ambulance. Get . . . sedate . . .'

'The old lady in the conveyance with the light on top?' asked Suzy, but she was really only talking to distract Leaf, as she whipped out the truncheon and tapped her on the shoulder. There was a sharp crack and a river of blue sparks ran up and down Leaf's body, from toe to head. Every muscle in her body spasmed and her eyes rolled back.

'You've killed her!' cried Michaeli from the doorway. She'd picked up a broom from somewhere and was brandishing it with a technique that suggested past lessons in kendo or perhaps a role in a stage musical of *Robin Hood*.

'No, I haven't,' protested Suzy, keeping a wary eye on the broomstick. 'You're Arthur's sister, Michaeli, right?'

'Yes . . .'

'I'm Suzy Turquoise Blue. You might say I'm Arthur's chief assistant.'

'His what? What is going on?'

'No time to explain,' said Suzy airily. 'Could you nip down to the . . . what d'ye call it, ambulance, outside and tell the old lady that Leaf needs to be taken care of. I must hasten away.'

'But . . .'

Michaeli lowered the broom a little. Suzy took this as an invitation and gingerly edged past, her wings flapping a little. A few feathers brushed Michaeli's face, making the other girl jump.

'Those wings . . . they're real!'

'I should hope so,' said Suzy. 'Best you can get. Hopefully, the owner won't miss 'em before I get back. Which way is the Eastern Hospital?'

'Uh, East Area? Kind of that way,' said Michaeli, pointing.

'Thank you,' said Suzy. 'And your roof garden lies beyond that door?'

Michaeli nodded, bewilderment plain on her face.

'Where are you going?' she asked.

'Back to the House, first creation of the Architect and epicentre of the Universe,' said Suzy. 'If I can find the Front Door, and if the Skinless Boy and his minions don't stop me. Goodbye!'

Michaeli gave a tentative wave. Suzy bowed, clapped her wings behind her back and ran up the stairs to the roof garden.

Behind her, Michaeli looked at Leaf to see if she was still breathing, but didn't go any closer. Then she went across to her own room and looked out of the window. There was an ambulance in the street. She hesitated for a moment, then ran down the stairs.

Suzy patted the ceramic iguana that stood in the roof garden on the head, jumped on its back and launched herself off it into the sky with a few strong wingbeats. Thirty feet above the roof, she caught an updraft and quickly soared to a height of several hundred feet.

The wings, besides being exceptional examples of their kind for flying, were also imbued with several other properties. Suzy was counting on one of them to make the return trip to the House uneventful. According to Dr Scamandros, who had reluctantly helped her borrow them from Dame Primus's dressing room, flying with the wings would generate a sorcerous effect that would make mortals unable to look at her. The wings also had some protective qualities, but again, only when in use for flight. Suzy had thought this rather shabby, and still thought so, even after Dr Scamandros had explained that it was the nature of sorcery to never live up to expectations.

Not that Suzy anticipated anything other than flying. She intended to fly to the manifestation of the House, which she had seen through Seven Dials was located above the hospital. Then she would fly right up to the Front Door and, if necessary, hover in front of it while she knocked. Then it would be straight back to Monday's Dayroom with the pocket. From there she would work out how to get it to Arthur so he could throw it in sufficient Nothing to get rid of it and the Skinless Boy.

A very straightforward and satisfactory job, Suzy thought to herself. Even Dame Primus could hardly complain – though she would of course, and carry on about the Original Law, but Suzy was used to that. It would be a small price to pay for saving Arthur's world from the Spirit-eater.

Suzy was three-quarters of the way to the hospital, and could clearly see the House ahead, when she also saw the flaw in her plan. From the lack of interest from various official-looking mortals she had flown above, it was probably true that the wings shielded her from the gaze of humans. And while this would not work on Nithlings, both she and Dr Scamandros had thought it very unlikely that the Skinless Boy had a set of wings.

What they hadn't given full thought to was the fact that someone had made the Skinless Boy in the first place and had helped it get through the Front Door to Earth, in defiance of numerous laws of the House. Anyone who would raise a Spirit-eater would not hesitate to use more common Nithlings. There could easily be other Nithlings here, sent to help the Skinless Boy achieve whatever he had been sent to do.

And now here they were. Suzy flapped her wings hard to gain height as she saw them. Three winged shapes, slowly flying in a circle about five hundred yards out from the Front Door. Currently, they were playing a game with one of the mortal's flying machines, taking it in turns to dive in front of it as it came around on its orbit of the hospital, its spinning top part chattering away. The fact that the mortal pilot couldn't see them and wouldn't know what he'd hit if one of them miscalculated was obviously the main attraction of the game.

Suzy didn't know exactly what kind of Nithlings they were. They were roughly human-sized, but one had the head of a rodent, one had a head like a snake and the third had a head that resembled a partially squashed avocado with eyes and a toothy mouth. They all had normal-enough limbs, save for great variety in the number of fingers. All three wore Denizen cast-off shirts, waistcoats and breeches, similar to the clothes favoured by Suzy herself, though these Nithlings did not have hats. They also had very fine-looking red-feathered wings, not the cheap paper ones. The wings probably had similar properties to Suzy's own, though Nithlings also had a native ability to remain unseen in the Secondary Realms.

They were armed with tridents, which suggested they might have once served Drowned Wednesday, but that was surely misdirection. Suzy knew too much about Drowned Wednesday to fall for that one. The sad, food-obsessed Trustee would not have employed Nithlings. These three had to be in the service of one of the four remaining Morrow Days.

Suzy continued to gain height as she watched them, circling to put the sun behind her. The Nithlings were busy with their game, but at any time they might remember their duty and look up and around. The sun would hide her to some extent.

The Commissionaire's truncheon would not be much use if it came to an aerial fight, Suzy thought. She couldn't see from her current distance, but the tridents were bound to be sorcerous in nature, either glowing red-hot or emitting electric effects or, if she was very unlucky, firing projectiles of Nothing.

I can't fight three armed Nithlings, Suzy thought.

She peered down at the House, trying to see if there were any more Nithlings or anything else near the Front Door. It was hard to see from so high up. She was now at least three thousand feet above the House, and there were deep shadows from the many bizarre overhangs, abutments, projections, crenulations, awnings and afterthoughts.

Her only chance would be to dive straight down, checking her flight at the last possible instant right in front of the Door. If she timed it right, did it fast enough and didn't break her neck, she might be able to get into the Door before the Nithlings could intercept her.

Suzy tucked the precious container with Arthur's torn pocket deeper into the fob pocket of her third-inside waistcoat, buttoned up the two waistcoats she wore over that and did her coat up all the way to her throat.

The Nithlings were still playing with the chattering flying machine. Suzy hovered for a moment, her chin almost resting on her chest as she made sure that she had a clear flight path straight down.

'Hey ho, it's any fool's go,' Suzy muttered to herself. She clasped her hands above her head in a classic diving posture, threw herself forward and down, and stopped flapping.

For an instant her outstretched wings held her in position, though her body was almost perpendicular to the ground. Then Suzy folded her wings all the way back and she fell like a meteorite from the heavens, straight down.

CHAPTER EIGHTEEN

Arthur got a very accelerated Not-Horse riding lesson that night. He and Fred, after the enormous surprise of a handshake and some nice words from Sergeant Helve, were hustled from the Mess Hall by the lieutenant. They were marched to the Orderly Room, where Colonel Huwiti informed them that they had been given battlefield graduations from Fort Transformation and congratulated them on their assignment to GHQ as privates in the Regiment. He shook their hands too. In return they saluted and did the smartest about-turns they could manage. Then they were marched off to the Quartermaster's Store, where they signed over all the recruit equipment they'd left in the barracks, handed back the Legionary gear they were wearing, and were issued Horde field riding armour and equipment, which they quickly had to put on.

From the Q Store, they limped after the lieutenant in their knee-length Horde hauberks and stiff leather boots, trying not to groan under the weight of their winged helmets, saddles, stuffed saddlebags and the curved swords the Horde called lightning tulwars.

The riding lesson was given in the Post Stables by a Horde NCO they had not met before named Troop Sergeant Terzok. He was considerably less wide across the shoulders than most of the other sergeants, but had the most amazing moustache, which Arthur was sure must be fake. Close up it looked like it might be made of wire, and it certainly stuck out at right angles from his nose in a way that hair surely couldn't manage.

They almost felt better when Troop Sergeant Terzok, rather than being strangely friendly, immediately shouted at them and proceeded to impart a long list of facts about Not-Horses and the riding of them, interrupting himself every minute or so to quiz the two of them on what he'd just said.

Arthur was tired, but also buoyed up by having survived the battle, without really having to think about it yet. The prospect of going to GHQ was a relief as well. So the first few hours of the Not-Horse lesson were bearable.

By the third hour, which was when they finally got to go into the Not-Horse stable, he was losing any feeling of relief. Then he made the fatal error of actually yawning, as Troop Sergeant Terzok was showing them the finer points of a Not-Horse that was standing quietly in its stall, its glittering ruby eyes quiescent.

'Am I boring you, Trooper Green?' shouted Terzok. 'Not exciting enough, hey? Want to get straight on a Not-Horse, do you?'

'No, Sergeant!' shouted Arthur. He was suddenly very wide awake indeed.

'No, Troop Sergeant!' yelled Terzok. He pushed his wire-brush moustache almost into Arthur's nose. 'You are going to ride a Not-Horse like a trooper in the Horde, not a private, and I am a Troop Sergeant, not some plodding ordinary sergeant. Is that clear?'

'Yes, Troop Sergeant!' shouted Arthur and Fred, who figured that it would be best for him to join in as well.

'If we had a few more Not-Horses here, I could have taken a troop after those Nithlings,' Terzok continued. 'None of 'em would have got away then. Right. I will repeat the basics for the fifth and final time. This here is Mowlder, the oldest Not-Horse on the post. Made up more than four thousand years ago and still going strong. He is a typical Not-Horse, with three toes on each leg, not the four-toed variant that is occasionally seen. Each of these toes has been fitted for combat purposes with a four-inch steel claw, as you can see. The Not-Horse's skin is a flexible metal, but the creature is itself a Near Creation based on an original design of the Architect. It has living flesh under the metal skin, which serves as a very useful armour. Like us Denizens, the Not-Horse is extremely hardy and heals well. Not-Horses are also smart and must be treated properly at all times. Any questions so far?'

'No, Troop Sergeant!'

'Right then. I will now demonstrate the correct means of approaching a Not-Horse to fit a bit and bridle. Watch closely.'

Arthur watched closely as Terzok demonstrated how to get all the harness on a Not-Horse. It looked straightforward provided the Not-Horse cooperated, but was not quite so easy when Arthur got to do it himself. Getting up into the saddle and actually riding the Not-Horse also proved to be more difficult then he'd thought.

Six hours after the lesson began, in the cold, dark early time before the dawn, Terzok pronounced Arthur and Fred as capable as they were going to get in the time available. Which was not capable at all, but he hoped they would stay on long enough to learn from experience. Before they left, he whispered in the ears of the two Not-Horses chosen to carry them.

By this stage, Arthur in particular was so tired that he didn't care if he was tied across the saddle like a blanket. He just wanted to rest and not have to listen to – or watch – Troop Sergeant Terzok and his moustache ever again. He'd thought he was used to being exhausted and had become much better at staving off the swimming vision and loss of coordination. But now even the proximity of a sergeant couldn't stop him swaying on his feet.

But he wasn't allowed to go to sleep. Another unknown lieutenant, this one unwounded and wearing Horde armour, arrived as the lesson concluded and announced that he would be leading them to GHQ.

'I'm Troop Lieutenant Jarrow,' he said. 'Seconded from the Horde to Fort Transformation. We'll be riding out in fifteen minutes, after I've checked your weapons, equipment, harness and mounts. Which of you is Gold and which Green?'

'I'm Priv . . . Trooper Gold,' said Fred.

Arthur mumbled something that sounded like it might be 'Green'. Jarrow frowned and stepped closer to him.

'I know there's a medical advice about you, Green,' he said, 'but the file's gone missing. Are you fit enough to travel?'

'I'm just tired, sir,' said Arthur. 'Very tired.'

He was so tired that he wasn't entirely sure that he'd actually said anything aloud. And he was also confused about where he was and what he was doing. Surely if he was meant to be going anywhere, it was school. School with Leaf and Ed.

Arthur shook his head. What was this school he could see in his mind's eye? Who were Leaf and Ed, and why were they looking down at him with the blue sky behind them?

'Have you shown these two the Horde method of carrying wounded, Troop Sergeant?' asked Jarrow.

'No, sir!' snapped Terzok. He looked at Arthur. 'Should I sling him up, Troop Lieutenant?'

'Yes, do,' said Jarrow.

Three Not-Horses had been readied for the ride ahead and were standing patiently outside the stable door. Terzok took what appeared to be a large canvas bag with leather straps and steel buckles from behind the stable door and hung it between two of the Not-Horses. Muttering something to them quietly, he buckled one side of the sack to the leftmost Not-Horse's saddle and the other to the Not-Horse in the middle. Thus strung, it made a kind of hammock between the two mounts.

'This here's a double-ride sack,' said Terzok. 'Not-Horses are able to perfectly match each other's stride, unlike other mounts. But the double-ride sack's only to be used when ordered because the mounts can't gallop with it fixed.'

Arthur stared at the sack between the two Not-Horses. He was so tired it took a few seconds for him to understand that it was for him.

'How do you get in?' asked Fred.

'If you're fit enough to climb in then you should be riding,' said Terzok. 'If you're not –'

He picked Arthur up under his arm, walked to the front of the horses and shoved him in the open end of the sack, armour, weapons and all.

'If the soldier being carried is very badly hurt, you do up these laces here,' instructed Terzok.

'But I don't want to be –' Arthur started to say.

'Silence!' snapped Terzok. 'You have been ordered to ride in the sack! Now go to sleep!'

Arthur shut up and wriggled around so the hilt of his lightning-tulwar wasn't sticking in his hip quite so much, and reached down to untuck a fold of his mail hauberk that was bunched up on his thighs.

Then, because a sergeant had ordered him to, he shut his eyes and fell asleep.

It was not a deep sleep at first. Through slitted eyes, Arthur was dimly aware of activity around him as Lieutenant Jarrow checked over the Not-Horse's harness. Then the sack he was in began to jiggle up and down and the steel claws of the Not-Horses' toes struck sparks on the flagstones outside the stable for a moment, before becoming muffled as they walked on to the dusty bare earth. The jiggling increased as they broke into a trot, then became a kind of swaying roll as the two Not-Horses carrying the sack changed pace into a perfectly matched canter.

As the Not-Horses continued to head out of the Fort at a steady pace, Arthur sank into a deeper sleep and began to dream.

He was standing in a vast, marble-lined room, surrounded on all sides by incredibly tall Denizens, each easily twelve feet tall, measured by their relationship to the piles of weapons, armour and Nithling bodies beneath them. Yet despite their height, Arthur was taller still, looking down on them from a position of lofty eminence. He was looking at a ring on his finger, a crocodile ring that was slowly turning from silver to gold. Only the last portion of it remained silver, and as he stared, it too turned to gold. The tall Denizens began to applaud and Arthur felt himself grow taller still, until he was suddenly no longer in the marble-lined room, but was a giant standing above a green field that a little voice in his mind said was the school oval. Children were running around his feet, pursued by dog-faced creatures that he somehow knew were called Fetchers. Then he was suddenly child-sized himself, and the Fetchers were twice his size, pinching and grabbing him. One tore the pocket from his school shirt and took the book that had been in it.

'Got you!' said a horrific, rasping voice.

Arthur shrieked and woke up, threshing about in the grasp of something leathery and horrible. A vicious creature had taken *A Compleat Atlas of the House*!

That's it. A Compleat Atlas of the House. *I had A Compleat Atlas of the House. My name is Arthur Penhaligon. I am the Rightful Heir.*

Arthur tried to hold that thought, but it slipped away. He gave up on it, opened his eyes and looked around. He was still in the double-ride sack, but the Not-Horses were standing still. The sun was coming up, a thin sliver of its rosy disc showing above the ochre-red hills to the east. Stunted trees with pale trunks and yellow triangular leaves were dotted around, too sparse to be called a forest.

Fred was standing in front of Arthur, massaging the insides of his thighs and muttering something about the iniquities of Not-Horses. Lieutenant Jarrow was sitting on a nearby stone, consulting his Ephemeris.

It was very quiet, the only sound the whirring breath of the Not-Horses and the occasional tap of their toes on a loose stone as they shifted their weight.

'What's happening?' asked Arthur sleepily. He pushed his arms out of the top of the sack and pulled himself part of the way out. He would have fallen the rest of the way if Fred hadn't caught him and restored his balance just long enough for both of them to collapse under limited control.

'What's happening?' asked Fred indignantly. 'You get to snore your way across half a dozen tiles, while I wear the skin off my thighs and bruise my tailbone – that's what's happening.'

'That's what has happened,' corrected Arthur, with a smile. 'What's happening now?'

'We've stopped for a rest,' said Fred. He tipped his head towards Lieutenant Jarrow. 'That's all I know.'

Jarrow closed his Ephemeris and walked over. Arthur and Fred scrambled to their feet, stood at attention, and saluted.

'No need for that – we're in the field,' said Jarrow. 'Are you fully rested, Green?'

'Yes, sir,' said Arthur.

'Good,' said Jarrow. 'We have a fair way to ride and there is a strong possibility we may have to run from New Nithling forces.'

'New Nithlings, sir?' asked Arthur.

'That's what we're calling them now,' said Jarrow. 'We'll avoid them wherever possible. Just stay close to me and stay on your mounts and we'll out-run them. They haven't got any cavalry.' He paused for a moment then added, 'Or at least we haven't seen any yet. Any questions?'

'What do we do if we're separated from you, sir?' asked Arthur.

'Give the Not-Horses their heads,' replied Jarrow. 'They'll find the nearest friendly force. But so you know, we're headed today for Tile 268/457. It's scheduled to move at dusk to a position only ten miles from the Citadel. We're currently on tile 265/459. We're going to go east for three miles and then south two miles. The tiles east are bare hills, grassy steppe and jungle with clearings; go south from the jungle and you get a ruined city and then lake and marsh, which is the tile we want. We'll have to be extra vigilant in the jungle, the ruined city and the marsh. Easy to be surprised in all three and hard to ride away. We'll take another thirty minutes' rest and then ride. I'll stand watch on the rise there. Keep the harness on our mounts, but you should give them a rubdown. Don't want them to rust.'

Arthur and Fred obediently got wire brushes, cleaning cloths and bottles of solvent from their saddlebags and began to work on the knee joints and other areas where the Not-Horses were prone to rust. The creatures nickered and whinnied slightly, enjoying the attention, and Arthur found himself warming to them. Out here in the field, with the sunlight dimming their red eyes, they seemed altogether different to the cold, ruby-orbed beasts of the dark stables.

'I wonder why they want us at GHQ,' said Fred. 'Lieutenant Jarrow said the order came from Sir Thursday himself.'

'He probably found out I was here as a Piper's child,' said Arthur, without conscious thought.

'What?' Fred looked under his Not-Horse's belly to stare up at Arthur.

'He probably found out I was here as a Piper's child,' repeated Arthur slowly. His words had the ring of truth, but he didn't know what they meant. He just couldn't remember . . .

Before he could think any further, Jarrow came scrambling down the slight slope.

'Mount up!' he called softly, cupping his mouth with his hands, so his voice did not travel. 'New Nithlings!'

Chapter Nineteen

At her current speed of over one hundred and eighty miles per hour, Suzy was only nine hundred feet and four seconds away from the Door when one of the Nithlings finally spotted her. It shrieked, surprising its comrade, who crashed into the helicopter it was playing chicken with. The Nithling, invisible to the pilot, smashed through the canopy and caused enormous damage as it thrashed around the cockpit while trying to get out again. In the process it accidentally killed both pilots. The attack helicopter reared up on its tail, hung there for an instant then plunged down into the car park and exploded, showering the hospital front, the surrounding soldiers and NBA agents with burning debris.

Suzy spread her wings at eight hundred feet, the shock of their opening momentarily blacking her out. Too effective, the wings brought her to a hover within a second, still a few hundred feet above the Front Door, with two Nithings flapping up towards her as fast as they could manage.

Suzy dived down again, straight at the Nithlings as if she were going to attack. They stopped to receive her assault, raising their tridents, but at the last second Suzy dipped one wing, slid sideways and down through the air, and landed on one foot on the hospital roof. The Front Door was right in front of her, but with the Nithlings now diving after her, Suzy didn't think there was time to knock.

She angled towards the Front Door, shut her eyes – and went straight through it.

Expecting an impact, Suzy wrapped her arms around her head. But after a few seconds of not hitting anything, she cautiously opened her eyes and lowered her hands.

She was floating, or possibly falling, in total darkness. Her wings weren't moving, but she had a sensation of movement in her inner ear. She couldn't see a thing, not even when she frantically craned her neck around to see if she could catch sight of the Front Door she'd just come through.

'Uh oh,' she whispered. Not having used the Front Door before, she'd thought that she would just come out the other side on Doorstop Hill. Evidently it was not as simple as that.

Suzy thought about her situation for a moment then whispered, 'Wings, shed light.'

She was relieved both to be able to hear herself and, a little later, to see herself, as the wings slowly began to glow, casting a pearly nimbus of light all around her.

Even with the light, there was still nothing else to see. Suzy looked up, down and all around, hoping for some indication that there was somewhere . . . or even something . . . else in this strange absence.

Seeing nothing, Suzy experimentally flapped her wings. Again, she felt the sensation of movement, but without any way to get her bearings, she couldn't be sure that anything was happening. For all she could tell, she might be stuck like a fly in jam, flapping her wings and getting nowhere.

Suzy shrugged, chose a direction at random and started flapping her wings in earnest. A considerable time later – perhaps hours – Suzy started to wonder if she had managed to get herself seriously lost somewhere inside the Front Door, or some area in between the House and the Door that wasn't Nothing but wasn't much of anything else either.

She stopped flapping her wings. The sensation of movement remained and Suzy thought about the situation. Just flapping about aimlessly had produced no results, so she had to do something else.

'Hey!' Suzy called out. Her voice sounded very loud in the quiet. 'Lieutenant Keeper! I'm lost in your stupid Door! Come and help!'

There was no answer. Suzy crossed her legs and took a cheese, mustard and watercress sandwich out of her hat. Like the hat, the sandwich was rather squashed, but Suzy ate it with gusto. She had rarely had access to any food at all as an Ink-Filler. Since becoming Monday's Tierce and gaining greater access to the larders of the Dayroom, she had rediscovered the enjoyment of food, even though it was not a necessity for life.

'Miss Turquoise Blue.'

Suzy jumped up and dropped her crust. Whirling round, she saw a tall, extremely handsome Denizen in a high-collared dove-grey morning coat, his black trousers knife-edge-creased above shining top-boots. His top hat was so glossy it reflected the light from Suzy's wings like a mirror. He held a silver-topped cane in his kid-gloved hand. His wings, furled behind him, were of beaten silver.

'Who are you?' asked Suzy suspiciously.

'That would be asking,' said the Denizen pleasantly. His tongue, Leaf noted, was an even brighter silver than his wings. 'I'll trouble you to hand me our Spirit-eater's treasure. We can't have his work interrupted, can we?'

'Your Spirit-eater?' Suzy's eyes flickered from side to side, hoping to see where this Denizen had come from or some other potential point of escape.

'Ours,' said the Denizen. His voice was extremely musical and pleasant to listen to. 'Come now. Give me the pocket and I shall show you a point of egress from the Door.'

Suzy blinked, and found her hand reaching under her waistcoats.

'I'm not giving it over to you!' she said through gritted teeth.

'Yes, you are,' instructed the Denizen. He yawned and patted his mouth with his left glove. 'Hurry up.'

'I'm not!' insisted Suzy, but to her horror, she found that she was taking out the container with its scrap of precious material.

'Very good,' said the Denizen approvingly. He reached out his hand to take the box as Suzy stared at it and tried to will herself to move away, to withdraw her hand.

Just as his fingers were about to close on the box, the Denizen's wings suddenly exploded out behind him and he twisted up and away, snarling in rage. Suzy fell back and somersaulted over twice before her own wings spread out and steadied her.

High above her, the silver-winged Denizen was in a furious duel with an electric-blue winged Denizen that Suzy did not at first recognise as the Lieutenant Keeper of the Front Door. His blue-fire sword was met by the silver flash of the other Denizen's sword cane, the two of them swooping, turning and diving as they exchanged lunges and blows and blurringly fast parries and dodges.

Suzy watched open-mouthed as the two combatants fought. They used their wings as much as weapons as a means of movement, blocking swords, slicing with the tips and delivering buffets that if they hit sent the targeted Denizen somersaulting through space. Sometimes the two were upside-down relative to Suzy, or perpendicular, and she got quite dizzy trying to re-orient herself before she gave up and just watched.

The swordplay was very fast and very dangerous. Many times one or the other only just managed to parry or weave aside or leap backwards as a thrust went home. Steel clashed on steel so quickly it sounded like a constant jangle of fallen coins. Suzy, who was being taught to fence by Monday's Noon, felt her eyebrows going up and down in constant surprise as she saw wing-assisted feats of sword-fighting that were in none of the manuals Noon had lent her.

Apart from watching, all Suzy could do was stuff the container with the pocket back into her waistcoat and stay out of the way. She contemplated trying to intervene, but the two combatants moved too quickly and were so focused on the fight that she concluded any move on her part would only put the Lieutenant Keeper off.

Then, as the Lieutenant Keeper went on the defensive, continually retreating upward, Suzy wondered whether she should try to get away. But she still couldn't see anywhere to retreat to. Instead, she followed the combat, her wings straining to keep up.

Suddenly, the Lieutenant Keeper stopped retreating and flung himself forward. The other Denizen tried for a stop-thrust but missed, and the two closed, blades locking. The Lieutenant Keeper was the slighter and shorter of the two, but his wings must have been stronger, for he pushed his opponent back at least twenty feet. At the same time he shouted something, a word that Suzy couldn't understand but still felt through every bone in her body, like a ripple of ague.

With that word, a circle of white light appeared directly behind the silver-winged Denizen. He must have sensed it, for his wings thrashed even harder to keep his place – but the Lieutenant Keeper was too strong for him.

'This does not end –' shouted the Denizen as he fell back into the circle of light. It was a doorway out, Suzy saw, with a gold-panelled room on the other side and an elephant's-foot umbrella stand. Once the Denizen was through, the circle closed like a bursting soap bubble. Again there was nothing but featureless space all around.

'Cripes,' said Suzy. 'Who was that?'

'Superior Saturday's Dusk,' said the Lieutenant Keeper. 'We are old adversaries, he and I. Not all the Days or their servants follow the compact of the Door to the letter and Saturday's minions are the slipperiest of all.'

The Lieutenant Keeper brushed back his long white hair with his fingers and wiped his face with the sleeve of his blue coat. He still looked harried; his waders were dripping with water and there were more dried blue bloodstains on his right sleeve. 'Doubtless he will return soon, possibly with others. I have closed many of the doors in the House, but this is of little avail when Saturday orders them open again and Sunday does not say yea or nay. Where do you wish to go, Suzy?'

'The Lower Hou—' Suzy started to say. Then she stopped.

'Can I go anywhere within the House?' she asked.

'The Front Door opens in all parts of the House, in various guises,' the Lieutenant Keeper informed her. 'Not all those doors are safe. Some are stuck and some are locked, and some are lost, even from me. But I can show you a door to any of the demesnes, within certain bounds.'

'Do you know where Arthur is now?' asked Suzy. She'd planned to take the pocket back to Monday's Dayroom, but it would be better to get it straight to Arthur so he could destroy it without delay.

'I do not,' said the Lieutenant Keeper. 'Come, decide where you would go. My work is never done and I cannot tarry.'

'The Great Maze,' said Suzy. 'I want to go to the Great Maze.'

'The only door I might open there is in the Citadel. That is where Sir Thursday resides. Are you sure that is where you want to go?'

'Sure,' said Suzy.

'There is great trouble in the Maze,' warned the Lieutenant Keeper. He looked directly at Suzy, his pale ice-blue eyes meeting hers. 'It is possible that soon all doors to and from the Maze will be closed. Elevators too.'

'Why?'

'Because a Nithling army stands on the brink of conquest there. If they defeat Sir Thursday's forces then the Great Maze will be cut off in order to save the rest of the House. So I ask again: are you sure you want to go there?'

'I've got to get this to Arthur,' Suzy answered, patting the container under her waistcoats. 'So I reckon I do have to go there. Besides, it can't be as bad as all that. I mean, Nithlings never get on with each other, do they?'

'These ones do,' said the Lieutenant Keeper. 'Here, as you insist, is the door to the Great Maze and Sir Thursday's Citadel.'

He gestured with his sword and once again spoke a word that made Suzy's stomach flip over and her ears ring. A circle of light formed and through it she could see a wooden walkway along a stone wall. A Denizen in scarlet uniform was marching along the walkway with his back to her, a musket on his shoulder.

'Thanks!' said Suzy. She flapped her wings and was about to dive head-first into the hole when she felt herself held back by her tip-feathers.

'No wings in the Great Maze,' said the Lieutenant Keeper. The wings detached themselves from Suzy, dropping into his hands. 'They attract too much lightning. Something to do with the tile changes.'

'But I have to give them baaa–'

Before Suzy could finish talking, the doorway moved forward and she fell through, emerging into late afternoon sunlight and a cool wind, high on the battlements of one of the bastions of the Star Fort, an inner defence of Sir Thursday's Citadel.

As Suzy clattered on to the walkway, the sentry suddenly stopped, stamped his feet and did an about turn. He took another two or three paces, staring right at Suzy, before the sight of her percolated into his brain. He stopped and fumbled with his musket, eventually bringing it to bear as he stuttered out, 'Halt! Who goes there! Call the Guard! Alarm! Guard! Corporal!'

CHAPTER TWENTY

The New Nithling patrol was easily evaded, the Not-Horses stretching their legs to gallop without the burden of the double-ride sack. Arthur, experiencing this for the first time, was at first terrified and then, after it became clear he wouldn't just fall off, exhilarated.

The Not-Horses had much greater stamina than Earthly horses, but even they could not sustain a gallop for long. After the Nithling force was nothing but a distant speck on the horizon, beyond the low hills of the current tile, Lieutenant Jarrow raised his hand. His Not-Horse slowed down to a canter, then to a brief trot and finally a walk, with Arthur and Fred's mounts following their leader.

They continued at a walk for the rest of the day, with half an hour's rest at noon, amid the ruined city of the last tile they needed to cross. It wasn't much of a ruined city. There were only outlines of old buildings, one or two bricks high, and grassy barrows that might or might not contain interesting remnants. Lieutenant Jarrow explained that there had never actually been a city there. It was built as a ruin, when the Architect had made the Great Maze to be a training ground for the Army.

The officer also showed them how to recognise a tile border – an important thing to know because anyone within a few yards of a border at sundown ran the risk of having different portions of their body simultaneously transported to different places.

Not all tile borders were marked in the same way, Jarrow explained, but most borders were obvious from a change in the colour of the vegetation or the soil, showing up as a continuous line. The border from the jungle to the ruined city, for example, was very clear, as every vine-hugged tree on the southern edge was almost yellow instead of a healthy green.

The border from the ruined city tile to the marsh was not as evident, since there was no clear line of colour change or difference in vegetation. But Jarrow pointed to a low cairn of white stones in the middle of an area where the ground slowly changed from a short green grass to low shrubs that were almost blue. Significantly, the cairn was a semi-circle, round on the northern side, and sheer on the south. It had been built to show the southern border of that tile.

The marsh proper began soon after. Jarrow let the reins slack and his Not-Horse picked a way through the spongy sedge and the tea-coloured pools of water, the others following in single file.

In the middle of the tile, or near enough by Jarrow's estimation, they found an island of slightly drier, somewhat higher ground, and here they set up camp. Jarrow again kept watch as Arthur and Fred removed the Not-Horses' harnesses, wire-brushed and oiled them, and polished their ruby eyes. Then they rubbed down their lightning-charged tulwars, sharpened them, and rubbed grease on their boots and their mail hauberks. All in all, this took till dusk.

Deep in the marsh, with the sun dipped below the horizon, they could only see one of the changed tiles around them. Looking to the east, where there had been nothing to see, there was now an imposing mountain, a dark silhouette against the starry sky.

'We ride to the Citadel in the morning,' said Jarrow. He'd used the last of the sun to consult his almanac, choosing not to show a light after dark. 'I'd like to ride now, and if we had different tiles we might have done it. But there's a mountain pass to go through now, and a forest, and the Eastern Water Defence.'

'The *what* water defence?' asked Arthur.

'It's part of the Citadel, and doesn't move. A dry lake that can be flooded by opening sluice gates from the subterranean springs below the Citadel hill. It should still be dry, but . . .'

Jarrow's voice trailed off. The three of them sat in the star-lit darkness, listening to the sounds of the swamp. Their Not-Horses stood quietly nearby, also occasionally talking to each other in their soft, dry language that perhaps only the oldest of troop sergeants might understand.

'Should be dry, sir, but perhaps won't be?' asked Fred after a while, greatly daring.

'Yes, it may have been filled,' said Jarrow. 'While tectonic strategy has proved masterful as always, there are so many New Nithlings around that some were bound to end up near the Citadel, and the different groups have been joining up on the plain below the hill . . . a nuisance really. Not a siege, not by any means.'

'What exactly is the Citadel, sir?' asked Arthur.

'It's a mighty fortress, Green. Four concentric rings of bastions, ravelins and demi-lunes, all sited to support each other with cannon and musket, and the approach ramps covered by firewash projectors. Then, within the third ring, there is the Inner Citadel, a Star Fort built upon a hill of hard stone. The Inner Citadel has earthen ramparts seventy feet thick abutting walls forty feet high and it is armed with sixteen royal cannon, thirty-two demi-cannon and seventy-two small cannons the artillerists call sakers. Though there has been a terrible shortage of powder for them ever since Grim Tuesday was deposed by this new Lord Arthur –'

Jarrow stopped talking as Arthur suddenly whimpered in pain and clapped his hands to his head. He felt as if a missile had struck the centre of his brain, exploding into a vast array of memories. Images, sounds, smells and thoughts reverberated everywhere within his skull, so many that he momentarily felt disoriented and sick. Every significant memory from the day he lost his yellow elephant to the approach of the three Bathroom Attendants was overlaid all at once in a crazy mish-mash of instant recollection.

The pain disappeared almost at once and the memories slowly retreated deeper into his head, sorting themselves out as they went, though not in perfect order. However, he did know who he was and what had happened, and that he was in great danger from Sir Thursday.

'Are you all right, trooper?' asked Jarrow.

'Yes, sir,' whispered Arthur.

'Memory pain,' said Fred. 'I punched myself in the mouth once because of it. Got a fat lip. Did you remember anything useful, Ray?'

'Maybe,' said Arthur guardedly. He was in a tough position. He wanted to tell Fred everything, but that would only put his friend at risk as well. 'I've got a few more things to think through anyway.'

'You two rest,' said Jarrow. He stood up, loosened his tulwar in its scabbard and began to pace quietly around their small island. 'I'll keep watch.'

'Don't you need some rest too, sir?' asked Fred.

'I have much to think about,' said Jarrow. 'And I do not need to rest yet. Piper's children need more sleep than drafted Denizens, and those Denizens need more sleep than regular soldiers like myself, who were made for the profession of arms by the Architect. But even I need to sleep more than our red-eyed comrades here, who sleep only in their stables and then no more than once a seven-day. I will rouse you before the dawn or if there is the suggestion of trouble.'

There was no alarm in the night, though Arthur woke several times, disturbed either by some night noise or by a twinge of discomfort, born from sleeping on the ground with only a saddle for a pillow and a rough, felted blanket for bedcovers.

Arthur was woken properly by Jarrow before any sun was visible, but as the higher stars began to fade. Without the need for breakfast, and being forgiven shaving as they were in the field, the trio quickly saddled the Not-Horses and went on their way, the two boys working hard to bear in silence the aches and pains that had come from the previous day's ride and their night on the ground.

Arthur did not spare too much attention to these pains or to the swamp he was travelling through. His mind was fully occupied thinking about what he was going to do, and what Sir Thursday might do to him. The Trustee had to know who Arthur was because either Lieutenant Crosshaw or Sergeant Helve would surely have reported his presence. Or possibly Sir Thursday might have known all the time and had Arthur drafted on purpose, rather than by bureacratic accident.

But why would Sir Thursday summon all the Piper's children in the Army to the Citadel if he only wanted to get Arthur? There had to be more to it, Arthur believed. There was also the question of what he was going to do if the opportunity presented itself for him to try to find the Will or get hold of the Fourth Key. Should he take it and put himself at risk of retribution? Or should he be a good soldier and follow orders and not give Sir Thursday any excuse to put aside Army Regulations and do something horrible to him? If he just tried to be a good soldier, he might end up having to serve his hundred years and he'd never get home –

Home. The Skinless Boy. Leaf. The –

'The letter!' Arthur suddenly said aloud, slapping his head again. He'd just remembered the letter from Superior Saturday, the one threatening his family. As Ray, without his proper memory, he'd dismissed it as a hoax. But now he remembered everything, it brought home everything he had feared would happen with the Skinless Boy.

'We must be quiet from here,' ordered Jarrow, wheeling his horse to address Arthur and Fred directly. 'The pass ahead should be clear, but we cannot count on it. Close up on me and ready your swords. We will charge through if the way is blocked.'

Arthur rode close enough to almost touch knees with the lieutenant, while Fred did the same on the other side. If they had to charge, they would do so as a tight mass of Not-Horses, a wedge that should punch through any New Nithling ranks that stood against them.

As they advanced, Arthur looked around properly for the first time in at least ten minutes. They were leaving the swamp, heading west, and the tile ahead was dominated by two rocky hills, with a shallow gorge between them that was perhaps half as high. The rough road they were on led into the gorge.

'Can't we go around?' he asked. He couldn't see anything too formidable to the north or south.

'There are mud pools to the north today,' said Jarrow, tapping his Ephemeris. 'And thistle-scrub south. Very slow for the Not-Horses. This way is somewhat steep, but the road is wide and good. Beyond the pass, there is grassland and a bucolic village. After that is the easternmost fixed tile, which is the Eastern Water Defence. If we are not waylaid, and the water defences are dry, we should be at the Citadel by late afternoon.'

They were not waylaid, but well before they saw it, they knew the Eastern Water Defence was not dry. It had been flooded and some of its water was spilling over into the adjacent tile, running down the main street of the bucolic village, a lovely but uninhabited collection of narrow lanes and charming houses that surrounded a large village green bordered by several pubs, a blacksmith's forge, four or five small shops and an archery range.

'Was there ever anyone here, sir?' asked Arthur as the Not-Horses waded up to their fetlocks in the water streaming down the main street, their noses held high to show their dislike for the stuff.

'Not permanently,' replied Jarrow. He spoke quickly and his eyes were never still, darting this way and that as he looked all around. 'But in the past, whenever this tile came close to the Citadel, the White Keep, Fort Transformation or one of the other fixed locations, the taverns would be manned and a fair established for the day. We should be able to see the Citadel in a minute. Once we are past these buildings.'

The road began to rise after the town, then levelled out again. There were stands of tall cypress trees at intervals along it, but the view was clear straight ahead. As they reached the flat, Jarrow stopped and gazed out, shielding his eyes with his hand.

Arthur and Fred did not look so much as stare, their mouths open wide enough to catch any small insects that might have been about.

There was a broad, mile-wide lake ahead of them, stretching north and south on to other tiles and on out of sight. Its eastern shore lapped the edge of the village tile, which was marked by a line of tall pines, many of them shorn of western branches.

Beyond the lake was a giant wedding cake of a fortress, spread over many miles. The outer line of angled bastions – which to Arthur looked like short, broad, triangle-shaped towers – formed the bottom of the cake, one hundred and fifty yards in and fifty feet higher there was the second line, and one hundred and fifty yards in from that and up fifty feet again, was the third line. Beyond that line was a hill of stark white stone, and on the hill was a star-shaped fort, each of its six points a bastion that held half a dozen cannon and perhaps two hundred defenders. Right in the middle of the Star Fort was an ancient keep, a square stone tower one hundred and fifty feet high.

A huge cloud of green smoke hung above the outermost defence line to the southwest.

'Firewash smoke,' said Jarrow grimly. 'There must have been an assault some time this morning. But I heard no cannons . . . We must be very low on Nothing-powder. We must go back to the village – we will have to build a raft.'

'Can't we signal the Citadel somehow?' suggested Arthur. 'Sir?'

'I have no communication figures,' said Jarrow. 'None could be spared for me. If we signal with smoke or mirror, the New Nithlings may see it and send a raiding party. They must be established in force on the western plains. I have never seen a firewash cloud as big as that one.'

It was not as difficult to make a raft as Arthur had thought. They simply took a dozen barrels from the nearest pub, three of its doors, and a quantity of rope, cordage, pitch and nails from the blacksmith's, along with some of the tools. Under Jarrow's direction, the barrels were lashed together, the doors nailed to the top and the likely places for the barrels to leak smeared with pitch.

The raft was assembled by the lake's edge, very close to the tile border with the bucolic village. Arthur was acutely aware of this, though he managed to stop himself looking at the position of the sun all the time, and he didn't ask Jarrow where the village was going to go at sundown.

But he got more nervous as the afternoon progressed. It was perhaps half an hour short of dusk when they finished, with the final touches being three oars from planks ripped out of the pub's benches.

It was a fine-looking raft, but it didn't look big enough for three Not-Horses, a Denizen and two Piper's children.

'Get all the harness and gear off the mounts and on to the raft,' said Jarrow. He too looked at the setting sun. 'We'll give them a quick brush and oiling before they go.'

'Where will they go, sir?' asked Fred. He had become very attached to his Not-Horse, who, according to the name engraved on its steel toecaps, was called Skwidge.

'They'll find their way to friends,' said Jarrow. He took the saddlebags off his mount and dropped them on the raft, which was now half in the water. 'Hurry up! We have to be away from the tile border before the village moves!'

The sun was little more than a sliver, barely visible on the horizon, between the Star Fort and the Inner Bastion, when the last Not-Horse went on its way with a farewell whinny. Arthur and Fred hastily threw their brushes and cleaning clothes on the raft and started to push it completely into the lake.

'Put your backs into it!' urged Jarrow, once more looking at the setting sun. But the raft, despite being two-thirds in the water, with the barrels on the far end already floating, was stuck fast in the mud.

Arthur and Fred got down lower and really heaved, and this time Jarrow joined them. The raft slid a few inches but stopped again.

'What's that noise?' gasped Arthur, in between shoves. He could hear a high-pitched whistling, like an ultrasonic dentist's drill.

'Tile moving!' shouted Jarrow. 'Into the water, quick!'

He grabbed Arthur and Fred and dragged them away from the raft and into the lake. Within a few steps it was up to the chests of the Piper's children, but Jarrow kept dragging them on, even though Arthur and Fred had their heads back and were gasping for air, their feet scrabbling to touch the ground as their heavy Horde hauberks and gear threatened to drag them beneath the water.

CHAPTER TWENTY-ONE

Just as Arthur and Fred thought they were going to drown, which was no improvement over death by dismemberment when the tile changed, the high-pitched whistle stopped. Jarrow stopped too and turned around, but he didn't immediately head for the shore.

'Help!' gurgled Arthur.

'Can't reach the ground,' gasped Fred.

Jarrow still didn't do anything but stare back at the shore. Then he slowly dragged Arthur and Fred back out and dropped them next to the raft. After a frenzied minute of coughing and gasping, the two boys recovered enough to notice that the raft was intact – and the bucolic village was still there. Jarrow stood near them, flicking through his Ephemeris, the pages held close so he could read them in the twilight.

'The tile didn't move,' said Arthur.

'No,' said Jarrow. He shook his head. 'But it should have. This is very serious. Only tectonic strategy has kept the New Nithlings from massing an overwhelming force against us for a decisive battle . . . We had best get to the Citadel at once!'

He threw himself against the raft with new fervour, weakly assisted by Arthur and Fred. This time, their makeshift vessel slid all the way into the lake and bobbed about almost as well as a proper boat. Or at least a proper boat that permanently suffered from a fifteen-degree list to starboard.

Though it was slightly less than a mile across the lake, Arthur and Fred were very tired before they had reached halfway. Jarrow kept up a punishing paddling pace and would not let them rest.

'Sir, if we could take a few minutes –' Arthur began to ask.

'Paddle!' shouted Jarrow. 'You are Soldiers of the Architect. Paddle!'

Arthur paddled. His arms and shoulders hurt so much that he had to bite his lip to stop himself from whimpering, but he kept paddling. Fred kept paddling too, but Arthur didn't really notice. His world had become small, containing only pain, the paddle and the water he had to cleave and push.

The moon began its shaky ascent as they approached one of the outer bastions that thrust out into the lake, small waves lapping the stone wall that faced the earthen embankment. The moonlight caught their helmets and hauberks, and that caught the attention of the sentries.

'Who goes there?' came the cry across the water, accompanied by the flare of a quick-match as someone readied a musket or small cannon to fire.

'Lieutenant Jarrow of the Horde and two troopers!' shouted Jarrow. 'Requesting permission to land at the water-dock.'

'Cease paddling and await our word!'

Jarrow stopped paddling. Arthur almost couldn't stop, his muscles set in a repetitive pattern. When he did lift the oar out of the water and laid it down across the raft, it took several seconds to get his hands to unclench.

'Advance to the water-gate!'

'Commence paddling!' ordered Jarrow.

Arthur and Fred mechanically took up their oars again and dipped them into the water. The raft, having stopped, was very difficult to get moving again. Fortunately, it was not far to the water-gate, a grilled gate of old iron some thirty yards further along the bastion's lake wall.

This portcullis was raised just enough to allow them to get the raft and themselves through and into a flooded chamber within the bastion. The grille came crashing and splashing back down as soon as they were inside.

There was just enough room inside to paddle the raft to a spot between two small boats, which were tied up against a low wooden quay or wharf. There was a reception party arrayed along the wharf: a lieutenant, a corporal and two dozen Denizens in regimental scarlet, with bayonets fixed to their Nothing-powder muskets. Jarrow climbed up and, after an exchange of salutes and the presenting of arms, talked quickly with the other lieutenant. Arthur and Fred wearily gathered up all the gear and Not-Horse harness.

'Gold! Green! Leave that!' instructed Jarrow. 'We have to report to Marshal Noon's Headquarters. You're the last two Piper's children to arrive.'

Arthur and Fred looked at each other and happily dropped the saddles, saddlebags and other gear. Then they helped each other climb up on to the dock, remembering to salute the other lieutenant.

'Better get 'em in Regimentals before they go to the Marshal,' said the other officer. 'Unless they're permanent troopers.'

'They aren't yet,' said Jarrow. He clapped Arthur and Fred on their sore backs, and they both nearly fell over from the sudden pain. 'But they have the makings. Let's be off. Troopers, atten-hut! By the left, quick march!'

Jarrow obviously knew the Citadel well. From the water-gate, he led them up a ramp and out on to the top of the bastion. They marched along its length, passing sentries and cannons, all staring out. Then they passed through a guardhouse with some formality between Jarrow and the officer of the watch, continued down another ramp and along a covered walkway lined with small cannons on swivels, climbed up through another guard-house, went down a spiral staircase, marched across a cleared space between the third and second defence lines, entered another bastion, and ultimately found themselves in a Quartermaster's Store that was so identical to the one at Fort Transformation that the two weary Piper's children wondered if they'd ever left.

In the space of fifteen minutes their Horde hauberks and helmets were stripped off and replaced by the much lighter and more comfortable scarlet tunics, black trousers and pillbox hats of the Regiment. They were issued familiar white belts with pouch and bayonet frog, and bayonets but not muskets.

'Only got powder for the sharpshooters,' said the Quartermaster Sergeant, a grizzled Denizen who had at some time been shot through the cheeks with a Nothing-laced bullet, so the wound would not completely heal.

As he spoke, air sucked through the holes and made it hard to understand his speech.

Jarrow did not change, presumably because he was a permanent Horde officer, but he did take the time to give his armour and boots a quick clean, earning the Quartermaster Sergeant's approval for doing it himself. Then he waited patiently while Arthur and Fred got sorted out. When they started to examine their bayonets, he called them to attention and marched them out again.

This time, they left the outer bastions behind, crossing the bare area to the second line and taking a zigzag path along various ramps, through several guardhouses and up four sets of stairs. On the far side of the second defence line, they crossed an even wider expanse of bare earth and a greater complexity of ramps, stairs and guardhouses, before exiting the third line bastion to arrive at the bottom of a narrow stair that wound its way up the side of the white stone hill.

'Where are we going, sir?' asked Fred.

'Marshal Noon's headquarters are in the Star Fort,' said Jarrow. 'Up these stairs, now!'

The hill was not as high as Arthur had thought it was when he'd been out on the lake. Perhaps no more than three hundred feet. He felt so much better after shedding the heavy weight of the hauberk, helmet and lightning-charged tulwar that it was almost a pleasure to climb the steps, though he knew he would be sore later. His time in the Army of the Architect had helped him discover numerous muscles he had not previously known he had; unfortunately, this discovery was always painful.

The bastions of the Star Fort were smaller versions of the ones in the lower defence lines. At the top of the stairs, Jarrow called out and did not proceed until he was answered by the sentry. Then, clearly illuminated by the greenish moonlight, they marched across the bare earth, crossed a ditch on a gangplank and entered a sally port in the face of the bastion.

'Reckon you could find your way out of here?' asked Fred a little later as they waited for Jarrow to finish talking to yet another lieutenant in yet another guard room – though this one was nicer than the ones below as it had panelled wood walls rather than bare stone, and a blue and red carpet on the floor.

'No,' said Arthur. That thought had occurred to him too, probably because unlike Fred it was quite possible he might really need to get out again.

'You're going into Marshal Noon's reception room,' said Jarrow, turning back to them. 'Apparently, there's already a number of Piper's children waiting and the Marshal will address you soon. Remember to stand at attention at all times unless ordered otherwise, and do not speak unless you are spoken to. Is that clear?'

'Yes, sir!' shouted Fred and Arthur.

Jarrow winced.

'You don't have to shout like that here. Save it for the parade ground. You've done well, Green, and you too, Gold. Good luck for the future. I hope we serve together again.'

He shook hands with them and was gone. Arthur and Fred turned nervously to the other door. A corporal grinned at them and opened it, gesturing for them to go inside.

Arthur felt an anxious, fluttering pain in his stomach. It didn't look like this was going to be the prelude to Sir Thursday revealing his identity and doing something horrible to him. But he was nervous about whatever was to come, for it was an unknown, both to his soldier-self and his secret role as the Rightful Heir.

They marched in together in perfect step. The room was large, but not as expansive as the round-table room in Monday's Dayroom. This room was much more spartan. It had a polished timber floor, with a spindly-legged desk in one corner, a black lacquered standing screen with maps pinned to it, several weapons mounted on the walls and the preserved head of a monster – possibly a fish, as it looked like it might have come off a thirty-foot long piranha. There were also twenty Piper's children in two ranks of ten, standing at ease. Most were in scarlet Regimentals, but there were four Legionaries in dress armour, three grey-coated Artillerists and two Borderers in green. They all turned their heads to look as Fred and Arthur entered the room and marched over to form up on the left of the parade.

'Wait for it,' whispered Arthur as they neared the ranks. 'Fred and Arthur, halt! Left turn!'

They executed the movements perfectly. The other Piper's children looked to the front again. All except for one of the Borderers, who stepped back behind the parade and sidled down the line. Then she came over and stood at attention next to Arthur.

'Hist! Arthur!'

Arthur slid his eyes to the left. The Borderer, a corporal no less, was Suzy!

Arthur's head moved two inches in sheer surprise before he whipped it back in place. Even so, his eyes nearly left their sockets with the effort of peering at his friend. He felt incredibly relieved by her appearance and at the same time his anxiety ratcheted up a notch. Suzy's arrivals normally anticipated serious mayhem and difficulties only by minutes.

'Suzy! They let you join after all?' he whispered out of the corner of his mouth. 'And you've already made corporal?'

'Not exactly,' said Suzy. 'It's a bit complicated, but basically I got here and they had a bit of trouble working out what to do with me. For a couple of hours they were going to shoot me as a spy. But it turns out I *was* in the Army before. I did my hitch four hundred years ago and been on the Reserve ever since! Not that I can remember it, though a few bits and pieces are coming back now. I told them I'd just got cleaned between the ears and was a bit confused, and then this order came for all Piper's children to report, no exceptions, so the Major who was in charge said "good riddance" and sent me along. The important thing is, Arthur, I've got the –'

'Atten-hut!'

An immaculate Regimental Sergeant-Major, her scarlet sleeves adorned with laurel wreaths and crossed swords, had entered the room. She marched over to the Piper's children, ramrod straight, her boots clicking in perfect rhythm on the floor, a silver-pointed ebony pace-stick under her arm.

'Close up that gap, soldier!' she snapped, pointing to the hole Suzy had left. She halted in front of the two lines, did an about turn and saluted the Denizen who had just followed her in.

He was considerably less splendid than the RSM, wearing what looked like exactly the same kind of Regimental private's uniform as Arthur's, with the addition of two black epaulettes which were each

266

adorned with a circle of six tiny golden swords. This struck Arthur as odd, since *The Recruit's Companion* said a marshal was only supposed to have five. The only other alteration to the private's uniform was that instead of a pillbox hat he wore a kind of black beret with a golden sword badge pinned to it. The badge looked too big for the beret, perhaps because it depicted a very old-fashioned hand and a half-sword, with a serpent coiled around the hilt.

He had small, deep-set eyes and was not particularly handsome for such a superior Denizen. He wasn't all that tall either, being only six foot six or so, and was perhaps half as wide across the shoulders as Sergeant Helve. All in all, he was not physically intimidating. But there was something about those dark eyes, the flat-lined mouth and the lift of his chin that made Arthur immediately fear him.

'Stand them at ease,' this Denizen ordered the RSM.

'Stand at ease!' repeated the RSM at several times the other Denizen's volume.

The Piper's children stood at ease, none of them out of time. Even Suzy got it right.

'I am Sir Thursday,' said the Denizen. The faintest ripple went through the ranks as he said that, but no more.

Arthur stared at the air in front of him, not even daring to move an eyeball. But though his body was still, his mind was racing, trying to work out what might happen and what he could do.

'I am going to explain a plan I have to you,' continued Sir Thursday. 'Then I am going to ask for volunteers.'

He paced up and down as he spoke, then suddenly stopped and looked out of the window on the far side of the room.

'Marshal Noon was to explain the plan, but he has suffered an indisposition. He may be joining us later. Sergeant-Major! The mapboard.'

The RSM marched across the room and picked up the black screen, carrying it back to a position in front of the Piper's children. Then she marched round to stand near Suzy, so she could also watch the presentation.

Sir Thursday walked over to Arthur and took the bayonet from the bayonet frog on Arthur's belt. Arthur didn't move and didn't look, even as he heard the foot-long blade slide free.

Surely he won't stab me in front of everyone, he thought desperately. *Dame Primus said he would obey his own regulations. He won't stab me –*

'I shall borrow this for a moment, Private,' said Sir Thursday. 'To use as a pointer.'

He turned to the mapboard and flourished the bayonet. A glowing yellow line appeared where he indicated, and another. Quickly, Sir Thursday sketched a square.

'This is the Great Maze,' he said. He added an 'X' down in the lower right corner. 'This is the Citadel.'

Then he drew a small circle right in the middle of the square.

'And this is the absolute centre of the maze, a point called 500/500. Who can tell me the only possible way to get a strike force from the Citadel to point 500/500 by midnight tonight, given that the tiles have stopped moving? It is three hundred miles away and there are perhaps two hundred and fifty thousand New Nithlings in the way.'

He turned to face them.

'Anyone? How about you, Private? Green, isn't it?'

'Yes, sir,' croaked Arthur. He wasn't sure if he should play stupid or give an honest answer, because he had immediately thought of one way to get there. 'I suppose . . . that the only way would be via the Improbable Stair.'

'And the natural conclusion one would draw from that?'

'That very few . . . uh . . . Denizens even know about the Improbable Stair, and fewer still can travel it,' said Arthur. He had a bad feeing about where this was going. 'I don't know how many soldiers someone able to use the Improbable Stair could take with them.'

'Very good,' said Sir Thursday. 'You are commissioned herewith as Second Lieutenant Green. In the Regiment, unless you have a preference for the Horde.'

'No, sir,' said Arthur.

What is he up to? he wondered. *He's setting me up for something.*

'The obvious question is, why would a force need to be sent from the Citadel to point 500/500?' Sir Thursday continued. He started to tap the mapboard with the bayonet. 'The answer is simple. Because ultimately I must obey my political superiors in the House, this campaign year I was compelled to change my plans and allow a vast number of Nithlings into the Great Maze. Nithlings who, unbeknownst to me, are New Nithlings, practically Denizens. They are trained, disciplined and well-equipped, and they are led by someone powerful and very clever, someone probably assisted by traitors within my very staff, someone who has uncovered one of the secrets of the Great Maze and with a lot of treacherous help has managed to put a great big spike of stabilised Nothing straight into the master position at point 500/500!'

Sir Thursday drove the bayonet into the mapboard with his last words, ripping and tearing at the wood with unbelievable ferocity. When he had reduced it to pieces, he impaled the remains with the bayonet, leaving the weapon quivering in a broken board.

He took a deep breath before turning back to face the parade.

'I find this annoying, as you can see. That spike has sorcerously frozen a tile at point 500/500. This is the master position of the Maze and if it is unable to move, no tiles can move. Consequently, I will be leading a force via the Improbable Stair to point 500/500. As the vast majority of Denizens are simply rejected by the Stair, I must take Piper's children, whom the Stair always accepts, and I am looking for twelve volunteers. We will go via the Stair, destroy the spike and return on the Stair. Sergeant-Major!'

The RSM marched back out the front, drew in a deep lungful of air and bellowed, 'All those wishing to volunteer for a special assault via the Improbable Stair take one pace forward!'

CHAPTER TWENTY-TWO

Arthur was too recent a product of recruit school. Even as his mind tried to tell him to think about it, his legs reacted like a galvanised frog to the word of command. He took one pace forward. So did Fred and, after a slight hesitation, Suzy. Peering across from the corner of his eye, Arthur could see at least another ten had stepped forward too. But that meant half the Piper's children hadn't volunteered.

'Dismiss the rest,' ordered Sir Thursday. 'Get them out of my sight! If any of them hold rank, strip it from them! And find some stars for Mister Green.'

As the RSM bellowed commands at the non-volunteers, the Trustee paced to the narrow slit window and looked out. Arthur couldn't see what he saw, but since it was a westward-facing window and they were high up, it was likely to be a huge host of New Nithlings, preparing for another assault on the outer bastions.

Arthur was probably going to see a lot of New Nithlings soon. But he was less worried about that than he was about Sir Thursday. Anyone capable of the berserk rage he'd just displayed after merely talking about something that made him angry was dangerous to be around. Even if you weren't the Rightful Heir, intent on removing him from his position and taking his Key.

No sign of the Key, anyway, thought Arthur. *Or the Will, for that matter. The Key is probably a weapon, I would think. The Will could be anywhere, maybe not even in this demesne of the House.*

'Mister Green's stars, sir,' said the RSM to Sir Thursday, interrupting Arthur's train of thought. The sergeant-major handed Sir Thursday a small velvet box.

'Four paces forward please, Second Lieutenant Green,' said Sir Thursday. Arthur marched forward and halted. Sir Thursday came up close, opened the box and took out two diamond-shaped badges of gold. He pressed them to the epaulettes on Arthur's shoulders, which instantly turned black and grew gold buttons, the 'stars' stitching themselves in near his shoulders.

'Congratulations,' said Sir Thursday. 'You will be my second-in-command for this assault on the spike.

Now, stand to my left and two paces behind me. You can't go back in the ranks now.'

Arthur marched round and stood at attention behind Sir Thursday. Suzy slowly dipped one eyelid in what might have been a wink. Fred stared at a point above Arthur's head and the other Piper's children looked directly at him without apparently seeing him.

Now that he was able to see them, Arthur noticed that several of them were corporals and there were even two sergeants. They would not be happy to discover that he was really only a partially trained recruit with one battle under his belt and that after a mere six weeks training.

'My plan is straightforward,' said Sir Thursday. 'We will emerge as close to the spike as is possible. I will need several minutes to destroy it, and must not be interrupted in that time. You will hold off any enemy that may interfere. When the spike is destroyed, we will return via the Improbable Stair to the Citadel. Given that we will have complete surprise, we have a very good chance of success. Any questions?'

One of the sergeants, a serious-looking boy with flaxen hair and what appeared to be a painted-on yellow moustache, snapped to attention and raised his hand.

'May we equip ourselves with our choice of weapons, sir?'

'The central armoury is at your disposal,' said Sir Thursday. 'Nothing-powder weapons included. Though I must ask that you do not overburden yourselves. I cannot carry a dozen soldiers and a cannon up the Improbable Stair.'

He smiled to show this was a jest and there was a ripple of dutiful laughter. Arthur smiled too, a bit late, but the smile was wiped off his face as Suzy snapped to attention and raised her hand.

No, Suzy! thought Arthur. *Don't ask him anything that'll make him mad!*

'Sir, this spike. It's made of Nothing? A lot of Nothing?'

'Yes,' said Sir Thursday. 'I believe I already said that.'

Don't say anything more! Since Arthur was behind Sir Thursday, he made a quick zipping motion with his hand over his mouth, only to turn it into an odd little nose-scratch as he saw the RSM's eyes flicker in his direction.

Wisely, and for possibly the first time since Arthur had met her, Suzy held her tongue.

'Any other questions?' asked Sir Thursday. There was barely repressed menace in his voice. He did not want any more questions. He wanted instant, unthinking obedience.

Arthur shivered. He would not want to be the bearer of bad news to Sir Thursday. Or any news for that matter, since it would be impossible to know how the Trustee would react.

There were no more questions.

'Sergeant-Major McLameth, carry on!' snapped Sir Thursday. 'Second Lieutenant Green, follow me!'

Arthur looked at Suzy. She rolled her eyes up several times but he had no idea what this meant. Fred, on the other hand, gave him a smile when the RSM wasn't looking, the smile of someone who is pleased by the success of a friend.

I hope Fred doesn't get killed, thought Arthur as he marched after Sir Thursday. *He doesn't really know what he's getting into, with his dreams of being a general. That one battle, we were shielded from the worst and it was still awful –*

'Marshal Noon's study,' said Sir Thursday, opening the door to a smaller room.

Noon's study was a surprisingly small room, only thirty feet long by fifty feet wide. To Arthur it looked more like an armoury than someone's study, as every wall was bedecked with weapons. Interspersed with the weapons were paintings and etchings of martial scenes, battles and skirmishes with Nithlings. All of them featured the same red-haired, debonair Denizen who Arthur understood must be Thursday's Noon.

There was a large mahogany desk, supported on three pedestals in the middle of the room. The desktop was bare, save for a gold and ivory-inlaid marshal's baton right in the middle.

'There are some matters we need to speak of Second Lieutenant Green,' said Sir Thursday. 'Or perhaps I should say Second Lieutenant Penhaligon?'

'That is my real name, sir,' said Arthur. He stood at attention, but his eyes flickered to the walls. If Sir Thursday attacked him, he would spring that way, grab that savage-sword off its pegs there . . .

'I did not plan to draft you,' said Sir Thursday. 'Indeed, I did not know about it until the recruiting officer made his report through his chain of command. He should have come straight to me, of course. He is Private Crosshaw now.'

After the furniture-demolishing episode I can see why he didn't go straight to you. I bet no one ever does if they can avoid it.

'As soon as you were drafted and became one of my soldiers, I was limited in what actions I might take against you,' Sir Thursday continued. He began to pace around the room, but he kept looking back at Arthur. 'But then it occurred to me that you were similarly limited in what you might do to release the Will and claim the Fourth Key. You see, Arthur, we find ourselves in a curious position.

'I am a soldier. Even though I command the Glorious Army of the House, I am not the ultimate

277

commander-in-chief. The Architect was, and when she disappeared I was convinced that Lord Sunday had the proper authority to assume this role, with Superior Saturday as his deputy. Saturday passed on Sunday's orders for me to take a portion of the Will and hide it and to assume custodianship of the Key. As always, I followed those orders. Until I hear otherwise from Lord Sunday or his deputy, those remain my orders.'

He paused and took a clockwork axe from the wall. Arthur tensed, ready to grab a weapon to defend himself, but Sir Thursday didn't move to attack. He started to bend the haft of the axe backwards and forwards, even though it was made of gravity-condensed steel. The axe's clockwork mechanism shrieked in protest as the cogs and gears within the haft were bent, and the flywheel at the end of the haft burned itself to a stop, smoke wafting around Sir Thursday's arms.

'I have followed those orders for the last ten thousand years,' said Sir Thursday, speaking through gritted teeth. 'Even though the Will constantly seeks to escape, and is always complaining and scheming and I can never ... never rest!'

The axe broke apart and springs richocheted around the room. Arthur ducked reflexively, but immediately stood at attention again.

'I can never rest, for if I rest, the Will may escape,' continued Sir Thursday. 'It makes me a little irritable.

But I have my orders. So you see, Lieutenant, I am not going to release the Will and I am not going to give you the Key until I am directly ordered to do so. Which, though I do not have a lot of communication with the Upper House, seems extremely unlikely.'

Sir Thursday brushed his hands to remove the last bits of powdered metal and stalked over to Arthur, leaning close.

'You may have plans, Arthur, to try to free the Will yourself. But you are not Arthur Penhaligon here, Master of the Lower House, the Far Reaches and the Border Sea. You are a commissioned officer in my army and I am ordering you to do nothing to free the Will. Do you understand?'

'Yes, sir,' said Arthur.

'Disobeying orders on active service is considered mutiny,' said Sir Thursday. 'For which the penalty is death. Do you understand that?'

'Yes, sir!'

'Then the matter is concluded, at least for the remainder of your service.' Sir Thursday's mouth curved up on one side in what he probably imagined was a grin. 'Much can happen in ninety-nine years, Mister . . . Green.'

'Yes, sir!' said Arthur, thinking, *More like the next twenty-four hours. You're going to get me killed on this suicide mission.*

'You had best join the assault unit and prepare yourself,' said Sir Thursday. 'We shall enter the Improbable Stair in eighteen minutes. Dismiss!'

Arthur saluted and did an about turn. But as he spun around on his heel, he heard a distant voice speaking directly into his mind. It was very faint, but clear, and he recognised the tone. All the Parts of the Will had a kind of monomaniacal directness, even in mental speech.

Arthur, I am here, bound to the Key. I can free myself if Sir Thursday's attention and power is sufficiently diverted.

Arthur gave no sign he had been contacted. He continued marching, his mind juggling many plans, fears and notions, constantly dropping, picking up and throwing them about.

To hear what was said and to speak to his mind, the Will must have been in the room with Sir Thursday. It said it was bound to the Key, so that must have been there as well. But Sir Thursday carried no visible weapons. He wore a private's uniform, but without a cartridge bag or bayonet frog to put anything in.

But there was that badge, Arthur thought. *That weirdly oversized badge on his cap. A sword with a snake wound around the hilt . . .*

CHAPTER TWENTY-THREE

Arthur found a sergeant waiting for him. It felt strange to be saluted by him instead of being shouted at, but it was a pleasant kind of strange. Arthur thought he would quickly get used to being an officer. The sergeant led him down a winding stair to a vast, echoing armoury that occupied a cavern hewn from the rock under the Star Fort. There were racks and racks of weapons and armour, in eight rows that each stretched for at least a hundred yards. The twelve Piper's children were clattering about, collecting their equipment. They were watched with resigned suspicion by three grizzled Denizen Armourer Sergeants. One of the sergeants, catching sight of Arthur and his new badges of rank, shouted, 'Stand fast!'

The Piper's children stood at attention, but not very fast or very smartly. One of them was even on the brink of slouching. Arthur ignored this.

'As you were,' he called. 'Carry on. Corporal Blue!'

Suzy appeared from behind a rack of bell-barrelled musketoons. She had a savage-sword buckled on to a wide, non-regulation leather belt. On the cross-belts above she carried four small Nothing-powder pistols in holsters.

Arthur gestured at her to go back behind another rack then joined her there, where they were shielded from the others by a line of eight-foot-high arrow shields known as pavises.

'Arthur, I've got the pocket!' whispered Suzy. She tapped her tunic.

'The pocket? My shirt pocket?' asked Arthur, taken aback. He'd been about to tell her about Sir Thursday. 'You mean the one used to grow the Skinless Boy?'

'Well, I ain't talking about just any pocket,' said Suzy. 'Do you want it now? I reckon you can stick it in that spike thing, if it's made of Nothing.'

'Yes,' Arthur said quickly. He held out his hand. 'But how did you get it? Did Leaf . . . is my family all right?'

'Dunno.' Suzy rummaged around inside her tunic and pulled out a clear plastic box with the scrap of material in it. 'Leaf got the pocket, but she couldn't get back to the House. She telephoned from your home and I nipped through the Seven Dials, but by the time I got there that brain fungus had taken her over. I didn't have time to stick around, so I flew into the Front Door. Only I got stopped by Superior Saturday's Noon, who would have had my guts for garters if the Lieutenant Keeper, bless his white hair, hadn't lobbed in –'

'I'll have to get the full story later,' Arthur interrupted. He was desperate to hear all the details, but he had to concentrate on the problems immediately at hand. 'We've only got a few minutes. Sir Thursday knows who I am. He's ordered me not to free the Will, which I think is in that cap badge he wears. The snake. And the Key is the sword.'

Suzy scratched her head. 'That's a bit of a poser. I thought he'd be the sort who'd just cut your head off.'

'He follows orders and regulations,' said Arthur. 'But I reckon if I show any insubordination he will kill me. Besides, I think he's planning to get me killed anyway, during this attack on the spike.'

'He's bound to,' agreed Suzy, which wasn't very encouraging. 'What are you going to do?'

Arthur looked around to check that no one had come within hearing distance.

'The Will spoke to me, in my head. It said it could free itself if Sir Thursday is sufficiently distracted. Once

it's free, I guess it can help me get the Key. Only . . .
I have to admit, even if I do get the Key and the Will
helps, I'm a bit . . . nervous . . . about taking on Sir
Thursday.'

'I know what you mean,' said Suzy.

'Also, since I've been ordered not to try to free the
Will, I can't even try to distract Sir Thursday myself,'
said Arthur.

'Why not?' asked Suzy. 'Just disobey orders. I do it
all the time with Old Primey.'

'I don't think I can,' Arthur explained. 'I can feel
a sort of pressure in my head when I think about
disobeying orders, and find it hard to even imagine
going against a direct order from Sir Thursday. I think
it's from recruit school and it's got even worse since
I was commissioned. That must be why Sir Thursday
made me an officer.'

'I'll distract him,' said Suzy. She had a thoughtful
look in her eyes. 'I reckon I've had so much practice
disobeying orders I can manage.'

'It's not as simple as that,' said Arthur hurriedly.
'We have to wait until Sir Thursday has destroyed the
Nothing spike. If it isn't destroyed, we won't have a
chance against the New Nithlings . . . though now I
think about it . . .'

'What?' Suzy took a power-spear from a rack and mimed throwing it, to test its weight. Arthur ducked as she swung it around, but kept talking.

'I wonder if anyone has tried talking to the New Nithlings and their commander,' said Arthur. 'I know they're the enemy, but they're not like normal Nithlings that just want to kill and destroy. Who knows what these ones really want? Maybe I could negotiate with them.'

'Negotiate with Nithlings?' asked Suzy. 'You can't negotiate with Nithlings –'

'Five minutes!' called the sergeant who'd shown Arthur to the armoury. 'Five minutes!'

'Five minutes!' repeated Arthur. 'I'd better get ready.'

He ran over to a rack of Legionary armour and, after a moment's hesitation, pulled out a junior centurion's bronzed cuirass rather than the segmented armour of an ordinary Legionary. He put it on and wedged the plastic box with the sorcerous pocket into the sheath under the armhole of his cuirass, meant to hold a last-resort dagger. 'Can you get me a savage-sword, Suzy? One of the medium-sized ones.'

'Yes, sir!' said Suzy, snapping a salute.

'You don't have to –' Arthur started to say. He stopped when he saw Suzy's eyeline. She was looking over his shoulder. At the same time, someone shouted, 'Atten-hut!'

Arthur spun around, cuirass straps flapping loose. Sir Thursday had entered the armoury. He was still wearing his scarlet Regimentals, but had on an iron Legionary helmet instead of a beret. He was holding a very long, broad sword that Arthur instantly knew was the Fourth Key. He could feel its power through his bones, a kind of shivery ache that travelled from his fingers to his backbone and down his legs.

The sword had a very wide hilt and handle, so it could be swung with two hands ... or by one if the wielder was very strong. There was a decorative metal snake wound around the plain brass hilt. All in all, the sword was a much larger twin to the one that had been on Sir Thursday's cap badge.

'Mister Green!' snapped Sir Thursday. 'Fall the troops in and check their equipment.'

'Yes, sir!'

Arthur hurriedly fastened the cuirass straps up under his arms, buckled on the savage-sword that Suzy handed him and slapped on an officer's helmet, complete with its scarlet horsehair crest. For a few seconds after that he wasn't sure what to do. Then he remembered what the officers always did: *tell a sergeant to take care of it*. He looked around and located the closest Piper's child sergeant, a Borderer with three black chevrons on her arm. Arthur quickly marched over to her.

'What's your name, Sergeant?'

'Quicksilver,' said the sergeant. 'Sir.'

'You'll be the troop . . . platoon . . . whatever-we-are sergeant, Sergeant,' said Arthur. He was a bit flustered, talking to a sergeant like this, after his weeks in recruit school on the receiving end of orders. 'Have everyone fall in and we'll both check their equipment.'

'Very good, sir,' said the girl. She looked quite a lot like Suzy, Arthur noticed. She had the same kind of narrow face, though Sergeant Quicksilver had very short black hair and her eyes were brown. 'Suggest we call the unit a raiding party, sir.'

'Good – carry on, Sergeant,' said Arthur. That was what officers said when they didn't know what to do.

'Raiding Part-eeeee!' yelled Quicksilver. 'Fall in! One rank!'

The Piper's children quickly formed up, automatically sorting themselves into line in order of height and shuffling sideways to get the right separation, measured by holding out a clenched fist against the shoulder of the soldier to the right. They were an odd-looking bunch. Nearly all of them had combined different kinds of armour, weapons and equipment from the various standard items used by soldiers of the Regiment, Legion, Horde or the Borderers. Arthur realised that all of them except for him had at least two weapons, and often three or four. He also realised that none of the Artillerists had volunteered, which perhaps explained why that unit was called the *Moderately* Honourable Artillery Company.

'Raiding party ready for inspection, sir!'

Arthur exchanged salutes with Quicksilver then walked along the line, looking over each soldier. If he'd felt more confident he would have commented on their weapons or equipment, but instead he just asked their names. He didn't feel like a real officer, but even as a fellow soldier he wanted to know who they were. After the battle at Fort Transformation, he knew that at least some of them would probably not be coming back. He wanted to know the names of his comrades and he tried to fix their faces in his mind as well, so he would have something to remember if he survived the coming battle and they did not.

He repeated the names in his head as they were spoken, memorising them. He'd always had an excellent memory, particularly for words and music.

The twelve Piper's children apart from himself, Suzy and Fred, were Quicksilver, Gluepot, Yellowbristle, Awning, Jazebeth, Halfcut, Sable, Fineold and Ermine.

They didn't tell him their first names. Five were girls and four were boys, and they looked between the ages of nine and thirteen.

At the end of the line, Arthur wheeled around and marched over to Sir Thursday, who was waiting patiently. Again, there was an exchange of salutes as Arthur declared the raiding party ready. Sir Thursday nodded then marched over to address the soldiers directly.

'I will enter the Improbable Stair first,' announced Sir Thursday. 'You will bring up the rear, Mister Green. The soldier following me will hold the back of my belt, and the soldier behind him his belt, and so on. If anyone lets go, they will fall out of the Improbable Stair wherever we happen to be at that instant, and anyone holding on will also go. Therefore it is essential that everyone keep a good grip.

'The Improbable Stair is … improbable … so though we are travelling a very short distance within the House, it is possible that we may emerge upon a landing of the Stair, which may be anywhere and anywhen. If this occurs, do not let go! We shall embark upon the Stair again immediately. No one must let go until I give the order. Is that clear?'

'Yes, sir!' shouted the raiding party.

CHAPTER TWENTY-FOUR

Sir Thursday didn't waste any time. As soon as he'd finished talking, he walked over to the right-hand side of the line of Piper's children and took his place.

'Raiding party!' he ordered. 'Right turn! Take hold of the belt of the soldier in front of you!'

Arthur hurriedly joined the end of the line as everyone turned right. He barely had time to grab Fred's belt before Sir Thursday sketched out a series of steps with his sword, its point leaving glowing lines in the air.

'No need to stay in step!' called out Sir Thursday as he raised his boot and improbably trod on the first of those glowing, insubstantial steps he'd just drawn. 'You may find it helpful to shut your eyes – but you must hang on!'

Though Arthur had used the Improbable Stair before, he'd never seen anyone else disappear into it. When he'd travelled on the Stair he had been totally focused on imagining a stair where there wasn't one, a series of steps made of brilliantly white marble, stretching up forever.

But that wasn't what he saw now. Sir Thursday ascended the glowing steps he'd drawn and then his head disappeared as if it had been suddenly erased, and then his shoulders too, and, all too quickly, the rest of him. The Piper's child following gasped as her arm disappeared, then shut her eyes and was dragged onwards, apparently into disintegration.

It was hard being last, though the line moved very quickly. Arthur noticed that not one of the Piper's children held back, though most of them turned their heads at the last second as if to avoid something happening to their faces. And their eyes were closed.

Arthur kept his eyes open. He wanted to be aware of any tricks Sir Thursday might try on the Stair.

He should have been relieved to find himself surrounded by white light, with the marble steps under his feet and a curling line of soldiers ascending the Stair ahead of him. But he wasn't.

The Stair had not been a spiral when he'd climbed it before. Now it was tightly coiled.

Arthur realised he'd stopped for a second when he was jerked forward. For a horrible instant he thought he was about to lose his grip on Fred's belt. But his fingers were jammed through and he closed them again tightly, looking only at the steps as he staggered forward.

'Hang on!' exclaimed Fred, as quietly as he could while still being emphatic. 'Sir.'

Arthur hung on and concentrated on the steps under his feet. For the first twenty or thirty or so he kept expecting Sir Thursday to do something, but then he remembered how hard it had been for him to lead just Suzy Blue up the steps. The Trustee wouldn't be able to do anything unless he put himself at risk of falling off the Stair as well – and in the case of the Improbable Stair a fall meant ending up somewhere you'd almost certainly not want to be.

This realisation allowed Arthur to start worrying about what was going to happen when they came out at the other end. Even if Sir Thursday did only need five or six minutes to destroy the Nothing spike, a lot could happen in that time. In the battle at Fort Transformation, scores of Denizens and New Nithlings had been killed or wounded in the first thirty seconds, let alone the first five minutes.

There was also the possibility that something would happen to Sir Thursday. If he wasn't able to lead them into the Improbable Stair then they'd be trapped, easy pickings for the New Nithlings.

Unless I can lead everyone back into the Improbable Stair, thought Arthur.

He wondered if using the Stair would increase the sorcerous contamination of his blood and bone. The crocodile ring was in his belt pouch, but there was no point thinking about it or about the contamination. Arthur knew he would have to do whatever it took for them to survive.

Something caught Arthur's eye and he looked up. The Stair stretched on forever, disappearing in a haze of bright white light. But Sir Thursday was gone, as were the two Piper's children behind him. The third was disappearing in mid-step.

'We're coming out!' said Arthur. 'Hold on!' He felt a bit silly as he said 'hold on' because almost everyone had disappeared by the time he said it, so only Fred heard and he knew Arthur was the one who hadn't been holding on properly.

Then Fred was gone and this time Arthur did instinctively shut his eyes. When he forced them open only a microsecond later, he saw the line of Piper's children ahead of him, with Sir Thursday at the head.

Only a few feet beyond Sir Thursday was a huge, rapidly spinning cone of utter darkness, shot thought with occasional coruscations of blinding white.

It was the spike – and not only was it spinning, it was bigger than Arthur had thought it would be. The part he could see was about thirty feet high and twenty feet in diameter at the top, but it looked like it was half-buried in the ground, the point having long since bored its way through the topsoil and into whatever material lay beneath the organic layer of the 500/500 tile.

'Let go!' roared Sir Thursday. 'Take up defensive positions.'

Arthur let go and looked around. They were on an earthen ramp reinforced with cut timber that had been built to emplace the spike. It was ten feet wide and perhaps sixty feet long. The raiding party was at the top of it, right next to the spike.

The other end of the ramp joined a dusty, well-trodden road lined with white rocks that stretched to the tile border, half a mile away. On either side of this bare road there were rows and rows of bright yellow bell-shaped tents. Hundreds and hundreds of tents, each one about twenty feet in diameter, occupying a forty-foot by forty-foot square.

There was also a parade ground, a square of bare earth two hundred feet long on each a side. A unit of a thousand New Nithlings was drawn up there, in the process of being inspected by a very tall, very imposing New Nithling – or perhaps even a Denizen because he was human-shaped and was wearing a pale yellow uniform greatcoat of many toggles and considerable gold braid, topped by a Napoleon-style hat worn sideways over what from a distance Arthur thought was either his own metal-masked head or some kind of horrible metal replacement. This very tall commander was trailed by a dozen officers, or Superior Nithlings, and in the mere second that it took Arthur to look down at the parade ground, he realised that this must be the mysterious leader of the New Nithlings.

He had no further time for thought. Sergeant Quicksilver was yelling and the Piper's children were arraying themselves in a line across the top of the ramp, preparing their Nothing-powder pistols and carbines and power-spears and, in Quicksilver's own hands, a muscle-fibre longbow.

'Very good, ah, Sergeant,' said Arthur. He had to struggle to keep his voice even. The whine of the spinning spike was very disturbing, rather like a human child complaining at an impossible pitch. The

New Nithlings on the parade ground had noticed the intruders. The tall commander turned to look at them – and though he did not appear to say anything, there was a sudden flurry of activity among the officers behind him and shouted commands.

'Take 'em five minutes to get here,' said Quicksilver with a practised glance. 'All those tents in the way –'

She stopped talking as big kettle drums began to pound, in that same rhythm Arthur had heard in the attack on Fort Transformation. With the drums, New Nithlings emerged from almost every tent, like ten thousand hidden bees suddenly emerging from an innocent-looking square of honeycomb.

Arthur looked at Sir Thursday. He was next to the spike, his sword raised above his head. Suddenly, he shouted a battle cry, a sound that rose above the noise of the spike and sent a jangling vibration down Arthur's spine. Sir Thursday cut down at the whirling Nothing, slicing off a huge piece that hurtled clockwise through the air and came down on a bell tent, destroying it instantly, so all that remained were some sagging guy ropes hanging down a hole in the ground.

But the spike did not stop spinning, nor was there any notable hole in it, as if the Nothing it was composed of had simply filled the gap.

Sir Thursday scowled and cut at the spike again, with similar results.

'Here they come,' said Quicksilver. 'Do you want to give the order to fire, sir?'

It took Arthur a second to comprehend that she was talking to him. He was staring down at the mass of New Nithlings who were being shouted and cajoled into ranks as they raced towards the bottom of the ramp to make up an assault force. There were lots of less organised Nithlings on the sides of the ramp as well, some of them trying to climb the sides, with some success, though it was thirty feet to the top.

All the New Nithlings were uniformed, armed with the crackly lightning spears Arthur had seen before and clearly well led. Though it was true they had greater physical variety among them than the Denizens, with extra limbs and distorted features, they bore no resemblance to the half-mad rabble Nithlings were supposed to be like.

'Yes, I'll give the order,' said Arthur as calmly as he could. 'Musketoons first then the power-spears. Quicksilver, you cover the left side and shoot the climbers. Suzy, you take the right and do the same with your pistols. Fred, you load for Suzy.'

Arthur drew his sword and moved to the centre of the line, with only half a glance back at Sir Thursday.

Even that was enough to know that the Trustee was not making any real progress against the spike, though at least he was timing his cuts so that the pieces of Nothing flew off into the camp rather than cutting a swathe through the Piper's children on the ramp.

'Wait for the order!' called Arthur as musketoons were levelled and power-spears raised.

A formation of New Nithlings twelve across and ten ranks deep was almost at the foot of the ramp. Arthur looked at them stomping forward and knew there was no way they could stop them or hold them off, or even survive. They'd have time for perhaps two volleys from the five musketoons, a cast of three power-spears and that would be it. They would be overrun.

Overrun, thought Arthur. *Just another way of saying that we'll all be killed. Unless Sir Thursday can do something with the Key. Or we could try to get back on the Stair . . . only there's no time. We'd never make it. They'd charge and cut us down . . . the last few for sure . . . which means me. Maybe that's what Sir Thursday planned from the start.*

The enemy drumming suddenly changed tempo, getting faster. The New Nithlings shouted and began their charge up the ramp. Suzy's pistols went off, and Quicksilver's bow twanged and twanged again as Arthur counted to three and shouted 'Fire!' The musketoons banged and Nothing-powder smoke billowed up. Arthur shouted, 'Throw!' and the power-spears flew, and Arthur shouted, 'Hold fast!' and moved into the front rank to be with the others, to try to hold the initial shock even if only for a few seconds, and then –

A strange and unearthly sound filled the air. A breathy, high-pitched single note that sounded a little like a flute and a little like a whale singing, and something entirely new and different as well.

The note stopped everything. In the case of the Piper's children, they literally stopped, frozen in mid-action. All of them save Arthur, who looked at Fineold with his savage-sword half out of its scabbard and Jazebeth's hand stopped with her fingers pulling back the lock of her musketoon.

Suzy was a statue on the brink of the ramp, a small snaphance pistol in each hand, pointed down the right-hand side of the ramp. Quicksilver was just as still across from her, her bow dropped in favour of a triangular-bladed poniard.

The New Nithlings were not frozen, but they had stopped their charge and their climbing. Those on either side of the twelve-Nithling-wide ramp assault force were turning around and withdrawing, and the rest were moving apart to create an avenue of clear space up the middle.

The tall commander was striding up that avenue, holding a simple wooden pipe to lips that were invisible behind a metal mask of dull steel, playing that one impossibly pure, impossibly sustained note.

Arthur heard movement behind him and twisted around. Sir Thursday was there, his face red and screwed up in rage.

'Traitors!' he screamed. 'Five minutes is all I asked!'

Before Arthur could do anything, Sir Thursday's sword sliced through the air and connected with the frozen Private Fineold at Arthur's side, cutting off his head with a single stroke. Then Sir Thursday rolled his wrists and, without stopping, swung the blade back again, straight at Corporal Jazebeth.

Without thinking, Arthur parried the blow. He got his savage-sword in the way, but it was as if the gravity-condensed steel was a mere twig. Sir Thursday's sword snapped it in half, the impact making the broken sword fly from Arthur's hand. Sir Thursday's blow was hardly slowed, continuing to thunk horribly into Jazebeth's neck.

Arthur half-fell and half-jumped back as Sir Thursday swung at him, changing the blow in mid-air from a cut to a thrust, flicking the point at Arthur. But the Denizen didn't follow through. Instead he leaped to the right and began to draw steps with the blade, beginning to enter the Improbable Stair.

Arthur's stomach muscles burned as he flipped himself fully upright. He took one swift glance around. The Nithling commander was twenty feet away, slowly walking up the ramp between the Nithlings, still playing that unearthly pipe.

Sir Thursday had one foot on his glowing step, his back to Arthur.

Arthur grimaced and reached alongside his cuirass under the armhole, feeling for the emergency dagger. But his fingers closed on a small plastic box. He had it out and in his hand before he remembered what it was.

I'm going to die, he thought. *But I can save my family*

He threw the box at the spike and threw himself on Sir Thursday's back just as the Trustee disappeared into the Improbable Stair.

CHAPTER TWENTY-FIVE

Arthur got his legs wrapped around Sir Thursday's waist and his arms around his neck as he took his first step on the treacherous marble of the Improbable Stair itself.

'Don't try anything!' warned Arthur. 'If you do anything but move on the Stair, I'll throw both of us off!'

Sir Thursday growled something, a sound so inarticulate and full of anger it might have been a beast's noise. But he kept plodding up the stair, carrying Arthur's weight as if the boy was no more than a light rucksack.

After twenty steps, the Trustee spoke again.

'You'll die for this. Mutiny is mutiny, no matter who commits it. You have sealed your own end, Lieutenant.'

Arthur did not reply. He kept all his attention on Sir Thursday's movements, not his speech. The Trustee had his sword in his hand, and he could easily angle it back and slide it into Arthur without warning. Arthur knew he had to be ready to throw all his weight to one side, even if it ended up being a dead weight. At least Thursday would be thrown off the Stair, hopefully to somewhere horrible where it would not be easy to get back on again.

Justice will be served, said a voice in Arthur's head. The quiet, telepathic voice of the imprisoned Part Four of the Will. *I nearly had him back there. You must make him angry again.*

Make him angry? Arthur thought back. *Are you as crazy as he is? I don't want to make him angry. I don't know how I'm going to survive as it is.*

It is the only form of distraction that will work on Sir Thursday, replied the Will. *Distract him, and I will free myself and deliver the Fourth Key to you, Lord Arthur. Then he may be brought to justice.*

I'm not making him angry here, Arthur thought back at the Will.

He considered where the least worst place would be to make Sir Thursday angry for a moment. Then he spoke aloud.

'There must be a big briefing room at the Citadel. For the marshals and so on, to keep up with what's going on. Particularly with the siege happening.'

'There is my operations room,' snarled Sir Thursday. 'There is no siege. It is only an inconvenience.'

'I want to come out in the operations room then,' said Arthur. 'Take me there. Or I'll throw us both off.'

'My revenge ... will be all the ... sweeter for your insults,' said Sir Thursday. Arthur could hear him grinding his teeth between words. 'It is merely delayed.'

Arthur opened his mouth to answer, but he never had the chance as unexpectedly, to him at least, they left the Stair and suddenly re-entered the House. Immediately Sir Thursday struck back with his free hand, his bony fist smashing Arthur off his back and on to the floor. Dazed, the boy struggled to his feet. Before he could do any more than stand up, Sir Thursday was bellowing orders and there were plenty of Denizens rushing about to follow them.

'Hold that traitor! All is revealed! The enemy is led by the Piper, and all Piper's children must be executed before they can conduct any traitorous activity. Marshal Dawn, see to it immediately!'

Arthur felt his arms pulled back behind him. He struggled to lift his chin, finally managing it with the

unintended help of someone who jerked his head back
so they could get an arm around his neck.

He was in a large domed room full of officers. The
three standing with Sir Thursday were the tallest and
most splendid, so they had to be Marshals Dawn,
Noon and Dusk. All three sported black eyes, and Noon
had a bandage around his right hand as well, which
suggested that they had been in recent fighting or that
they did not always see things Sir Thursday's way.
Arthur thought the latter was more likely.

'We're not traitors!' Arthur croaked as he was
hauled backwards toward a door. 'Sir Thursday killed
two of his own soldiers! He's not fit to command! I am
an officer in the Glorious Army of the Architect too and
I demand to be –'

He got no further, as Sir Thursday crossed the room
in a single leap and punched him in the stomach. It hurt
worse than anything Arthur had ever felt, worse even
than his broken leg. He couldn't breathe and for several
seconds thought he never would breathe ever again.
It was more frightening even than an asthma attack
because his chest felt actually broken, not just tight.

But after ten or twelve awful seconds, he did get a
breath, as Sir Thursday's attention was diverted by
Marshal Dawn. Clad in the green of the Borderers, she
stood out in a room dominated by scarlet headquarters

uniforms, and also because unlike everyone else she strode towards Sir Thursday, rather than edging away from him.

'The lieutenant is correct. He has levelled a serious charge and it must be heard.'

Sir Thursday's eyes narrowed to slits and he glided like a snake across the floor towards the Marshal.

'Must be heard? I have issued *orders*, have I not, Marshal Dawn? I want those Piper's children *killed*.'

'Regulations state –'

Sir Thursday slapped her in the face. She rocked back, but did not try to defend herself, merely spitting out a tooth. Then she started again.

'Regulations state that a court of enquiry –' The next slap knocked her down and back on to her knees. But she stood up, and this time the other two marshals marched forward to stand with her.

'Sir, this is neither the time nor the correct –' began Marshal Noon.

'Orders!' shrieked Sir Thursday. He turned and pointed at Arthur. 'I am ordering my soldiers to kill all the Piper's children, starting with this one! Is there no one here who knows their duty?'

'Nobody move!' snapped Marshal Dusk, his voice cold and penetrating. 'That is not a legal order. We are soldiers, not gallows-hands.'

'You are nothing!' screamed Sir Thursday. 'I demote you to nothing. I will carry out my orders myself.'

He twirled, lifted his sword so that it pointed straight at Arthur's heart and ran straight at the boy.

Arthur tried to throw himself forward to the ground, but he was held too fast. He could not avoid the thrust.

But the sword did not strike home. Sir Thursday had only taken a single step when the snake wound around the hilt suddenly uncoiled and reared back. It was made entirely of words, and one line that ran down its back suddenly shone silver. The letters grew to the full width of the reptile, spelling out a single phrase: *Let the Will be done!*

The snake's fangs gleamed in the silver light and it struck before Thursday could take another step, its top jaw snapping down on the back of his hand, biting deep. Sir Thursday's hand jerked, lifting the sword so that the blade whistled well above Arthur's head, sliced the ear off the Denizen holding him and then embedded itself in the wooden panelling of the wall.

Arthur heard the Denizen behind him scream and felt him let go. Sir Thursday was trying to rip the snake that was Part Four of the Will from his hand. The Marshals were drawing their swords. Everyone else was huddling back against the walls, some drawing weapons, but most just watching in stunned amazement and fear.

Arthur knew what to do. He spun round, reached up and, exerting every last ounce of his strength, pulled the sword out of the wood. It clanged on to the ground because it was too heavy for him to hold up. Arthur knelt beside it and gripped the hilt.

Then he spoke in the clearest voice he could muster.

'I, Arthur, anointed heir to the Kingdom, claim this Key and with it . . .'

Sir Thursday howled in rage, plucked the snake from his hand and threw it across the room. Then he snatched a sword from the nerveless hands of a staff major and, still howling like a beast, ran at Arthur.

His path and his swordplay were blocked by the marshals. It took all three of them to do it, their blades clashing and weaving as they fought to hold off the ravening monster that Sir Thursday had become.

Arthur spoke faster and faster, his gaze on the lightning-fast interplay of swords.

'With it command of the Glorious Army of the Architect and Mastery of the Great Maze. I claim it by blood and bone and contest. Out of truth, in testament and against all trouble!'

Something touched his leg and Arthur shrieked, rather spoiling the momentary silence that had fallen as he finished claiming the Key. He looked down and saw the snake spiralling up and around his leg.

The marshals took advantage of Sir Thursday's momentary distraction, backing him into a corner, but he was neither disarmed nor defeated. It was all the three marshals could do to keep him there and protect themselves from his lightning lunges and cuts. He might no longer have the Fourth Key, but he was still extremely dangerous.

'Point the Key at him and order him to stand to attention,' hissed the Will. It had coiled most of its body around Arthur's upper arm and stretched up from there so its diamond-shaped head was unnervingly close to his ear.

'I don't want to use the Key,' whispered Arthur.

'What?!' hissed the Will. 'I know you're the Rightful Heir! I can tell!'

'Yes, I am,' Arthur whispered back. 'But ... look, we'll talk about it later.'

'So you have my Key,' called out Sir Thursday. He lowered his sword, but the marshals did not press home their attack. 'However it takes more than that to command my Army, particularly when the enemy is at the gates. I take it the enemy is still at the gates?'

'Yes, sir,' said a colonel uncertainly. 'But we are confident that when the tiles start to move again, the enemy will lose heart –'

'The tiles will not move,' said Sir Thursday. 'Due to treachery, I failed. The spike was not destroyed.'

His words were met by gasps, suppressed moans and even one or two outright cries of despair. Several officers looked away; only a very few looked to Arthur. Their behaviour indicated that the situation was very bad, and now that Arthur thought to listen, he could distantly hear the sound of battle, though there was no cannon fire. Which was either good or bad, depending on whether it was due to lack of Nothing powder or because whatever attack was in progress wasn't that serious.

'I am Lord Arthur, the Rightful Heir of the Architect,' Arthur announced. 'I am assuming command. Marshals Dawn, Noon and Dusk, I want you to disarm and arrest the Denizen formerly known as Sir Thursday.'

'I command the Army by order of Lord Sunday, conveyed in writing by Superior Saturday,' countered Sir Thursday. 'Perhaps I was hasty in demanding the Piper's children be executed, but we are at war. Surely you all know that I am the only one who can lead us to victory over the New Nithlings. Arrest this Arthur, and in due course we can look into his claims and hold a proper court of enquiry.'

'Use the Key!' hissed the Will.

'The Will of the Architect has chosen me,' said Arthur desperately. He raised his arm to show the snake. 'This is Part Four of Her Will.'

He could feel the mood of the Denizens in the room changing. They would so easily fall back into the familiar pattern of obedience to Sir Thursday.

'What Will?' asked Sir Thursday. He took a step forward and the three marshals stepped back, their weapons lowered. 'That is merely a sorcerous snake, a thing of the Upper House. An embellishment to the Key. Colonel Repton, you are close there. Arrest Lieutenant Green, as he actually is. You see that he cannot use the Key, don't you?'

'Use the Key!' hissed the Will again, desperation coming through in its soft serpent voice.

CHAPTER TWENTY-SIX

'I am the Rightful Heir, you know,' said Arthur, with weary resignation. He lifted the Fourth Key. It shrank as he raised it, transforming itself from a sword into a slender marshal's baton of ivory wreathed in tiny golden laurel leaves.

The baton began to glow with a green light reminiscent of the Great Maze's moon as Arthur held it up. He levelled it directly at Sir Thursday, keeping it in line with the Trustee's now strangely yellow-tinged eyes.

'Atten-hut!'

Everyone in the room stood at attention, except for Arthur and Sir Thursday. The Trustee's eyes grew even more yellow, and a vein stood out and began to throb upon his forehead as he tried to resist the power of the Key. Then, ever so slowly, his boots began to slide across the floor, coming together with a loud click of his heels. His hands went to his sides and the sword he'd taken angled back to rest on his shoulder.

'You are stripped of all rank and privileges,' said Arthur. His voice echoed with power, sounding deeper, stronger and much scarier than any boy's should.

Sir Thursday's epaulettes flew off and his buttons rained upon the floor. His sword snapped into three pieces and the hilt became rusty powder in his hand.

Arthur lowered the Fourth Key.

'Marshal Dawn, take whoever you need with you and get Sir Thursday locked up somewhere safe. Make sure he can't escape, but also make sure he is guarded from outsiders too. Somebody is killing all the former Trustees.'

'Yes, sir!' snapped Dawn. She took off her belt and used it to bind Sir Thursday's hands. He did not resist, but he glowered at Arthur, his deep-set eyes staring at the boy with undisguised hatred. Dawn gestured at two colonels to help her and together they led Sir Thursday from the room.

'Good riddance,' said the Will. 'Now, Lord Arthur, the situation is quite grave. I believe that our first step should be to try Sir Thursday in a properly constituted court, so that he can answer for his many crimes –'

'Marshal Noon,' said Arthur, using two fingers to hold the snake's mouth shut, 'has anyone tried negotiating with these New Nithlings?'

Marshal Noon looked at the frustrated Will coiled on Arthur's arm, then back at the boy. 'No, sir. It has never been possible to negotiate with Nithlings.'

'My brother is a soldier,' said Arthur. 'An officer. He told me once that every army always fights its current war as if it were the previous one, learning no lessons from what is actually happening.'

'Yes, sir,' said Noon – but he looked puzzled.

'What I mean is that we are being attacked not by the old kind of Nithling. These are New Nithlings. Everything is different about them. And they are led by the Piper. At least I guess it's him. Sir Thursday thought so and he'd have no reason to lie about that. Which makes me wonder what the Piper and his Nithlings actually want.'

'To destroy us, sir,' said Noon.

'That's what Nithlings usually want,' said Arthur wearily. 'But like I said, everything is different about these New Nithlings. Otherwise we wouldn't even be in this situation. Which reminds me, what is the situation?'

'It's serious,' Noon reported. 'We should view the battlefield, but in essence, the New Nithlings around the Citadel continue to be reinforced. There was an assault half an hour ago, which nearly carried the outer southwest bastion. We are low on firewash, have very little Nothing powder and the garrison is not up to full strength. The New Nithlings are constantly reinforced, while we are not. We have a force of 17,286 at last report in the Citadel, and about another sixty-two thousand troops at the White Keep, Fort Transformation, the Cannon Arsenal and Irontoe Hold. But with the tiles stopped, there is no way we can be reinforced in time by marching as it is too far. Besides, they will be beset themselves, since there are so many enemy in the Maze. The enemy force against us here numbers at least seventy-five thousand, with tens of thousands more on the march. Without tectonic strategy, we cannot prevent their arrival.'

'Lord Arthur,' interrupted the snake, whom Arthur had let go. 'If the Citadel is in danger of falling then we should leave, being sure to take our prisoner so he may answer to justice –'

'Shut up!' ordered Arthur. 'What is it with you Parts of the Will? You can't see the forest for the trees. Besides, even if I was going to leave – which I'm not – I'm sure there's no way out except the Improbable Stair, which I am not going to take because I do not want to use the Key! Is that clear?'

'Yes, sir,' mumbled the snake.

'That reminds me.' Arthur fumbled in his pouch and took out the crocodile ring, sliding it on his finger. But he didn't dare look at it straightaway and he welcomed an interruption from Marshal Dusk.

'Pardon me, sir,' said Dusk. His uniform was a dark grey with black epaulettes and black buttons. Like all Dusks, he had the reserve and inner quiet characteristic of a late evening. 'There is a way out. An elevator from Sir Thursday's study goes up to the Middle House and down to the Lower House.'

'An elevator?' asked Arthur. 'Do we have telephone connection with the rest of the House as well?'

'Yes, sir,' said Dusk. 'Do you wish to place a call?'

Arthur tapped the Fourth Key on his thigh, wincing when it actually hurt. The ivory baton was a lot harder than it looked and the gold leaves were pointy.

His mind raced as he tried to work out what to do. Amid the big question of how to defend the Citadel, he had a constant nagging fear for the safety of Suzy and Fred and the other Piper's children in the raiding party. They'd been frozen or turned into statues or something, which suggested the Piper didn't want to kill them. He had brought them to the House in the first place, after all. But Arthur couldn't be sure they'd be all right.

The biggest puzzle was the revelation that the Piper was the leader of the New Nithlings. As far as

Arthur could remember, the Piper was one of the three children of the Old One and the Architect, born to a surrogate mortal mother. But he didn't really know any more than that.

Why would the Piper be leading an army of almost-Denizens against the House? His older brother was Lord Sunday, wasn't he?

'OK,' he said finally. He paused as everyone in the room looked at him respectfully, anticipation in their faces. 'How big is Sir Thursday's elevator? It's not a stupid little one like at Fort Transformation is it?'

'It is of variable dimension, I believe,' said Dusk. 'Perhaps the size of this room at its largest extent.'

'How long would it take to get to and from the Lower House?' asked Arthur.

'It depends upon the elevator operators and the local authorities. Minutes, hours, days . . . I could not say.'

'Right,' said Arthur through clenched teeth. 'I hope it turns out to be only minutes. I want to try to negotiate with the New Nithlings. One other thing my soldier brother once said was that it's always best to negotiate from a position of strength. So I am going to call on the Lower House, the Far Reaches and the Border Sea to use that elevator to send through as many Commissionaires, former Overseers, Midnight Visitors, sailors and so forth as we can round up, with Monday's,

Tuesday's and Wednesday's Dawns, Noons and Dusks, and as much Nothing powder as we can get together.'

'Civilians,' said Noon in a disparaging tone. 'Though the powder would be useful.'

'They're all used to fighting Nithlings of one kind or another,' Arthur reminded him. 'Besides, I bet most of them did their time in the Army and are on the Reserve.'

'Reservists are little better than civilians,' sniffed Noon. 'Reintegrating them into our forces is never easy. Besides, I don't believe even you have the authority to call up the Reserve. That is a function of the Upper House. Sir.'

'I think in the current circumstances we will take whatever reinforcements we can find and be extremely grateful,' said Dusk. He looked pointedly at Noon, who did not meet his gaze. 'And Sir Arthur is not calling up the Reserve. Just bringing in . . . volunteers.'

'Who had better be welcome,' said Arthur. Sometimes the lack of common sense among Denizens drove him crazy. 'Where's the phone?'

A captain hurried across the floor holding a small wickerwork suitcase that looked rather like it might have a picnic set inside it. He flipped it open to reveal a telephone handset on a cradle. Arthur picked up the handset and the captain started cranking a little handle on the side of the suitcase.

'Can I help you?' said a crackly voice that sounded very far away.

'Get me Dame Primus,' ordered Arthur.

'She's not taking calls,' said the voice. 'I had one for her not long ago.'

'This is Lord Arthur, Rightful Heir of the Architect. And it's urgent, please.'

'Pardon?'

'I said, this is Lord Arthur –'

'No, not that bit, what did you say at the end?'

'Please,' repeated Arthur. 'Look, it *really* is urgent.'

'Putting you through now, sir,' said the voice. In the background Arthur heard her add, 'He said "please", and him higher than all them rude nobs.'

There was some louder crackling, then a voice Arthur recognised as Sneezer's spoke.

'Monday's Dayroom. May I help you?'

'Sneezer, it's Arthur. Put Dame Primus on please, straightaway.'

'Very good, sir.'

'Lord Arthur?'

The snake on Arthur's arm jumped as Dame Primus's voice echoed through the room. Not for the first time,

Arthur wondered why all the superior Denizens did that on the phone. It was probably just so they sounded important.

'Yes. I haven't got much time so listen carefully. I want every available Commissionaire Sergeant, Metal Commissionaire, Midnight Visitor, the former Overseers from the Far Reaches, the regular sailors and all our superior Denizens to come through to the Citadel in the Great Maze with weapons and as much Nothing powder as is available, as quickly as possible. Oh, and Dr Scamandros and anyone else who might be useful in a battle, including you. There'll be an elevator in the Lower House. Any questions?'

'Yes, Lord Arthur, I have numerous questions,' said Dame Primus in a peevish tone. 'What is going on? Are you planning to fight Sir Thursday? That would not be a sensible course. Even with all our forces, we would be no match for the Army –'

'I have the Key and Part Four is free,' interrupted Arthur. 'Sir Thursday is under arrest –'

'And will be judged!' blurted out the snake.

'And we are about to be attacked by a vast army of New Nithlings led by the Piper. So hurry up, will you?'

'Indeed,' said Dame Primus, her tone quite changed. 'It shall be as you say, Lord Arthur. I do not know how quickly we can come, but we will do our best.'

320

'That's that then,' said Arthur. 'Let's have a look at the battlefield, and while we do that, somebody can find a big white flag. And an olive branch. You could do that, Marshal Noon. Lead on, Marshal Dusk.'

As they walked to the door, Arthur lifted his hand and took a surreptitious look at his crocodile ring. He did not need to hold it close to see that the gold had washed past the fourth marker and was a third of the way towards the fifth.

CHAPTER TWENTY-SEVEN

High on the battlements of the Star Fort, it was easier to see just how much trouble the Citadel and all those who sheltered behind its walls were in. There was a blackened, churned-up borderland that stretched for about three hundred yards beyond the western bastions. After that, there were numerous diagonal trenches dug in a complex pattern that ran for miles to the west and to the north and south. These trenches were heavily populated by New Nithlings and New Nithling siege equipment, including scaling ladders, bundles of fascines for filling trenches, battering rams, and many large mantlets that were like portable roofs they carried to protect themselves from arrows and musketry.

'So that's what seventy-five thousand New Nithlings look like,' said Arthur. He tried to sound nonchalant, but there were so many of the enemy, and everything about their position looked so organised, from the trenches to the way that each unit was formed up within the earthworks, each with its own colourful banner above it, spread by the breeze and bravely lit by the afternoon sun.

'More like ninety thousand,' said Dusk, looking at a strip of parchment in his hand. 'The Borderers report another column has just arrived. There – you can see its dust in the distance.'

Arthur looked where Marshal Dusk was pointing.

'How far away is that?'

'Four miles,' said Dusk. 'Off the fixed tiles. They'd normally be moved far away at sunset.'

Arthur didn't say anything, but everyone glanced at the downward-lurching sun and there was an unspoken note of regret that the mission to destroy the spike had failed.

'They're preparing for another assault,' said a colonel at Dusk's side.

'That's unusual,' said Dusk. 'They've only just failed in their last attempt. Normally, they wait a day or so, to really build up their numbers. I wonder why the hurry now?'

'They were close to taking the southwestern corner bastion,' answered the colonel. 'Perhaps they think a quick assault will finish that task.'

'I had best go to see to the defences, sir,' said Dusk. 'If I may suggest, sir, it would be wise to send Marshal Noon there too. He is a tremendous fighter and always greatly cheers the troops.'

'We'll all go,' said Arthur. He licked his lips, which had became suddenly dry.

Just the wind, Arthur thought.

'I'll go out with the truce flag,' he said. 'I don't suppose the Piper will be there . . . though I guess he can probably use the Improbable Stair too . . . so maybe he will be . . .'

Arthur paused for a moment, thinking before he continued.

'I'll ask for him. If he's not there and they're prepared to talk, it will win us some time. If he is, I'll try to drag things out as long as I can, to give Dame Primus time to get the reinforcements here.'

I just pray she's not as slow and bureaucratic as she normally is, thought Arthur. He hoped this doubt did not show on his face.

'They may simply try to kill you,' said Marshal Dusk. 'The Key will protect you to some degree, but we do not know the extent of their Nothing-based sorcery or powers. And the Piper . . . I know little about him, but he was always rumoured to be a most powerful and unusual sorcerer himself.'

'When did you last hear about him?' asked Arthur.

'We do not pay much attention to what goes on elsewhere in the House or the Secondary Realms,' Dusk explained. 'But of course new recruits bring rumours, and letters come from their civilian homes. Now that I think on it, I suppose I have not heard anything of the Piper's exploits for several hundred years at least.'

'And now the Piper's back, apparently from Nothing, with an army of New Nithlings.'

'With your permission, I will personally choose and lead your bodyguard,' said Dusk.

Arthur shook his head and pointed down.

'I'll go alone. To the middle of the firewash-burned zone there, between those two bastions. You can cover me from there. If too many of them come for me, I'll back off. But I hope when they see the white flag, they'll send just one messenger. They are very military . . . I think they'll do the right thing.'

'They are good soldiers,' Dusk said slowly, as if it were hard for him to say this aloud. 'Perhaps they will send a herald. But in case they do not . . . we have a troop of the Horde here, sir. So, again with your permission, I will have them stand ready near the southwest sally port. In the event a rescue is required.'

'Sure,' Arthur said. 'But no one is to do anything unless I give a clear signal or I'm being literally dragged away or attacked. I don't want everything to go off the rails because someone shoots the herald or something.'

He hesitated then spoke again.

'You'd better assign soldiers to watch the Piper's children too. The Piper might be able to make them do things. I don't want any of them hurt or locked up or anything. They should be allowed to carry out their duties. Just have them watched, and if they do act strangely, they can be restrained. But not hurt, all right?'

'Yes, sir,' said Dusk. 'Here is Marshal Noon, with the truce flag.'

Noon stomped grumpily out on to the battlements, a staff with a furled white flag in his hand.

'Thank you, Marshal.' Arthur felt a bit guilty for sending the marshal to get a white flag. It was because the Denizen had annoyed him and he felt ill that he had behaved in such a way. His mother and father would be horrified at his misuse of power. If he wasn't careful, Arthur thought, he'd not only turn into a Denizen, he'd turn into one like Sir Thursday. 'I should have sent a junior officer. I apologise.'

'Yes, sir,' said Noon stiffly. 'Do you have further orders, sir?'

'I want you to take personal charge of the defence of the outer bastions,' said Arthur. 'I am going to try to get us time by talking, but it may not work and the New Nithlings are apparently preparing to attack again.'

Noon looked out over the crenellated wall and back again.

'Within the hour, I would say,' he said. 'At sundown.'

'I suppose I should change into something more impressive,' said Arthur. He looked down at his dusty cuirass and the torn and bedraggled uniform underneath it.

'You hold the Key and Part Four of the Will of the Architect rides upon your arm,' said the Will. 'You need no adornment to proclaim your authority. Now, Lord Arthur, I think that you might find ten minutes to hold a court and try Sir Thursday –'

'Please stop going on about a trial or whatever for Thursday!' exclaimed Arthur. 'I've got enough to worry about!'

'In my experience, if justice needs to be done, it should be done swiftly and visibly,' protested the Will.

Arthur wasn't listening. One of the officers around him had idly picked up a lead bullet or a small stone and was throwing it over the wall. Something about its arc made him suddenly wonder if he'd thrown the Skinless Boy's pocket far enough to land in the Nothing. If it had fallen short, as now seemed all-too likely, he would have to try to get that back from the Piper in order to destroy it.

'Sir Thursday will face trial,' he said, trying to refocus. 'He murdered Fineold and Jazebeth. But right now we haven't got time. Let's get down to the outer bastions. Marshal Noon, if you would lead the way?'

As with his journey into the Citadel, Arthur was led along, through and past a bewildering arrangement of tunnels, gates, walkways and guardhouses. But it was different this time. He was constantly saluted and his arm grew weary from raising his baton in reply. The Marshals spoke to the soldiers, encouraging them, talking to them by name, congratulating them for their exploits so far in the siege. But Arthur couldn't do that. Every time he was about to say something morale-boosting, he found the words he was thinking of sounded insincere. So he remained silent, striding along amid the crowd of marshals and other officers, but strangely alone, space always around him, no matter how confined they were.

He felt lonelier still as a small sally-port door was opened and a sergeant handed him the staff with the now unfurled white flag. It was huge, the size of a double-bed sheet, but Arthur found he could carry it like a pike, balanced on his shoulder.

'Good luck, sir,' said the sergeant as he helped Arthur and the flag through the doorway to the blasted earth beyond.

'Good luck, sir,' echoed Marshal Dusk and the dozen staff officers who seemed to do nothing but follow senior officers around.

Arthur stepped forward and raised the flag. The sally-port door shut behind him. He took another few steps and looked back up. The bastion's battlements were forty feet above, soldiers peering down through the embrasures at him.

Arthur turned to look at the enemy lines and walked forward, out into the middle of the firewash-blasted dead ground between the bastion and the forward trenches of the enemy.

'I hope this works,' hissed the Will. 'It is rather foolhardy of you, Lord Arthur. I suspect that the first three parts of myself have not counselled you as well as they should have. I suppose they are out of balance, being only three parts of seven. With the addition of myself, we will be four, and the scales will be a little better adjusted.'

'I want you to be quiet if we do get to have a meeting with the New Nithlings,' said Arthur. 'I don't want any interruptions. And don't attack anyone either. The last thing we need is a poisoned messenger.'

'I can choose to be poisonous or not,' said the Will. 'As the case requires. I can even choose my poison.'

'Well, don't poisonously bite anyone unless I ask you to,' said Arthur forcefully. He looked up at his flag and saw that it was fully spread. There had been no olive branch available, but the white flag should be an unmistakable request for a truce and negotiation, Arthur thought.

He'd been a bit concerned that the firewashed area was going to be a gruesome repository of dead Nithlings, but there were no bodies or even any bloodstains. Just a fine, grey ash that lay inch-thick on the dirt, puffing up under Arthur's feet as he strode out towards the trenches.

When he judged he was halfway, Arthur found a patch of loose earth, probably from where a cannon ball had struck early in the siege, and stuck the staff in the ground. Then he stood under the flag and waited.

He could see the front line of trenches very clearly, and the heads of the New Nithlings who were observing him as closely. They did not use muskets or any other distance weapon as far as he knew, but even so his skin felt tense, as if there would suddenly be a shot or an arrow would plunge down from the sky.

Nothing happened for a considerable time. The sun sank lower in the sky. Arthur even began to get bored, which surprised him. The New Nithlings continued to move about the trenches, carrying ladders and other gear, and pushing larger siege engines along further back. But they did not move out of their trenches and come forward.

Arthur almost missed it when something began to happen. The pattern of Nithling movement changed and all handling of large equipment stopped. It also became much quieter.

A tall figure climbed out of the forward trench and walked towards Arthur. A Denizen-tall figure in a voluminous yellow greatcoat that hid his body, topped by that Napoleon hat and the steely mask. He had no obvious weapons, but the greatcoat could conceal almost anything, and of course, he probably had his pipe.

He walked up to within two yards of Arthur and stopped. Then he gave a sketchy half-salute. Arthur, without thinking, returned it with an instinctive, smartly snapped salute at full attention.

'You are courteous,' said the Piper. His voice was light and somewhat strange, and it made Arthur feel like he was in a dream, not really understanding what was happening, but also feeling an overwhelming urge to agree with the Piper. He shook his head to clear it and gripped the Fourth Key more tightly.

'I see you are protected,' said the Piper. His voice sounded the same, but it didn't have the same effect. 'I suppose that is only to be expected.'

'Why are you here?' Arthur asked gruffly. His own voice sounded like a crow's rasping caw after the Piper's melodious tones. 'I mean, why are you attacking the Army?'

'Let us introduce ourselves first, surely,' said the Piper. 'Though I have now been told who you claim to be. I am called the Piper, and I am the son of the Architect and the Old One. I am the Rightful Heir to the House.'

CHAPTER TWENTY-EIGHT

'Uh,' said Arthur. 'Um, that's kind of . . . tricky. You see, I'm Arthur Penhaligon, and though I didn't want to be, I am the Master of the Lower House and the Far Reaches, Duke of the Border Sea, and Commander-in-Chief and Overlord of the Great Maze, and all because your mum's . . . the Architect's Will chose me to be the Rightful Heir.'

'The Will chose you because I was not available at the time,' said the Piper. 'That is regrettable, but it can easily be rectified.'

'Right,' said Arthur. 'Where were you?'

'I was in Nothing,' said the Piper, bitterness in his voice. 'Where I was cast by my turncoat brother, Lord Sunday, seven hundred years ago.'

'In Nothing? Shouldn't you be –'

'Dissolved?' asked the Piper. 'Very little of my corporeal flesh remains beneath this coat and mask. But I am the Architect's son. Even as the Nothing ate my flesh and bone, I shaped the Nothing. I built a place for myself, a small worldlet where I could recuperate, and there I lay for the first hundred years, regaining my strength. In my second century I made the wordlet larger. I created servants to tend me and began to fashion connections back to the House. In the third hundred I began to build an army, not of mindless Nithlings but of my New Denizens. Better ones than Mother made. More like mortals. Smarter and able to change. More in keeping with my father's vision. In the fourth century I made the spike, and in the fifth I began to plan how to re-enter the House through the Great Maze –'

He stopped and took a breath.

'But we are not here to talk of my past, but of my future. I did not believe any part of my mother's Will had been released until quite recently, Arthur, when my rats confirmed the news. But I am not displeased at your progress. You need simply hand over the Keys to me and I will continue in my campaign against my traitor brother and his minion Saturday. You may return to your own world in the Secondary Realms and live the life you should have had, as I believe you wish to do.'

Arthur opened his mouth then shut it again. He didn't know what to say or think. He was being offered a reprieve from the awesome and awful responsibilities that had been thrust upon him.

'It's not as simple as that,' hissed a voice near his elbow.

'And what, pray tell, do you have to do with it?' asked the Piper, bending down so his metal mask was close to the serpent's head, close enough that he could see the lines of type swirling about to create the illusion of snakeskin.

'I am Part Four of the Will of the Architect, as you very well know,' said the snake. 'And Arthur is the Rightful Heir. He can't just give you the Keys because you're not the Rightful Heir.'

'I am the Heir by right of blood and inheritance!'

'If that was all that mattered, it would be Sunday,' said the Will. 'He's the oldest.'

'I have proved I am Her inheritor,' said the Piper. He spread his arms wide to take in all the New Nithling army. 'Look what I have wrought from Nothing!'

'Very impressive, but it makes no difference,' said the snake. 'Arthur is the Rightful Heir. Now that he has the Fourth Key and is commander-in-chief, you are rebelling not against the traitor Sunday but against the legitimate authority of the House. Which makes you a traitor now. Not that your loyalty was ever quite as clear as anyone would wish.'

'Your tone is overly familiar,' said the Piper. He did not sound angry but rather more puzzled. 'Who are you to question my loyalty?'

'You are as much your father's son as your mother's,' said the snake. It uncoiled itself and stretched higher than Arthur's head. 'You never sought to free the Will yourself till you argued with your brother in quite recent times, as we count it in the House. Am I wrong in thinking that Sunday cast you into Nothing because you once again tried to free the Old One against his wishes?'

'That is not relevant,' said the Piper. 'Arthur, either you give me the Keys, beginning with the Fourth Key you hold there, or I will take them from you or whoever holds them.'

'What will you do once . . . *if* you get them?' asked Arthur.

'I shall rule the House.'

'I mean, will you set it to rights and get everything back in order so the House just watches and records the Secondary Realms and doesn't interfere?'

'It is not interference to tend something that has grown awry,' said the Piper. 'My mother was confused on this issue. Essentially, she did not want others to meddle with what she had made, but she "interfered" with the Realms herself if the mood took her. As shall I.'

Arthur shook his head.

'You don't care about all the life out there, do you? All the mortals. We're just the end product of the Architect's big experiment.'

'No,' said the Piper. 'That is true of my brother Sunday. It is not true of me. I love my mortals, the children I brought to make the House more interesting, and the rats who serve as my spies. I tried to make my New Denizens as much like them as I could. I succeeded too well perhaps, for they would prefer to farm and make things, even though they are excellent soldiers and wish to serve me well. Now, we have talked enough. What is your decision, Arthur? I must tell you that if you decline my generous offer, we will attack as soon as both you and I leave this ashen field.'

'What happened to the Piper's children who were with me on our attack on the spike?' Arthur asked.

'Two were slain by Sir Thursday, though I tried to save them. The others serve me now, as is right and proper.'

'Of their own free will?'

'They exist to serve me,' replied the Piper. 'It is their reason for being.'

Arthur looked down at the baton in his hand. He could feel the power of the Fourth Key like a constant low vibration and a warmth that was delicious to his skin.

I wonder if I'm getting addicted to the Keys, he thought. *I wonder if I'm making a really big mistake. One with untold consequences for everybody alive, here in the House and all those billions of humans and aliens and who knows what out in the Secondary Realms . . .*

'I would be happy to work with you against Lord Sunday,' Arthur said slowly. 'And I'm sure we could give your army part of the Great Maze to have for farms. There are even villages ready-built for them to move into. But I can't give you the Keys. Like it or not, I am the Rightful Heir and I think I have to keep going. To set everything to rights. To let the universe get on with itself, without . . . without your kind . . . toying with all our lives.'

'That's that then,' said the Piper. 'I shall play at your funeral, Arthur. You deserve no less, for all that you lack wisdom. It shall be soon, I fear, for the Citadel will not stand long against the might I bring to –'

Arthur was never entirely sure what happened then. The Will either spat poison at the mouth opening of the Piper's mask or struck at his mouth so swiftly that its passage looked like a spray of venom.

Whichever it was, the Piper staggered back and let out a cry of pain and anger that burned the inside of Arthur's ears, even after he managed to clap his palms to his head. The boy turned and bolted back towards the bastion. Behind him, the great kettledrums of the enemy beat out a staccato alarm, and tens of thousands of New Nithlings shouted out in rage at their enemy's treachery, a noise that was as loud as thunder and much more frightening.

Arthur sprinted to the sally port and through the open door. As soon as he was past, it was bolted with six huge bolts and then, when he had gone forward along the passage, a vast stone was swung against it and locked in place.

'I told you not to do anything!' Arthur shouted at the Will, which had coiled itself on his forearm, its head held low. 'That was dishonourable and stupid. The New Nithlings will go berserk.'

'You told me not to poisonously bite anyone,' said the Will. 'I did not. It was an acid. Unfortunately, the Piper will only be incapacitated, at best, for a day or so. If I got it in his mouth. If he still has a mouth.'

A clatter of footsteps and armour announced the arrival of Marshal Dusk and his entourage.

'What happened, Sir Arthur?' asked Dusk. 'We could not see clearly, but the assault has begun!'

'The Will spat acid at the Piper,' said Arthur bitterly. 'For some dishonourable reason of its own.'

'The Piper is a traitor to the Rightful Heir,' said the snake. 'And a very powerful enemy who now will not take the field against us for a day or more. Besides, the parley was finished.'

'Get off my arm,' said Arthur coldly. 'And get out of my sight.'

'As you wish,' replied the Will. It slithered off Arthur's arm and made its sinuous way across the floor, disappearing into a gap in the stones.

'Has any help arrived from the Lower House?' Arthur asked as he was led back through the outer defences. Even through the many thick stone walls that were now between him and the enemy, he could hear the drums and the shouting.

'Not yet, sir,' replied Marshal Dusk. 'Where shall you direct the battle, Sir Arthur? I suggest the Star Fort.'

'No,' said Arthur. 'Somewhere on the second line of bastions, where I can be closer to what's happening.'

'The central western bastion is the tallest in the second line,' Dusk informed him. 'Usually, it would be too noisy and clouded with smoke, for there are two royal and four demi-cannon mounted there. But without Nothing-powder . . .'

'Yes, I know,' said Arthur. 'Will that telephone work there?'

'I believe it will work anywhere within the Maze,' said Dusk as they emerged out into the fresh air on to a high catwalk that linked two of the second line bastions. 'Provided it is cranked at exactly the right speed. Fortunately, Captain Drury is an expert.'

'I'll call Dame Primus again and hurry –'

His words were lost in a titanic boom and blast of air, and a rumbling underfoot that shook the catwalk and made several of the officers lose their balance.

'What was that?' asked Arthur.

'A mine,' said Dusk grimly. He looked back at the outer line of bastions. The southwest bastion was no longer visible, hidden beneath a plume of dust and smoke that coiled up several hundred feet and billowed out horizontally as well. 'They must have tunnelled under in the last few days . . . and they have no shortage of Nothing-powder.'

Beyond the giant dark cloud, the sound of the drums increased in tempo and volume.

'They're assaulting through the breach!' said Dusk. 'We must hurry!'

He led the way at a run, with Arthur close behind. The cloud of smoke and dust quickly overtook them, shrouding them in its choking mass as they were admitted into the second defence line.

Behind them, the surviving bastions of the first line threw down their bridges, closed all connecting gates and doors, and prepared for the onslaught of seventy-five thousand New Nithling soldiers.

CHAPTER TWENTY-NINE

'There is no answer, sir,' said the operator. 'We cannot raise anyone in the Dayroom of the Lower House.'

Arthur handed the telephone back to Captain Drury and shook his head.

'No answer! I can't understand what's happening. There should be someone there. And we should have had help arrive by now!'

Marshal Dusk did not say anything. They were in the third line central west bastion now. There were still individual bastions holding out in the first and second lines, but the defences had been breached in numerous places, all in the space of an hour.

'Is it going to get worse at night?' asked Arthur, with a glance at the setting sun. 'Or better?'

'I fear it will make no difference,' said Dusk. 'The moon will be bright and there are fires enough to light their way.'

There were many fires burning below them. The New Nithlings had brought a new weapon to bear, a tube that squirted something like super-concentrated firewash in a tight stream. They had used this 'incandescent lance' – as it was quickly dubbed – to burn through thick stone walls as well as gates. The only thing that had saved the third defence line thus far was that the enemy appeared to have used up all their supplies of these tubes, which could only be used once.

'Has that runner come back from the Star Fort?' Arthur asked.

'No, sir,' replied one of the staff officers. His head was bandaged, the result of the last attempted escalade by the Nithlings against the central bastion. Their ladders had seemed too short up until the last moment, when they had thrown them against the wall and activated some mechanism that extended both ends by several yards. Arthur had fought himself in the effort to turn back that attack, an intense and horrible few minutes where New Nithlings seemed to be pouring over the walls like water.

Arthur's soldiers had repulsed the attack, but the New Nithlings were massing once more below. Thousands and thousands of them, filling all the space between the defence lines, safe now because the defenders had run out of firewash and even easily procured debris to throw at them.

'They're forming up!' warned Dusk. 'Stand ready!'

His order was echoed all around the walls of the bastion and out across to the bastions on either side, picked up and repeated by officers and NCOs.

'You had best get to the Star Fort now, sir,' said Dusk. He spoke very quietly, close to Arthur's ear. 'I do not think we will hold them this time.'

'I'm not going,' said Arthur. He looked at the crocodile ring on his finger and thought of his home and family. They all seemed so distant now, so far away. He could not easily even summon up their faces or voices in his memory. 'I will use the Key against them. We will prevail.'

He held up the baton and it caught the last light of the sun, transforming not into the unwieldy sword of Sir Thursday but a slim, needle-sharp rapier that caught the sunlight and reflected it back in a coruscation of beams that lit up all the bastions with a clean brilliance that cut through all smoke and dust.

'The Army and Sir Arthur!' shouted Dusk. Once again, his cry was picked up across the bastions, but it was louder now, more heartfelt.

'Sir Arthur! Sir Arthur!'

The Denizens below answered with their drums and their shouts. Rank after rank began to march towards the bastions, all abristle with ladders and hooked lines and smoking firepots to hurl.

'Sir Arthur!'

It was not a war cry. Captain Drury was tugging at his elbow. But he was not holding the phone. He was pointing to the far west, where the disc of the sun had finally disappeared, though some of its light still lingered in the upper sky.

'Sir! Look!'

Arthur blinked and blinked again. Through the drifting smoke, in the dim twilight, he couldn't at first make out what Drury was pointing at. Then he saw it. The skyline had changed. There was a mountain range immediately to the west, perhaps three miles distant.

A cheer rose up amid the shouts of 'Sir Arthur', the wild cheer of unexpected hope.

'The spike,' said Marshal Dusk. 'Sir Thursday lied. He did destroy it.'

'No,' said Arthur. 'I think maybe I did . . . I threw a sorcerous pocket in it.'

'A what?' asked Dusk.

'Never mind,' said Arthur. For a moment, he savoured an intense feeling of relief. The pocket was destroyed and the Skinless Boy with it. His family was safe. But the relief was very brief. Arthur looked out of the embrasure and, though he had not held much hope, was unsurprised to see that the New Nithlings, though they might have lost some of their reinforcements to tectonic strategy when the tiles moved, were unfazed.

I wonder what I can do with the Key, Arthur thought as he looked out at the solid tidal wave of New Nithlings. *I suppose I can use it to make me stronger and quicker and tougher than any Nithling or Denizen. But there's just so many of them, it won't make a difference in the end. They just keep coming . . . it is like being in a natural disaster. There's just nothing that can be done . . . and those New Nithlings just want to be farmers, it's all so crazy –*

A hand suddenly jerked Arthur back behind the merlon.

'Pardon,' said a familiar voice. It was followed a moment later by the sight of a barrel flying over the battlements, two burning fuses trailing sparks as it went past. Four seconds later, there was a huge explosion near the base of the wall.

'A grenado,' said Sunscorch, Wednesday's Noon, with a wide grin. 'Biggest we could make. And there's plenty more where that came from.'

'Sunscorch!' exclaimed Arthur. 'You came!'

'Aye, me and a few others,' said Sunscorch.

Arthur sat up as more explosions boomed beyond the walls. The bastion was suddenly packed with Denizens. There were blue-jacketed sailors lighting fuses on barrels of Nothing-powder and firing them out of squat wooden mortars they'd set up at the back. There were Commissionaire Sergeants and Metal Commissionaires forming up in ranks alongside the soldiers. Midnight Visitors flew overhead, raining long metal darts down on the New Nithlings.

A crowd of buff-coated Artillerists rushed past, wheelbarrowing smaller barrels of powder and piles of canister shot, discussing how low they could depress the bastion's cannons, ecstatic that they could once again use their weapons.

'Dame Primus is preparing to sally below,' said Sunscorch. 'She's going to use the Keys, and she's got the Monday superior Denizens and Wednesday's Dawn and old Scamandros and everybody we could bring who's ever fought a Nithling or who says they have. About five thousand all told, though they're still coming through.'

Sunscorch paused to look over the side.

'This lot don't look much like no Nithlings to me.'

'They're New Nithlings,' said Arthur. 'Almost Denizens . . .'

'You don't sound real happy, Arthur. I mean, Lord Arthur.'

'Just call me Arthur,' said the boy. He looked at the sword in his hand and it slowly changed back into a baton, which he thrust through his belt. Then he stood up and looked through the embrasure.

The New Nithlings were retreating in good order. Though Dame Primus had not yet attacked, she had stalked out of the sally port, with her varied troops fanning out behind her.

It was not the presence of her followers that made the Nithlings retreat. It was Dame Primus herself. Eight feet tall and clad in a greatcoat that was surprisingly similar in colour and cut to the Piper's, she was wreathed in a sorcerous nimbus of whirling blue and green sparks that lashed out every few seconds up to eighty feet away, striking down Nithlings. And that was just with her standing still. When she raised her Second-Key-gauntleted fists and crashed them together, a whole group of at least a hundred Nithlings was suddenly lifted into the air and smashed against the rear wall of the nearest second line bastion.

For the first time, Arthur saw what it really meant to wield the Keys. He cried out as Dame Primus took the trident of the Third Key from her belt and waved it negligently, all the fluid in the bodies of several hundred Nithlings leaving them in a ghastly spray that splashed on to a burning walkway nearby, almost extinguishing the flames.

'Let them retreat!' shouted Arthur. 'Let them go!'

No one could hear him. Even Sunscorch, only a few yards away, was busy shouting at the mortar crews, telling them to fire further out.

Arthur took the baton of the Fourth Key from his belt and held it up.

'Magnify my voice,' he said. 'And cast light upon the field.'

The baton did the latter first. It merely glowed itself, but in answer the newly risen moon shone suddenly brighter, its green light becoming bright enough in a few seconds to cast shadows.

'Let the New Nithlings retreat to their trench lines!' said Arthur, at normal volume. But as his words left, they became much, much louder, louder even than the booming mortars and cannons. 'Cease fire and let them go!'

His voice was so loud an echo came back from the new mountain range that had moved in at sunset.

'Go . . . go . . . go . . . go . . .'

The bright moon faded and there was sudden quiet.

'They are going,' said Marshal Dusk, relief in his voice. 'I wonder if they will be back.'

'It all depends on the Piper,' said Arthur, his voice heavy and slow with extreme exhaustion. 'But with Dame Primus here as well as me, and all four Keys, and our extra troops . . . I think he will either make peace or retreat back to where he came from and prepare for another go.'

'But with the tiles moving . . .'

'He has an Ephemeris,' said Arthur. 'I saw the corner of it sticking out of his greatcoat pocket. And we're in no shape to pursue them, are we?'

Suiting action to words, Arthur slumped down with his back against the battlements. Many followed his example, but Marshal Dusk remained standing and Sunscorch busied himself directing the mortar crews to swab out and clean their massive wooden barrels.

'Just a moment of peace,' muttered Arthur. 'Before Dame Primus gets here. Just one moment of peace, that's all I want . . .'

His voice trailed off and his head slumped forward, as sleep claimed him.

On his finger, the crocodile ring glinted in the moonlight.

It was now exactly one half pure gold.

CHAPTER THIRTY

Leaf woke in a panic, choking. Before she could work out where she was and what she was choking on, a stream of clear fluid gushed out of her nose and into a bucket that was being held in front of her, and her head was held over it.

'Keep still,' said a calm female voice. 'This will last about five minutes.'

'*Eerggh, ick, eurch,*' spat Leaf as the stuff just kept coming, flowing fast enough that some of it washed back down her throat. That was what made her cough.

'You've just come out of sedation,' the voice continued. 'This clear fluid is a mixture of an agent we've used to flush a foreign . . . well, fungoid out of you and the denatured fungoid itself. Once it's out, you'll be fine.'

'Oh ish sho horrigle,' gasped Leaf. She felt weak and flaky and very disoriented and her sinus cavities really hurt. She was in a bed, that was clear, but the roof was green and very low and kind of saggy, and there were clear plastic walls everywhere.

She turned her head and saw it was a nurse holding her head and the bucket. A nurse in a biohazard suit, her face indistinct behind a double visor.

'You're in a field hospital, set up on the oval at what I believe is your school,' explained the nurse. 'Everything is going to be OK.'

'How longsh 'ere?'

'How long have you been here?'

Leaf nodded.

'I think it's been a week. Things have been very hectic, though they're picking up now. At least they caught the terrorists who spread this thing.'

'Shwat?!'

'Well, not caught exactly, as they were all killed in the raid on their headquarters.'

Leaf shook her head in disbelief, till that motion was stopped by an even firmer grip.

'Don't do that, please. Keep it in the receptacle.'

A week, she thought in disbelief. *I've been under sedation for a week. But Suzy must have got the pocket to Arthur or I wouldn't be here . . .*

'Air ow my parents?'

'How are your parents?'

Leaf had meant 'where are my parents?' but she nodded gently anyway, making sure this did not disrupt the cascade of fluid.

'I'll have to check. No visitors here, of course. They probably are at home, I should imagine.'

'Ay woor in Est Eerea Hopital.'

The nurse's hand holding the bucket shook.

'They were in East Area Hospital?'

Leaf nodded slowly.

'I'll get a doctor to check for you,' said the nurse carefully. 'I'm sure they're OK, but there were a . . . a number of casualties at East Area. After the helicopter crash and the breakout attempt, the army . . . most of the people inside . . . most were fine.'

'Wat day iz?' asked Leaf, two tears running down her cheeks to drip unnoticed into the bucket.

'What day is it? Friday, dear. It's Friday morning. Oh, there's the doctor coming in the end now; she must be wanting to check up on you. You know, the funny thing is her name's Friday too and she only works Fridays! Doctor Friday, imagine that! We call her Lady Friday on the wards, because she's so . . . so beautiful and refined . . . Oh, do stay still!'

THE KEYS TO THE KINGDOM

continues in

LADY FRIDAY

For a taster,
please read on . . .

CHAPTER ONE

The Nithling soldier thrust its crackling, electrically charged spear towards Arthur's chest. At the very last moment, just as he was about to be impaled, the boy managed to block the thrust with his shield, the spear point scratching up and across with a horrifying shriek of metal on metal. Arthur stabbed back with his savage-sword, but the Nithling dodged aside and then leaped upon him, knocking him down as its taloned fingers ripped at his face –

Arthur sat up in bed, screaming, his hands scrabbling for a weapon. His fingers closed on a sword hilt and he picked it up and hacked at his attacker – who melted into thin air as the boy became fully awake. The sword in his hand transformed itself, changing from a slim rapier to a marshal's gold-wreathed ivory baton, the shape the Fourth Key appeared to prefer when Arthur was carrying it.

Arthur put the baton down and took a deep breath. His heart was still hammering as if a crazed blacksmith were at work in his chest, the fear from his nightmare only slowly fading.

Not that the waking world was all that much better. Arthur looked hopefully at the silver crocodile ring on his finger, the one that indicated just how much sorcery had seeped into his blood and bone. But it was no different than it had been the night before. Five of the ten marked segments of the ring had turned gold, indicating he was now at least half Denizen. Every time Arthur used a Key or some other sorcery he would be affected and the ring would measure the contamination. If the gold spread across just one more segment, the process would be irreversible and he would never be able to return home. Not without negatively affecting everyone and everything he loved. Denizens had a bad effect on life in the Secondary Realms.

'Home!' said Arthur. He was really awake now and every one of his many problems clamoured in his head, demanding he think about them. But foremost of them all was his desire to find out what was going on back home and to check that everyone was all right.

He slid out from under the heavy satin sheets and off the feather-stuffed mattress on its four-poster base of mahogany. Each of the posts was carved with battle scenes, which distracted him for a moment, so he found out the hard way that it was further to the ground than he expected. He was just getting up off the floor when a discreet knock came at the door.

'Come in!' Arthur called out as he looked around. He'd been so exhausted battling to defend the Citadel against the New Nithling army that he'd hardly noticed where they'd carried him off to sleep. Clearly it was the bedroom of some very superior officer – probably Sir Thursday himself – for as well as the ornate bed there were several gilded, overstuffed armchairs; a richly woven carpet that depicted yet another battle scene, this one a vast spray of orange-red firewash over a horde of misshapen old-style Nithlings; a washstand with a solid gold washbasin and several thick fluffy towels; and an open door leading to a walk-in wardrobe absolutely stuffed full of different uniforms, boots and accoutrements.

'Good morning, Lord Arthur. Are you ready to be shaved?'

To be continued . . .

About the Author

Garth Nix was born on a Saturday in Melbourne, Australia, and got married on a Saturday, to his publisher wife, Anna. So Saturday is a good day. Garth used to write every Sunday afternoon because he has had a number of day jobs over the years that nearly always started on a Monday, usually far too early. These jobs have included being a bookseller, an editor, a PR consultant and a literary agent. Tuesday has always been a lucky day for Garth, when he receives good news, like the telegram (a long time ago, in the days of telegrams) that told him he had sold his first short story, or when he heard his novel *Abhorsen* had hit the *New York Times* bestseller list.

Wednesday can be a letdown after Tuesday, but it was important when Garth served as a part-time soldier in the Australian Army Reserve, because that was a training night. Thursday is now particularly memorable because Garth and Anna's son, Thomas, was born on a Thursday afternoon. Friday is a very popular day for most people, but since Garth has become a full-time writer it has no longer marked the end of the work week. On any day, Garth may generally be found near Bronte Beach in Sydney, where he and his family live.

Thank you for choosing a Hot Key book.

If you want to know more about our authors
and what we publish, you can find us online.

You can start at our website

www.hotkeybooks.com

And you can also find us on:

We hope to see you soon!